YES, MASTER...

YES, MASTER...

TAWNY TAYLOR
ANNE RAINEY
VONNA HARPER

APHRODISIA

KENSINGTON PUBLISHING CORP.

www.kensingtonbooks.com

APHRODISIA BOOKS are published by

Kensington Publishing Corp.
119 West 40th Street
New York, NY 10018

All Kensington titles, imprints, and distributed lines are available at special quantity discounts for bulk purchases for sales promotion, premiums, fund-raising, and educational or institutional use.

Special book excerpts or customized printings can also be created to fit specific needs. For details, write or phone the office of the Kensington Special Sales Manager: Kensington Publishing Corp., 119 West 40th Street, New York, NY 10018. Attn. Special Sales Department. Phone: 1-800-221-2647.

Aphrodisia and the A logo Reg. U.S. Pat. & TM Off.

ISBN-13: 978-0-7582-8784-7
ISBN-10: 0-7582-8784-4

First Kensington Trade Paperback Printing: March 2013
10 9 8 7 6 5 4 3 2 1

Printed in the United States of America

CONTENTS

Stark Pleasure

TAWNY TAYLOR

1

"Check this out. It's the perfect job for you." My roommate, Jenn, tossed a copy of our school's newspaper at me from across the room. She was at the far end of our dorm room, which wasn't very far, boxing up her books and papers. She'd accumulated a lot of books and papers. She'd been boxing stuff up for days.

Me, I was pretty much done packing. I didn't own much. I liked to live light. No extra baggage.

Sitting at my desk, my back to her, I leaned to the side, out of the direct path of the flying missile. The folded paper smacked the wall in front of me and landed on top of my laptop.

"Thanks." I unfolded it, skimmed. At first glance, nothing stuck out. A few "opportunities" to make money from home, a job as a telemarketer, and another ad for models. "Which one?"

"The modeling one, of course."

Of course. At five-foot-nothing, I, Alice Barlow, was perfect modeling material.

I lobbed the paper back. "Ha, ha. Very funny. Next, you'll

be telling me I should try out for a women's professional basket-ball team."

"No, silly. It's not a joke. You didn't read the ad. It's for an artist's model. Not a fashion model." Another box loaded, Jenn half-carried, half-dragged it to the mountain we were building next to the door. Moving day was going to be hell. We lived on the third floor of our dormitory, and there was no elevator. "Artists like to use models of all shapes and sizes. Not that you're fat. With your tight dancer's body, not to mention your flexibility, I bet they'd love you." She lifted the box about waist high, which was roughly three feet shy of getting it on top of the pile. She staggered.

"Are you sure you can't get rid of some of this stuff?" I asked, as I ran to her rescue.

"No, absolutely not."

I glanced in the gap between the flaps as I grabbed one end. "You're graduating with a communications degree. When are you going to need a book about global economics?"

"You never know. I might need something to fall back on," she reasoned between groans and grunts. Once we had the box on top of Mount Useless-Crap-More, she brushed her hands off, smoothed the blond flyaway hairs out of her face. "So, are you going to apply for the job?"

"Artist's model? Don't they pose nude?" I asked, retreating to my desk.

Jenn shrugged. "Sure. But I've seen you naked. You've got nothing to be ashamed of." She patted her nonexistent belly—the one she was always complaining about. "Unlike me." She turned sideways, rubbed her stomach like a pregnant woman. "Check out this gut."

"Shut up." I dismissed her ridiculous exaggeration with a toss of my hand. "You don't have a gut. Or thunder thighs. Or arm fat."

"Yes, I do." She waved, pointing at her triceps. "See the arm fat jiggle?" Nothing was moving. But we'd had this conversation before. At least a few hundred times since freshman year. We were now a few weeks away from moving out of the dorm and into our own apartment. Graduation was in a little over two weeks. I think we were both equally excited and scared. Excited to be finally heading out into the "real" world, getting our first full-time jobs. Scared because the economy was in the toilet, and jobs in our fields were scarce. Thus, the conversation about the modeling job in the first place.

"I can't model nude," I stated. I was feeling twitchy just thinking about it. Naked? Me? In front of a stranger?

"How do you know you can't? Have you ever tried?" Jenn asked as she dumped a load of notebooks, textbooks, and miscellaneous crap in another empty box.

"No, but—"

"Did you see what they're paying? It's not a bad deal."

I hadn't gotten that far. The second I read the word *model*, I stopped. The paper was sitting right there, next to my computer. But I didn't bother looking. The point was moot. "If it's such a great opportunity, why aren't you applying?" I volleyed back.

"I am."

My jaw dropped.

Jenn?

I gaped.

Posing naked?

I gaped some more.

"What?" Jenn narrowed her big blue eyes to itty-bitty slits. "Close your mouth."

I shut my mouth.

Then I opened it, to speak. "You're a born-again, Bible-touting Christian who's taken a vow of celibacy."

Jenn sighed. "I'm posing for a *professional* artist. Posing. Not having sex. Not posing for *Playboy*. Not posing for a horny college guy who is pretending to be a serious photographer."

"What if your parents find out?"

She shrugged again. "So what? I'm an adult now. They can't punish me." She tossed the teddy bear she'd had since she was five into the box.

Adult?

"True, they can't punish you," I said.

"It'll be temporary, a way to get some income started. Once Channel Two hires me to anchor the six o'clock news, I'll retire. Then again, maybe I won't." She shut the flaps of the box and gave me a come-hither look. "Help me?"

"Sure." I hustled over and took one end of the box. Together, we added more useless junk to the mountain.

"We make a good team," she pointed out as she headed back to the stash of empty boxes. "We'll be okay."

"I hope you're right. I'm a little scared," I admitted. I knew we both were nervous. But until now, neither of us had admitted it.

"Me too, I'm scared. To be honest, that's the only reason why I'm even considering the modeling thing." She folded her arms over her chest, as if she were trying to hide herself. "I'm not crazy about getting naked in front of anyone except my husband someday."

Now, with that admission, I felt a little guilty. Here my best friend was willing to risk humiliation and shame so we could eat. I should be willing to do the same. "I'll put in an application too. But only if I don't hear back by the end of the week from the other companies I applied with."

"Thank you." Jenn hugged me. "We're smart, we're resourceful. We're going to be okay, one way or another. It won't be so bad. I promise."

"I hope you're right about that."

* * *

A week later, I was about to find out if it would be so bad. Unlike my other job applications, which had led me nowhere fast, I'd received a call back almost immediately after applying online. And that phone call had been from a woman. A very friendly but professional-sounding woman. She informed me there was no interview process; I would come in for my first session and if things worked out well, I would be asked to return.

Thus, I was on my way to the studio.

Yes, I was a wreck.

If only I'd received a call back on any of those other jobs. Even the part-time gig at J. C. Penney. But nope, nothing.

Just think about the money.

The drive wasn't long. My insides churned the whole way. I parked in the small parking lot in front of the huge industrial-looking structure, cut off the engine, and talked myself into getting out.

I felt sick.

The money. We need the money.

My legs felt heavy as I walked across the parking lot. I felt hot, nauseous.

I can't do this.

By some miracle, I made it to the door. I pulled it open, stepped inside. I was standing in a lobby, a very nice one, full of polished, gleaming wood and marble. Directly in front of me was a desk. It was curved like a smile. The girl sitting at it was smiling too.

"May I help you?" she asked.

"I don't know. I'm here to see . . . unit 700."

She stood. "Follow me." Walking on shoes that made me wince, she *click-clacked* to a bank of elevators. We went to the last one. She slid a key into a lock located just above the CALL button, then hit the button. The elevator chimed right away, the door *whooshed* open, and I reluctantly stepped inside.

The ride up was slow and a little herky-jerky. That did nothing to settle my herky-jerky nerves. When it finally stopped, and I was safe and sound on the seventh floor, I breathed a little sigh of relief.

I exited into a small foyer area that wasn't much bigger than the elevator. Directly in front of me was one set of glossy black-painted double doors.

I knocked.

Almost immediately, the door swung open, and I was face-to-face with a man, roughly in his midtwenties; short, stocky build; with very dark, curly hair, deeply tanned skin, and clothes spattered with paint.

The artist?

"Hello, I'm Alice. Alice Barlow. I'm the model."

"I'm Estefan. The artist." Estefan gave my hand a good, hard shake and waved me inside. "Welcome. Thank you for coming. I was just getting set up." As he pushed the door shut behind me, he asked, "Have you worked as an artist's model before?" He spoke with a heavy accent. Spanish, I guessed.

"No. Never."

His gaze flicked to my hands. Mine did too. I was wringing them, I realized. I let them fall to my sides.

"You're nervous," he said, hurrying toward the easel set up nearby.

"Very," I admitted as I glanced around. This place was huge and much of it wide open. The ceilings were high, as I would expect in a loft. The walls brick. The floor polished concrete. Gray and shiny. Not far from the easel was a raised, white-painted wooden dais with a white wooden chair and some of those photography umbrella lights circling it. I assumed that was where he wanted me. Behind the chair hung a crisp white curtain backdrop. The rest of the space was loaded with art stuff. Stacks of metal pieces, wood pallets, and towering metal industrial shelves loaded with other materials lined the two long walls flanking the model stand.

"If you're uncomfortable at any time, just speak up," Estefan said as he hurried around, gathering stuff.

"Okay."

Not even looking my way—he was gathering some pencils from one of the shelves—he said, "I'm a professional. If it makes you feel any better, when I'm sketching, I am studying the angles of your body, the curves. I don't really see you like I would if I were looking at you in another setting."

I went back to wringing my hands. "I'm not sure if that makes me feel better or worse."

He turned to me, grinned. His smile was charming. Sweet. It made me feel better . . . a little. "I'm going to finish getting set up. You can change in there." He pointed at a closed door not far from the main entry.

"Sure. Okay." I hurried into the changing room, which was the size of a closet. It was a small, tight space, but I didn't mind. At the moment, small, tight, and private was exactly what I needed. With shaking hands, I shucked my clothes and folded them into a neat stack. I pulled on the little robe Jenn had told me to bring, took a look in the mirror, and just about passed out.

I couldn't do this. No way.

I called Jenn. She answered on the third ring. "I did it. You can too." No hello. No how are you doing.

I swallowed my lunch for the second time. "I can't."

"You can. Just sit there and imagine you're lounging by the pool in our new clubhouse when we move—"

"Nobody's ever seen me naked. Not since I was . . . I can't remember how old." I knotted the belt on my robe super-tight. "Not since my mother stopped giving me baths."

"What?" Jenn said, sounding completely shocked.

"I said—"

"I know what you said. But what about . . . sex? What did you do when you and Brad had sex? Turn off all the lights? Keep your clothes on?"

I sat on the stool and grabbed my jeans off the floor. To hell with this. I couldn't do it. No way. "We didn't have sex. I lied."

"You lied to me?"

"I was embarrassed to admit the truth." I looked at my jeans, dropped them on the floor again, and closed my eyes. I knew what she was thinking. She was disappointed I couldn't go through with this when she had. But she was more hurt about the lie than anything else. "I'm sorry I lied to you."

Jenn didn't speak for at least ten minutes. At least that's how long it felt. I was just about ready to hang up when she said, "I'm really hurt you lied, but whatever. If you can't do this, don't. You can find another job. I'll help you."

She would. She always did.

Just like she had forked over half her bank account last year so I could eat too.

Just like she had "loaned" me the money to buy my books the year before that, and had never, not once asked me when I would pay her back.

And she'd stripped naked and let Estefan sketch her, so she could earn her half of our down payment on the apartment we both loved.

After all she'd done for me, how could I not at least give this a try?

"Alice? Did you hang up on me?"

"No, I'm here," I said, staring at the back of the door I would have to open soon. "I was just thinking."

"About . . . ?"

"I'm going to give the modeling a shot."

"You don't have to." Her voice was apologetic. "I'm not trying to force you to do something you can't do."

"I know."

"I swear it's not that bad. Estefan doesn't say much. He just works. That makes it easier to focus on something besides him."

"Focus on what?" I asked, still staring at the door. Could I really go out there? Could I really do this?

"For starters, he warms up by doing fast sketches. You hold a pose for a couple of minutes and then change. It's tough, coming up with new poses, so I spent those two minutes thinking about what I'd do next."

"Okay." I lifted my chin, took a deep breath. "I'll call you when I'm done."

"Good luck. Not that you'll need it."

"Bye." I clicked the button, dropped my phone into my purse, and, before I had another panic attack, opened the door. If I was expecting Estefan to notice I'd come out, I would have been disappointed. He was busy at work, drawing something on his easel.

I padded up to the raised platform, untied my robe's belt, and started easing it off my shoulders.

"Keep it on," he said. "You don't have to take it off until you're ready."

"O-okay." I watched him for a moment, thinking he'd look my way. He didn't.

He said, "I always start out doing some quick sketching exercises. I need you to hold a pose for about two to five minutes. Then change positions. The more interesting and unique, the better."

"Sure." Interesting and unique, I could do. I stretched one arm up over my head, lengthened one leg behind me, and looked up at the ceiling.

"Nice! But are you sure you can hold that position for five minutes?"

"I took dance for fifteen years," I told him.

"Good. Now, don't move until I tell you to."

I did just as Jenn suggested, and while I waited for his cue, I brainstormed the next pose.

"Good, now change," he said.

Had that even been two minutes? I took my second pose. My robe fell open. I didn't close it back up. A little tingle of exhilaration jolted through my body.

"Love this one. Most models need some coaching. You're doing great."

"Thanks," I said to the back wall. I couldn't look at him. If I did, I just knew I'd start hyperventilating again.

"And change."

Before I realized it, I'd gone through at least a half-dozen poses. And my robe was lying on the floor. I hadn't looked at Estefan. Not once.

"Okay. That's it for the warm-up," he said. "Did you need a break before we begin the longer part of the session?"

"How long will that be?" I asked as I stretched to loosen my arms, legs, and neck.

"A half hour."

"No, I'm good." Better to get the session done and over with.

"Great. Then let's begin." He flipped his page in his sketchbook. "This time, I need you to take a pose you can hold for longer. You don't have to stand. You can sit or lie down."

"Okay." I sat on the floor, took a pose that I hoped would be interesting, back arched, head tipped back like I was leaping through the air, and just for kicks, I wrapped the belt of my robe around my wrists. I asked, "How's this?"

"Gorgeous."

I stared up at the high loft ceiling, following the grid of iron beams holding it up, wondering how old the building was, what it might have been when it was first built. A door squeaked. My first instinct was to turn my head to see if someone had come in. I didn't. But I did slant my eyes in that direction.

And I wasn't sure whether that was a good thing or a bad thing.

Who is that?

My whole body went warm.

Then it went cold.

My heart hopped once, twice, as soft footsteps *tap, tap, tapped* across the polished concrete floor.

A man who looked like a god was coming my way. His gaze flicked to me for an instant, then jerked back to Estefan. He went to Estefan, whispered something to him, Estefan responded, then the god glanced at me again. This time his gaze was a little longer.

Once more I felt my skin warm, little prickles tingled all over, my stomach, my arms, my back. His lips pursed ever so slightly then he focused on the exit and started walking. I lost sight of him just before he reached the door. I didn't hear him leave. I didn't hear the door open or the echo of it slamming shut. Had he left? Or was he watching? Was that gorgeous man looking at me? *Naked* me?

My heart thundered in my chest.

Who was he?

"Would you like some music?" Estefan asked, his voice startling me a little.

"Sure. Thanks."

The sound of classical music filled the space. Tchaikovsky. "Dance of the Swans." Instantly, I felt more at ease as the familiar melody vibrated through my body. What felt like ten minutes later, he said, "That's it. I'm finished."

I looked at the door first. Why, I don't know. Okay, I did know.

Stupid.

Of course, the man was gone. He'd probably left right away.

"His name is Stark. Tristan Stark," Estefan said.

"Oh." My gaze snapped to him. I grabbed my robe, wrapped it around myself. "I was just—"

"Curious. I know. All the models are." His smile was rueful. "Don't worry. You aren't insulting me. I think he is a beautiful man too. He is my . . . would you say, benefactor? I was selling my work to tourists on street corners in Rio de Janeiro a year ago. Now, I am here, working in a studio larger than my family's home, receiving commissions for thousands of dollars per painting."

I tied the belt, tugging the bottom of the robe to cover my thighs. "That's wonderful, that you were able to find someone both willing and able to help you."

"Mr. Stark has helped more than me. I've been sending money home every month. Mr. Stark has changed the lives of dozens of people. My family. My family's friends."

My gaze wandered back to the door. "He's a good man, then?"

"Good, yes. Demanding, but fair. And generous, but strict." He went to a shelf, grabbed something, and returned. He handed me an envelope. "You are an excellent model. I have received a commission for a painting and would like to use you. It would pay more than this. I would need at least four hours."

I fingered the top of the envelope as I considered his offer. "That sounds . . . great. Thank you."

"You should know, the client has particular taste."

I wasn't sure where he was going with this. "Okay."

"Come. Let me show you." He motioned me toward a small desk tucked into a corner. I tugged on the back of my robe as I followed. He pointed to the chair. "Sit. I will show you."

I sat. He reached around me, waking the Macintosh in front of me with a wiggle of the mouse. An image of a young woman lying on a silky white sheet filled the screen. Her arms were stretched up, wrists bound, legs stretched long, ankles bound too. "This is a photo of my last painting for him. He wishes to have another, similar."

It was . . . kinky. It was sexy. It was basically bondage porn. A huge wad of something wedged in my throat. "I see. I'll . . ."

"It's too sexy? You feel uncomfortable?" he asked.

"A little."

"You think about it. Call me."

"I'll do that. Thanks."

He nodded, extended a hand. "I hope to hear from you soon."

We shook hands and then I took my little white envelope back to the dressing room. I shoved it into my purse and changed my clothes. When I exited, he was busy working. I quietly *tip-tapped* out into the hall, hit the elevator button, and waited. The bell chimed, the door rolled open, and . . .

He was there, in the elevator car. Tristan Stark.

His gaze flicked to my face. His lips curved slightly. It wasn't a smile. But it was a semi-friendly expression. He motioned me in. "Miss Barlow."

2

Tristan Stark knew my name?

Of course, he knew my name.

He'd probably written my check.

"Mr. Stark."

The door rolled shut, closing us in. I stood facing it, prickles of awkward awareness creeping up and down my spine.

My skin felt warm and cold at the same time. Crazy. I had no idea why this man made me feel so uncomfortable. Maybe it was because I found him so incredibly good-looking. Maybe it was because of the sharpness of his gaze. Or the way he stood silent behind me. Silent and strong.

All I knew was I'd had my share of boyfriends, and secret crushes. I'd never felt this way about any man. Especially a man I had just met.

The car jerked suddenly, dropping out from under my feet. I lost my balance, falling backward. Strong hands caught my waist, steadied me.

The lights cut out.

"Damn." That was Tristan Stark. His breath puffed on my neck. My skin erupted in goose bumps.

The craziest impulse flashed through me. I wanted to lean back, to get closer to this mysterious, sexy man. A lot closer. "We stopped. Should I be worried?"

"We've had some problems with this elevator," he said, still holding my waist. "I've had it serviced twice this week."

"Oh."

His fingers tightened on me. A *zing* of heat blazed through my body. "I'm going to help you sit. It can get extremely disorienting, being in complete darkness."

"I'm okay." I eased down, reaching one hand to find the floor. When he released me, I regretted refusing his help. I sat, then scooted on my butt until my shoulder nudged the wall.

The wall moved.

I was guessing that wasn't the wall. It was a man. Him.

"Sorry," I said.

"Not a problem." He was sitting too. I could tell by how close his voice sounded. Another wave of heat vibrated through me and my face warmed.

I was blushing like a silly little girl. It was so good he couldn't see me right now.

He sighed. The first sign of any emotion I'd seen thus far.

"Should we be pushing a special button? Calling for help?" I asked.

"No, the power cut out. The button doesn't work without power. And my cell phone doesn't get a signal in this building."

Blind, I fished in my purse, found my phone. I pushed the button, powering up the full color touch screen, and blinked and squinted. The brilliant light scorched my retinas. I checked my reception. Zero bars. "Nothing here either."

"It's okay. My assistant will realize I'm missing soon, will figure out what's happened and call the service company again.

Of course, it'll take some time before they can get out here. It could take a half hour or so. I hope that isn't too great an inconvenience—"

"A half hour is no problem," I reassured him. Secretly, I wasn't terribly disappointed, being shut in an elevator with Tristan Stark.

"Good."

Silence.

It would seem Tristan Stark wasn't the type to make small talk, so I decided to get things rolling. "Estefan seems to have a very special gift."

"His talent is evident. How was your session? He was quite pleased with your poses. He told me you are a dancer."

"*Was* a dancer," I corrected, wishing the lights hadn't cut out. It would be so much nicer, having Tristan's face to look at as we talked, rather than thick black nothingness. "I haven't danced in years. The session was good, thanks." I added, for some reason, "My first."

"You've never modeled before?"

"No." I felt myself blushing yet again. I felt like he was expecting an explanation. Why, I couldn't say. "My roommate and I are graduating, moving into our first apartment. We saw the ad in the paper. The pay was pretty good."

"Graduating?"

"Barnard College. Accounting."

"Hmm."

"Summa cum laude," I added. Why did I feel this overwhelming need to impress this man? He probably could care less what I studied, or how well I'd done.

"Interesting, accounting. Do you have a résumé?"

"I do. At home." Would I get a job referral out of this situation? Wouldn't that be great?

He said, "If you're looking for a position, I might know someone who is hiring. I could pass your résumé on to him."

"That would be great. Thanks."

"Then again"—his voice sounded different, a little looser—"Estefan would probably kill me, for stealing you away from him."

"I promise, I won't tell if you won't."

The lights flickered then illuminated, and my gaze jerked up to the lights then dropped to Tristan as the car jerked then started, once again, its downward descent. He was sitting on the floor next to me, very close. And his expression was much more relaxed and friendly than it had been when I first stepped into the car.

He pushed to his feet faster than I did, offering a helping hand as he straightened. I accepted. Our eyes met, and a jolt of heat blazed through me. It didn't take me entirely by surprise.

"Thank you," I said. "This has been the most pleasant elevator stranding of my life." I didn't mention the fact that it had been the only elevator stranding of my life.

His eyes glittered a little as he chuckled. "Mine too."

At the ground floor, the door slid open. He motioned for me to exit first. I stepped out into the lobby, a warm sensation vibrating up and down my spine. For some reason, I felt as if he were watching me. I glanced over my shoulder.

Our eyes met.

He had been watching me.

Inside, I gave a silent *whoop*. Outside, I smiled, waved. He acknowledged me with a slight nod.

I called Jenn the minute I was outside the building.

"That was a long time!" she practically screeched. "Don't ever do that to me again! I called you five times. Five."

"Easy, Mom," I joked as I strolled to my car. "I got stuck in the elevator on the way out."

"Oh. That sucks! You were stuck in an elevator? For how long?"

"I don't know. Five, ten minutes maybe. It wasn't such a bad thing. I'll tell you all about it when I get home." About halfway to my car, I glanced over my shoulder, wondering if he was still watching me. Somewhere, in there. Maybe through those windows there, the ones that were tinted.

"Oooh! What happened? You have to tell me now. That's just mean, making me wait."

I laughed. Having reached my car, I remoted open the door locks. "You are such a child sometimes." I could visualize her pouting right now, arms folded over her chest.

"Am not," she snapped. Then she laughed too. "I'll be waiting on pins and needles until you get home."

"Hmmm . . . You're running low on boxes. Maybe I should make a stop at—"

"Don't you dare! You come straight home, young lady."

"Okay, okay. See you soon." I clicked off, flopped into my car, and cranked the motor. The image of Tristan Stark's eyes as he'd reached for my hand flashed through my mind. My insides hopped around like scared rabbits.

Who would've thought getting stuck in an elevator could be such a thrill?

My roommate, Jennifer Nicole Wendell, aka Jenn, was sweet, and smart, and thoughtful, all good traits for a roommate to have. But one thing Jenn wasn't was patient. The second I stepped into our dorm room, she assaulted me with at least a dozen questions.

What happened?

Are you okay?

Did someone offer you a job?

Did you go through with the modeling?

Why aren't you saying anything?

Probably grinning like a complete dork, I stood mute, waiting for the verbal onslaught to stop. It didn't take Jenn long to get the message.

"Fine. I get the hint." She paused. "I'm being quiet so you can talk."

"Hmmm. Which question should I answer first?"

My roommate visibly bit her tongue. Her neck turned an interesting shade of pink.

I couldn't help laughing. "Okay, I've tortured you enough." We made ourselves comfortable on our little couch, sitting under the massive wood loft we'd built to hold our beds. I hugged a pillow to my chest. Jenn mirrored me. "I met someone."

Jenn's eyes bugged. "When?"

"After I finished with Estefan—who, by the way, has the most adorable accent ever—"

"I know! So sexy, isn't he?" Jenn's eyes sparkled. I'd seen those sparkles before. She was attracted to Estefan.

I hadn't thought he was sexy. But if Jenn thought so, who was I to argue?

"Sure, he is," I said. "Anyway, after I was finished, I met a man named Tristan Stark in the hallway outside of Estefan's loft. He's Estefan's host, discovered him in Rio de Janeiro, and has been helping him get started here in the States. There's something about him. He's really good-looking. Like, model good-looking. And . . . intense. He makes me a little nervous. We got in the elevator together and all of a sudden it stopped and the lights cut off."

"Oh God." Jenn leaned forward. "What happened? Did he kiss you?"

My cheeks got a little warm as I imagined him leaning in, brushing those oh-so-perfect lips of his over mine. "No, he didn't kiss me."

"Did he touch you? Or ask you out?"

"Um, no. Nothing like . . . *that*. We talked."

"Talked?" Her voice was flat.

"About school, about my résumé, which I need to send him."

"So he's helping you find a job?" At my nod, she said, "Ooookay." Clearly, she'd expected to hear something else.

"Yes, I think he is helping me find a job. But, even though it doesn't sound like it, I felt like we made some kind of connection. On a deeper level."

Jenn shook her head. "Honey, that's what you said about Ryan Maroney."

I had said that about Ryan Maroney. And I'd been wrong. The connection I'd felt only went one way. But now I could see the difference. I'd wasted so much time chasing a man who had absolutely no interest in dating me. Over two years. "This time, I'm right."

"Did this Tristan guy ask for your number?"

"No."

"Did he ask you to get in touch with him?"

"No. Well, except to say I could give him my résumé and he'd pass it on."

Jenn lifted one you-see-what-I'm-getting-at brow.

"It was the way he looked at me," I reasoned. "It wasn't a friendly look. It wasn't an I'll-pass-on-your-résumé look either. It was an I-want-you look."

Jenn pursed her lips. "Okay, if you think so, then who am I to say it isn't true? I wasn't there. How did the modeling session go?"

Relief. I was glad to have the inquisition over. "Good, I guess. Estefan asked me to model for a special project. And it pays more."

"Awesome!" Jenn gave me a quick hug. "See, didn't I tell you it wasn't so bad?"

"You were right. Though I kind of slowly worked up to going completely nude. And then I avoided looking at Estefan to keep from dying of humiliation. At least the time went pretty quickly."

My cell phone rang, and I checked the screen. "Speak of the devil." I answered, "Hello, Estefan."

"Hello, Alice. I'm calling to ask you a question."

"Sure, shoot."

Jenn gave me a what-does-he-want look, and I shrugged.

"You remember Tristan Stark, the man who came into the loft during our session?"

My cheeks started burning. "Sure."

"He called me, asking for your phone number and address. I thought I'd better ask your permission first before giving it to him."

"Oh, it's fine. Thanks! He's helping me find a job. A permanent job. Don't worry, I'll still work with you on your special project."

"Thank you. That's all I needed to know. As far as the next session goes, how about Thursday?"

"Thursday's fine. See you then."

"Bye."

I clicked off, gave Jenn a smug grin. "Estefan asked if he could give Tristan Stark my phone number."

Jenn lifted both brows this time. "Okay. We'll see what happens next. Just do me a favor. Don't let this guy hurt you."

"I promise, I won't. I have my eyes wide open, and I've packed away the rose-colored glasses for good."

3

The limo pulled up in front of our dorm building at exactly 6 P.M. on Saturday night, the exact time, to the minute, that Tristan had said he would pick me up for our dinner. As it turned out, the phone call hadn't gone exactly as I had expected. While the purpose for our meeting was still professional—I was going to give him a handful of copies of my résumé—he'd suggested we have dinner too. I was all too happy to have a chance to spend some one-on-one time with the fascinating man in a place that was fully illuminated.

Jenn was standing at the window, hopping up and down. "It's Tristan, the billionaire. He sent a limo. This is a date, Alice! You were right."

"I told you so." Extremely nervous—Tristan was so out of my league—I ignored Jenn's squeals and Ohmygods and paced back and forth until there was a knock on our door.

"Have fun!" Jenn gave me a bouncy hug and I headed for the door, opened it.

It wasn't Tristan Stark.

It was a man I'd never seen before. He was wearing a black suit, white shirt, and tie.

"Hello, my name is Dave. I've come to pick up Miss Barlow," Dave said, his mien very formal.

I wasn't sure how I felt about Tristan sending a lackey to pick me up. He hadn't come himself? Why not? Too busy? I glanced over his shoulder, thinking maybe Tristan was waiting in the hallway. No deal.

"Okay." Feeling a little let down, I sent Jenn a tense look over my shoulder.

She shrugged.

My expectations for the evening dimmed slightly, I looped my purse over my shoulder, waved good-bye to my roommate, and followed Dave down to the waiting car. Again, I looked for Tristan as I ducked inside.

No Tristan.

"Mr. Stark apologizes for not coming to pick you up personally. He was delayed and felt it was better to send a car to pick you up, rather than be late."

"I see." I made myself comfy, watching all the students' curious stares as the driver started the car and pulled away from the building. Minutes later, we were motoring down the freeway, headed in the opposite direction from where I'd anticipated. "Where are we going?"

"The airport."

"Airport?" I echoed. I had been expecting dinner at an expensive restaurant in town. Not a trip in an airplane. I called Jenn to let her know what was going on. She seemed a little quiet. I took that to mean she was nervous. I promised I'd call her later and let her know I was okay.

I clicked off and watched the scenery roll by as the car zoomed along I-94. We pulled up to a small airport out in the middle of cornfields somewhere in the outskirts of Ann Arbor.

The limo parked in front of a metal building, next to a tiny airplane that maybe carried two to four people.

Was Tristan really expecting me to get into that thing?

My heart started pounding.

The car's door swung open, and there was Tristan, offering a hand out.

"I apologize for not picking you up," he said, "but I had to handle a situation, and I didn't want to delay our flight."

I accepted his hand, and a little tingle swept through me. "Just tell me the 'situation' had nothing to do with that plane."

He chuckled. His eyes sparkled when he laughed. I liked his sparkles. "It had nothing to do with the plane. Come, let me show you. It's perfectly safe. My pilot has logged thousands of hours of flight time, both during daylight hours and at night."

His pilot. His freaking pilot.

This man was miles out of my league. Make that light-years.

"Is that a lot?" I asked, feeling a little stupid.

"It is. Which is why I hired him. He is a retired naval pilot."

"Okay." I accepted Tristan's help up into the tiny plane. While the pilot did his preflight checks, we buckled ourselves into our seats. I said a prayer.

"Okay, sir," the pilot said. He looked pretty young to be retired from anything. "We're clear for takeoff."

Tristan looked at me.

I tried to smile. The only good thing about this situation was my empty stomach. I'd been too nervous to eat lunch, and that was before finding out I would be taking a toy airplane to some unknown destination.

His brows furrowed. He took my hand. "It's a short flight. Have you flown before?"

"Never. Not even on a big jet."

"You're in for a treat, then."

The little plane bumped and rolled up to the end of the runway. The engine cranked up and we started to go faster, faster.

I squeezed my eyes shut and tried not to say or do anything embarrassing. I think I might have crushed Tristan's hand a little when I felt the wheels lift off the ground. And I know I did when we zoomed straight up into the sky. Then the plane tipped to the side, turning. For a minute, I became dizzy. It felt like I was on a carnival ride. I breathed slowly.

He leaned in to me. That was the only thing about the flight, so far, that I liked. We were close. Really close. "Are you okay?"

"Fine," I muttered.

Thankfully, we straightened out and if we were climbing higher it wasn't on such a steep angle. I heard myself sigh with relief. Then I looked out the window. Mistake. Once again, I squeezed Tristan's hand. "Tell me, Tristan, what do you like to do in your free time?" I asked, anxious for a distraction as I jerked my gaze toward him.

"I enjoy mountain climbing," he said. "Being outdoors, breathing fresh air. I feel alive." His expression reflected his words, and for a moment, I didn't care about the fact that we were miles above the ground and could crash to our death. I was drawn in, captivated. "Have you ever been?"

Me? Mountain climbing? That was funny. "The closest I've been to a mountain is an indoor rock-climbing wall."

"Maybe someday you'll go with me."

Was that an invitation? My heart did a little hop in my chest. "Maybe."

"I plan one trip a year," he said. His thumb skimmed back and forth over the back of my hand. It was a little touch, but wow, what an impact it had. My face was getting warm. Other parts too. "I go to a different location each time. Last year, it was Mount Tai, in China, one of China's Five Great Mountains. It was an experience of a lifetime, even though one climbs a staircase, rather than the natural face of the mountain."

"That must've been one heck of a long staircase," I said,

studying his features. His face was so perfect, right down to the little mole on his cheekbone. Eyes, and the thick, dark eyelashes framing them. Nose, straight and perfectly proportioned for his face. Lips.

Oh, those lips.

". . . over seven thousand steps . . ." He was talking about something, but I was mesmerized, captivated, not hearing much of anything.

I tried to shake myself out of my stupor. *Focus, you twit. A man like this expects a woman to be intelligent, well-spoken.* "Seven thousand steps. I can't imagine."

He continued, "There are temples along the way. I've never seen anything like it."

"Sounds fascinating." Of course, I was much more fascinated by the man sitting next to me, holding my hand.

"It was." His voice sounded a little less jubilant. I wondered why.

"You sound . . . sad."

"I'm not. I'm just . . ." He stared at me long and hard. "I went alone. I do a lot of things alone. There was a time when I believed that was best. But maybe not anymore."

What was he trying to tell me?

I had no idea how to respond. Was this billionaire, who owned so much, who had limos and private planes and Daves at his fingertips . . . lonely?

"Where are you going this year?" I asked.

"I haven't decided yet."

I didn't know anything about mountains. I couldn't make any suggestions. So, instead of giving some lame response, I said, "You seem very passionate about climbing. I'm sure it will be somewhere wonderful."

His gaze sharpened. It almost felt like he was trying to look inside me, to read my mind. "I'm sure it will. Tell me, Alice, do you have a passion?"

"A passion?" I repeated. "No, I don't think so. I enjoy dancing. I took ballet for many years."

"Dance." Some kind of expression flashed on his face for a moment, and then poof, it was gone. "You danced for years, and yet you don't consider it a passion?"

"No. I don't dance anymore."

"Why not?"

"I didn't love it enough to make it my life. And I wasn't committed, nor great enough to dance in a professional ballet company. And if you look outside of ballet, there aren't many jobs for professional dancers, at least not ones that allow you to keep your clothes on."

I swear, his gaze flicked south for the briefest moment, to my nonexistent chest. Yes, if I'd had any aspirations of being a Vegas showgirl, I would have had to pay for some boobs. Clearly, my super-duper Victoria's Secret push-up bra wasn't hiding that fact.

"I understand."

"Thus, I accepted the scholarship from Barnard and entered their accounting program. I had thought about continuing lessons while I was in school, but juggling both school and dance, both time-wise and financially, wasn't working. I had to give one up."

"What about now? You've graduated."

"I'm not graduated yet. But I am finished with classes. My graduation is in a week and a half."

His smile made my insides hop around. "Then you have a reason to celebrate."

"I do."

"We shall celebrate." He leaned closer, cupped my cheek. His thumb grazed my cheekbone. "I'd like to make a confession."

"What confession?" I asked, my gaze locked to his. I was breathless. Was he going to kiss me?

"Being trapped in the elevator was no accident."

"What do you mean, no accident? Did you stop it?"

"I did."

My heart jerked in my chest.

Nobody had ever gone to such extreme measures to spend time alone with me. It was romantic, straight out of a movie. And yet it was also slightly scary. Almost stalker-ish.

"Why did you do that?" I asked.

"I needed to talk to you, to find out if you were really as fascinating on the inside as you were on the outside."

Fascinating? He thought I was fascinating?

"And . . . ?"

He leaned closer still, and my eyelids fluttered shut. Just before they closed completely, I saw something dark flash in his eyes. Raw male hunger. His lips grazed mine, barely touching them. Little tremors quaked through my whole body.

When he didn't kiss me again, I opened my eyes.

He was still holding my face, looking at me. "Does that answer your question?"

"Not really. I think you might need to try again, and this time make your point a little clearer."

"Hmm." His gaze flicked to the pilot, sitting in front of us. His hand inched down the side of my face, his thumb stroking my bottom lip. "Later. We'll be at our destination soon." His voice was low, husky, and full of carnal need.

A quiver shimmied up my spine. There was no doubt where this was going. And I was excited and nervous, both. To think my first time doing . . . *it* . . . might be with a man like Tristan Stark. A powerful, rich, mysterious man who owned a private plane and traveled the world, climbing mountains and rescuing starving artists from third-world countries. I wondered if I was dreaming.

I must have been smiling to myself. Tristan squeezed my hand and leaned over to whisper, "What are you thinking about, little Alice? What's making you smile?"

I turned to him. "It's a secret."

His laugh made every nerve in my body rejoice.

I learned fairly soon after that that landing was not as harrowing as taking off. Nevertheless, I was extremely glad to have my feet back on solid ground. I immediately dismissed the notion of someday becoming a flight attendant. Wouldn't happen.

Not long after we landed, we were whisked away in another limousine, driven down a winding, hilly road, flanked by thick forest. Tristan made the time go by quickly, asking me questions about myself, my friends, my family. When we finally reached our destination, a gorgeous house hidden on a deep, wooded patch of land, I felt he knew just about everything there was to know . . . and then some. Me, I knew far less about him. Whenever I asked a question, he managed, somehow, to turn things around, and get me to talk instead.

He was a sneaky, clever man.

As the car rolled to a stop, Tristan said, "This is where I come when I need to get away. My sanctuary." He helped me out of the car. I'd never been so thankful to be on solid ground. And when we walked up to the house, he opened the front door for me too, stepping to the side so I could enter first.

Such a gentleman. I'd never been treated better.

The house's interior was unbelievably gorgeous, of course. The entry opened directly to a wide great room with soaring, vaulted ceilings. The floor was polished dark wood, almost black. The walls were crisp white. And the furnishings were a blend of new and old, rustic and sleekly modern. There were metal accents here and there. Steel light fixtures hung from the beamed ceiling; metal legs on tables; some metal boxes sat on the shelves flanking the huge stone fireplace.

I was in awe.

If someone had told me a few weeks ago that I would go on

a date with a man like Tristan, to a place like this, I would have laughed hysterically. I was still having a hard time believing it was all real.

"Dinner is ready. Are you hungry?" Tristan led me toward a door exiting out onto a huge covered deck. A table was set for us, drinks poured. But my gaze didn't linger on the table long, not when there was something far more amazing to look at just beyond it.

A lake. Still, blue waters glistening in the sun.

"Wow," I said. "What a view." A hawk swooped down, landing on what appeared to be a perch for it standing no more than ten feet from the end of the deck. "Is that . . . your pet?"

"I'd say, I'm more his pet," Tristan said, amusement making his voice light. "He comes to me when he wants something." Tristan lifted the cover off one of the plates, pulled a little bit of meat off, and, after donning a thick leather glove, offered the morsel to the raptor. It snatched it, consumed it in one swallow, sharp bird eyes staring at me.

If it was expecting me to do that, it was going to be disappointed.

"I think he's still hungry," I pointed out.

"No, he's just spoiled." Tristan pulled off the glove, returned it to its place, and pulled out a chair for me. "Please, sit."

I sat, thanking him when he pushed in my chair. I went for a drink first. It was wine. Very good wine. I didn't drink alcohol often, so I knew I didn't want to overdo it. I sipped again, and the cool, fruity liquid slid down my throat. That was delicious. It would be so easy to drink too much. I took another sip. Smooth.

My gaze traveled from Tristan's handsome face to the lake and back again. "This has been quite an adventure. I wasn't expecting something so extravagant. More, a nice dinner at a restaurant."

"I prefer privacy."

"I understand." At that statement, an alarm sounded in my head.

After a bad experience my freshman year, I'd become somewhat paranoid, suspecting every older man who showed an interest in me was married, looking for clues. Tristan was most definitely older than me. But up until now, I hadn't felt any reason to suspect he might be married. Now that I thought about it, that would be a good reason to throw me in a plane and fly me far, far away from home.

When he lifted his wineglass—he was a lefty—I checked his ring finger. No ring. No tan line.

"I'm not married. I'm just a private person." He looked at me over the rim of his glass.

My cheeks heated. Really, had I been that obvious? "A friend of mine was dating a man for a while, for almost four months. It got pretty serious. Or so she thought. She was expecting a wedding proposal down the road. Until she found out her boyfriend was already married. And his wife was pregnant."

"I'm sorry." He set down his glass, still studying me with those dark, sharp eyes of his. "Was he your first love?"

I blinked, trying to decide if I should even try to deny the truth. No, what point was there? Sure, it would make me look like an idiot, having failed to see the signs right away that Brad was married. But maybe that was okay. I'd never told anyone what really happened between Brad and me. Not even Jenn. I was too ashamed. Perhaps it was time to let it go. "He was." I quickly decided to try Tristan's tactic. "What about you? Who was your first love?"

"I haven't found my first love yet."

I wasn't sure how I felt about that. Tristan was at least five years older than me. If I had to guess, I'd say he was around thirty. How was it he hadn't fallen in love at least once in thirty years?

Was he that unattainable? Did he have commitment issues? Did he have intimacy issues?

"Like I said on the plane, I've primarily focused on my work." He lifted the cover off his plate and motioned for me to do the same. As he speared a potato with his fork, he added, "What relationships I have pursued, I've kept casual. No strings. No entanglements. No complications. My life is already fairly complicated."

As if he'd planned it—to illustrate his point—his phone rang. He pulled it from his pocket, checked the screen, apologized, and left the table.

That left me and the hawk sitting out there, for maybe twenty minutes. By the time he'd returned, I'd eaten as much of my dinner as I wanted and was ready to do something besides sit on the deck and stare at the lake.

He returned, apologizing profusely. His eyes flicked to my plate, which was covered once again. "Have you had enough to eat?"

"I'm finished." I patted my stomach. "That was a lot of food. Delicious, though."

"I'm through as well. Come, let's go for a walk." He took my hand, led me across the deck and down some steps to a path. It hooked to the left, cutting through a small patch of forest before ending at a private sandy beach.

I inhaled, smelling lush green life and dirt and water. "If I owned this property, I don't think I'd ever want to leave."

"I don't ever want to leave." He released my hand, angled himself to study me.

I felt his gaze on me as I kicked off my shoes. It had been a long time since I'd felt sand under my bare feet. Warm. Heaven. I padded down to the water's edge. It was colder than I expected. I did a little hop, then spun around as I heard a low chuckle.

"You move like a dancer." He said that as though it was the most amazing thing he'd ever seen.

I took it as a compliment. "Thank you."

He offered both hands, and I took them. Then he pulled me close, closer until my body was almost touching his. "I want to kiss you right now. I haven't stopped thinking about it since we got off the plane."

Then what was he waiting for? "Kiss me."

Something flashed in his eyes again. Hard male hunger, perhaps. Whatever it was, it made my body tingle all over. "If I kiss you, I won't stop there."

"What are you trying to say?"

His palm slid up my arm, up to my neck. Higher. His fingers curled into a fist, catching my hair. He gently pulled, easing my head closer to his. My insides did somersaults. When his mouth finally found mine, I actually moaned. His lips were soft, moist. His kiss was patient, an exploration. I explored too, slipping my tongue into his mouth, tasting him. A warmth flooded my body, and a pulsing need pounded between my legs.

I wanted Tristan Stark to be my first. I wanted him so badly, even though I knew he would probably break my heart. At the moment, I didn't care. All I could think about was how I felt as his tongue glided along mine, caressing me intimately, how thrilled I felt to be held in place, unable to move my head.

All too soon, he ended the kiss. His lids were heavy. His mouth was still close, temptation like I'd never known.

"Kiss me again, please," I whispered.

"Not yet." Still holding one of my hands, he turned, leading me back up the path, toward the house. "Let's go inside."

My legs were a little wobbly as I followed his lead. We went up the steps, across the deck—our dirty dishes were gone—back into the house, down a hallway.

We stopped at a closed door.

4

Tristan didn't open the door right away. He seemed to be hesitating. I wondered why. It couldn't be that he was embarrassed. What was there to be embarrassed about? Was he having second thoughts? Was he thinking I didn't want to have sex with him?

I was assuming the room on the other side of that door was a bedroom. I smiled, making it clear I had some notion what was about to happen, and I was happy about it.

Holding the doorknob, he leveled a serious look at me. "I need to show you something now. Before I open this door, I want to make it clear you are free to leave whenever you want."

"O-okay." Why the speech?

He gave me one final lust-filled look, then twisted the knob and pushed. Instead of going in, he moved to the side, allowing me to enter first. Reaching around my shoulder, he flipped a light switch and the room filled with soft light.

I took two steps in and stopped. My gaze meandered around the room, the walls papered with an elegant damask in shades of gray. Against one wall was a big wooden *X*, chains ending in cuffs bolted to the top and bottom of each end of the boards. In the center stood a huge wood table. Above the table—which I assumed was not meant for dining—hung the most beautiful crystal chandelier I'd ever seen. The twinkling light flickering off the crystals reflected on the glossy table's top. Against one side wall was a large armoire. And the other was a thing that looked kind of like the kneeler I remembered from my grandmother's Catholic church.

Overall, the room was both exotic and scary at the same time. I wasn't sure I wanted to know what happened in there.

"Do you know anything about domination and submission?" Tristan asked. He was standing a small distance away, watching me closely.

"Um, no. Nothing." I wasn't sure I wanted to know anything about domination and submission. My gaze flicked from one thing to another. Could I imagine myself in this room? Would I enjoy it?

My stomach knotted. My palms were sweating. I dragged them down the sides of my legs.

"When we were kissing outside, you wanted more," he said.

"I . . . yes, I did."

"This is what comes with 'more.'" He stepped a little closer. "I don't have sex, Alice. I don't make love. I play. I explore my submissive's limits, find that thin line between pleasure and pain, ecstasy and torture."

This explained why he'd never been "in love." "I never . . . would have guessed you . . . this . . ."

He stepped closer still. "Would you like to leave now, Alice? Have you seen enough? Or do you still want more?"

Did I?

My heart thudded against my breastbone and I felt a little disoriented, a little like Lewis Carroll's Alice when she'd fallen down the rabbit hole. "I . . . don't know."

A muscle in his jaw tensed for a brief moment. "I'll call for the car." He turned, heading back down the hallway.

That was it.

Our date was over.

He had shut down because I couldn't accept him, or rather, couldn't accept what he did in that room.

That was probably a good thing.

It was over.

I'd probably never see him again, never feel that secret thrill as he held my hand, never taste his kiss again.

It was over.

I'd never feel the pain of being paddled or whipped.

It was over.

And I was . . . conflicted.

Even now, my skin tingled where he'd touched me. And a pulsing throb ached between my legs. But I was scared. I didn't know what it felt like to make love, let alone fuck. This was way more than I was ready for. I knew it.

But something made me cry out, "Wait!"

Tristan stopped, turned. "You don't have to—"

"I know. It's just that I'm . . . this is so embarrassing."

"What is it, Alice?" His voice was softer now, inspiring me to trust him. As he came toward me again, his gait was smooth. He moved like a big jungle cat, every motion fluid.

"It's not just that I don't know about those kinds of things, bondage, or whatever it's called." I swallowed hard. There was something in my throat. And that something was huge. "I'm a virgin. I don't know *anything*."

He didn't respond right away. He was studying me, silent. Finally, he murmured, "I should take you home."

That was probably true. But I didn't want to go home yet. I wanted to understand this man, wanted to know him better. I wanted him to kiss me again, to hold me too. "Why do you do it?"

"It's hard to explain. It gives me great pleasure, having someone lay her trust at my feet and open herself up to me."

That big lump was still stuck in my throat. I think it was even bigger now. "I want to put my trust in your hands."

"You don't."

"Yes, I do. I've never felt the way you make me feel. I'm scared and excited all at the same time. I think I shouldn't want the things I want, but something inside me tells me to go for it anyway." I wrapped my arms around myself. My hands were shaking. They were shaking a lot. But that didn't change what I was saying or make it any less true. "And when you kiss me I melt inside."

He groaned, pulled me to him, enveloped me in his arms. He kissed the top of my head. "I melt inside too."

I reached up, traced the line of his jaw with a fingertip. "You're so beautiful and deadly at the same time. Like your hawk."

Dark hunger flashed across his face. "I could say the same thing about you." He palmed my cheek, glanced my lower lip with his thumb. Taking a gamble, I slid my tongue out, flicking it over his skin. He pressed his thumb between my lips, and I suckled. At the carnal hunger I saw in his eyes, my insides throbbed. My pussy clenched.

God help me, I wanted this man to make love to me. And then I wanted him to fuck me. I ached for him to show me the darkest side of himself.

"Tristan." I shuddered.

He pulled his hand away, released me, took one, two, three steps away. Inside, I shouted *no*. Outside, I stood mute and watched him.

He glanced over his shoulder, took one look at me, charged back to me, hauled me against him, and kissed me. His tongue shoved into my mouth, stroked, tasted, took. I trembled and gasped and moaned. Tiny flares were igniting everywhere. My

skin tingled. My nerves zapped. A rising tide of heat was building inside. Growing bigger with every stroke of his tongue.

When he broke the kiss, I whimpered. Would he walk away
again? *Please don't turn away. Please.*

"Dammit," he mumbled. His gaze slid down, to the vee of
my blouse. He placed one fingertip at the base of my throat, in
that little dip in the center. "You are so beautiful. I can picture
you lying on my table, writhing with need, begging for me to
take you."

I could picture that too. I kind of liked it.

"You don't have to protect me. I'm not a child. I'm a
woman." Aware my hand was trembling a little, I placed it over
his and pushed, moving it down the center of my chest. My
eyes remained locked to his. I wanted him to know I was serious, that I wanted what the heat in his eyes promised. I wasn't
completely afraid.

Down his hand traveled, between my breasts, lower, over
my stomach, farther, to the throbbing heat between my thighs.
I forced his hand down, made him cup my sex. The pressure
felt so good, so right.

A little moan slipped out.

He growled, low, like an animal's warning. I was playing
with something very dangerous. That only made my need that
much greater.

"There are rules," he said, his voice breathy, husky.

"Teach me."

"I've never had a virgin."

"Take me." I tipped my hips, pushing my burning tissues
against the hand that was still there. "I trust you."

Tristan took one, two deep breaths, mumbled something I
couldn't make out, then kissed me. This kiss was wild, a plundering. His tongue shoved into my mouth, filling it with decadent flavor. His hand rubbed back and forth against my crotch,
and spirals of tingling heat pulsed through my center, curling,

swirling. His other hand clamped over my breast, squeezing hard.

I was instantly a tight, trembling, whimpering mess of desperation. I'd never had anything in *there,* deep inside me, but I sure wanted something now. Stroking deep and hard. My body knew what it needed.

The kiss ended abruptly. Tristan took my hand, pulled me away from the room with the table and chains. Had he changed his mind? Was he sending me away?

"Tristan, please."

He walked down the hall to the closed door at the end, threw it open.

A bedroom. A gorgeous bedroom with an enormous bed.

He was taking me to his room.

He circled the small sofa positioned at the end of the bed, hauling me with him. We stopped. I was breathless. He was breathless.

"Dammit," he cursed.

"What's wrong?" I asked between little gasps.

"Nothing. I'm just . . . not prepared for this." He was looking at the nightstands.

"What do you mean?"

"Condoms. I keep them in the playroom."

"I brought some." I shook my shoulder bag.

"You . . . ? You brought condoms?"

I nodded. "I was hoping . . ." Blushing profusely, I set my purse on the bed.

He slid an arm around my waist and pulled me flush against him. At the feel of a hard bulge pressing against my stomach, my heart started trying to hammer its way through my breastbone. With his free hand, he cupped the back of my head. His fingers clenched a fist full of my hair. He pulled, forcing my head to tip to one side. "You're so beautiful. So innocent."

"Soon to be not so innocent," I mumbled.

Inside, my body tightened, blood gathered between my legs, creating the naughtiest tingling. I couldn't help tipping my hips back and forth in time to the steady beat pulsing in my flesh.

He nipped my neck, and little blades of stinging pleasure cut through me, making me gasp. My spine arched and my breasts smashed against his hard body. How I loved the way he touched me. Rough, but at the same time gentle. It was as if he knew exactly what I wanted, what I needed.

"If I make love to you today, it will be the first time for both of us," he murmured against my neck. A shudder of need crashed through me. I hooked my fingers, dragging them down his arms. My nails slipped along the crisp material of his shirt.

"I need you," I said.

"I'll go as slow as I can." He slipped his hands down my sides. Finding the bottom of my top, he pushed the material up, over my stomach, my chest, and finally over my head. I was still wearing my skirt, panties, and a black lace bra I'd bought just for tonight. All I could think about was getting them off. I tried to reach around my back and unhook the bra.

"No." His tone was sharp.

I dropped my hands.

He walked, his body forcing me back. My butt hit the wall, and in a second, I was smashed between it and Tristan's rock-hard body. "Arms up, over your head."

My heart did a few flip-flops as I did what I was told.

He clamped a hand around both of my wrists, holding them in place. "Yes, that's the way." He forced his knee between my legs, using his foot to kick my feet apart. "Hmmm."

Hmmm was right.

Still holding my arms in place, he tipped his head down to tease my nipple through my bra. The material did nothing to diminish the torment. He laved and nipped and suckled while his hand slipped under my skirt to finger the wet tissues between my legs.

"You're so wet."

I wasn't just wet. I was on the verge of collapsing. My heart was pounding so hard it almost hurt. My pussy was burning. I was breathless and dizzy. When, oh when would he take away the aching need?

"Please, Tristan." I swallowed a sob.

His fingers found their way under the cotton crotch of my panties. His fingernails grazed my nether lips. Instinct made me slide my feet wider, tip my hips forward. I wanted him to touch me deeper, to stroke where the burning was the worst.

"Is this what you want, baby?" A finger dipped between my labia.

It wasn't deep enough. It wasn't wide enough.

"More. Please."

"You ask so sweetly, Alice." His finger inched deeper, almost deep enough.

I quaked. I pulled on my arms, wanting to wrap them around his neck. I couldn't.

"No, you like it like this. You want me to take control."

He was right. I hadn't realized until now what all my secret fantasies had meant. I didn't know the term, but I craved this, a strong, powerful man taking control, touching and stroking and tormenting me. While I writhed and begged and pleaded. Yes, oh yes.

He added a second finger and my knees nearly gave out. He scissored his fingers, stretching my tight tissues. It hurt but it also felt so good. The little burn only amplified all the other intoxicating sensations pummeling my system.

The scent of his skin and my own need.

The pounding of my heart in my ears.

The sound of my sighs and whimpers.

And the taste of his lips still lingering on mine.

I couldn't take it anymore. The heat was unbearable. The need excruciating. "Tristan, please."

His finger left my pussy. His other hand released my wrists. "Come here." He led me to the bed. But before he let me lie down, he pulled off all my clothes. I stood completely nude before him, waiting and watching as his gaze wandered up and down my body. My skin tingled wherever he looked. As if I could literally feel his gaze. "You are beautiful. Perfect. It's no wonder Estefan can't stop talking about you."

"He can't?"

"No. He says your musculature is perfect. I see far more than your musculature."

"You do?" I was getting dizzy and giddy.

"I do. Like these sweet little nipples. They're the color of my favorite fruit. And my mouth waters when I look at them." He flicked one with a fingertip, and a sharp blade of need sliced through me. My legs started trembling. "And that ass." Using his hands, he turned me around. "Round and firm and smooth. I can't wait to see it pink from my spanking. To see your cunt glistening with your juices."

Oh God. Would he please stop talking? I bent over, placing my hands on the mattress. Would the sight of that inspire him to finally do something, rather than just talk about it?

"Hmmm. I like that. Move your feet wider apart."

I did as he asked. And I was rewarded with more strokes to my pussy. His fingertip circled 'round and 'round on top of my clit, and with each little circle, my body tensed more. I'd touched myself like that before. I knew it felt good. But it had never felt this good.

I felt like my body was soaring toward some unknown pinnacle. Hotter. Tighter. My need swelled. He pushed two fingers inside me, and something inside me snapped. A huge tsunami of erotic heat crashed through me, and it felt like every nerve in my body had fired. I was tingling all over, my inside muscles spasming around his fingers. My head was spinning too. I let it fall forward and rode wave upon wave of intense pleasure.

"Yes, that's it, Alice. You come so pretty for me."

I'd orgasmed.

So that was what a real orgasm felt like.

The intense sensations started fading, and I was already anxious to feel it again. I reached between my legs, thinking I'd cup the bulge in Tristan's pants. But my fingers didn't find linen. They found smooth, velvety flesh stretched over a hard, thick rod.

He looped an arm around my waist and leaned down, until his chest and stomach were pressed against my sweat-slicked back. "Hmmm. Stroke me," he said against my shoulder. He nipped me when I did what he asked. "Yes, like that." His breath warmed my nape, making goose bumps erupt all over my shoulders and back. I was hot and cold, tight and relaxed. Needy and satisfied. A bundle of contradicting wants and needs and desires.

But more than anything, I needed to be filled. To be stroked inside. Deep inside.

I tightened my fist, using it in the place of my pussy. He did most of the work, using his hips to thrust in and out, in and out. Slowly, gradually, I moved my hand closer to my vagina. The tip poked at my tender flesh with each inward thrust, teasing me and making me that much more desperate to finally have him inside me.

"Okay, my precious. I can't make you wait another minute. You've been such a good girl. Lie down." He maneuvered me around, forcing me onto my back. "Condom. Now."

At last, I would have what I wanted, what I needed.

5

My legs were trembling as Tristan eased them apart. He was standing up, and I was lying on my back, my ass on the edge of the mattress. I felt as if I had a fever. I was hot and cold, burning and shaking. Desperate and a little scared.

His gaze started on my face. It was dark, full of hard male need. It didn't stay on my face for long. It wandered lower, settling on the tender flesh between my legs.

A part of me longed to clamp my thighs together, to hide that part of myself from his eyes. My muscles twitched, tightening a little. I felt his hands resisting, holding my legs.

"You're beautiful," he murmured. "I won't have you hiding from me. Not if you're mine."

I wasn't sure what he meant by that. At this point, with such overwhelming need pounding through my body with every heartbeat, I didn't care. All I knew was I needed him to fill me, to stroke away the ache.

He fingered my pussy, flicking his thumb over my clit. My spine tightened. My legs and stomach too. My hips lifted toward his hand. "It's going to hurt. I'll go as slow as I can."

"Please," I mumbled. "I hurt now."

"I know, baby." He bent over me, dragged his tongue down my slit, and I swear, I saw stars. He'd told me the torment was over. Why wasn't he keeping his word? Before I found the strength to say something to him, he straightened back up, pulled on my hips so I was even closer, and slid the head of his sheathed cock up and down my pussy lips. "Open your legs wide for me. Yes, like that." My insides clenched, my breath hitched as I did as he asked, rotating my legs open, knees pulled up. "Relax, sweet girl." He fisted his cock, holding it against my entrance. With his other hand, he drew slow, deliciously sweet circles over my clit. Oh, so good.

I felt myself relax a little, enjoying the pleasant *whoosh* of heat each circle pulsed through my body. His cock inched into my opening then stopped. I tensed again. My pussy burned, the skin stretched. I clawed at the sheet. Tears gathered in my eyes. He'd hit my hymen, was pressing against it. I could feel my body resisting his invasion. "Oh God," I heard myself say.

"It'll hurt less if I go fast."

If I didn't ache for him so badly, I might have told him to stop. In fact, I almost did anyway. I felt like my insides were being torn open. I clamped my lips and nodded.

He shoved his hips forward and searing white heat blazed through me. A fullness followed. Uncomfortable. I lifted my hips, tried to pull away. But Tristan held me in place.

"Shhh. Give it a minute. Don't move."

"Hurts."

He pulled out a little, and the fullness eased somewhat, making it more bearable. "Better?"

I nodded.

"Open your eyes."

I'd closed them? I lifted my lids. He was standing over me, bent slightly at the waist. His gaze was locked on mine, his eyes searching, full of concern. "Are you okay?"

I nodded. It seemed that was all I could do.

His cock slipped out a little more. The movement inside produced a tiny spark of pleasure.

"Oh," I said.

"Good?"

"Yes."

He withdrew until it seemed only the tip of his penis remained. He shook as he moved. His arms, his chest, his stomach muscles. A fine sheen of sweat covered his skin, glimmering in the low light. He looked incredibly sexy, almost too beautiful to be real. I could hardly believe he was here with me, this man. Why me?

A sigh slipped from my lips, and his mouth curled into a hint of a smile.

"Now, that's more like it." Holding my knees, he eased into me again, one glorious inch at a time. As he glided deep inside, he stroked me *there*, where I'd been aching to be stroked. The tiny spark grew.

"Yes," I murmured.

"That's it, relax. Take me." His head fell back. "Damn, you feel so good. So tight." Moving with nearly excruciating control, he fell into a slow rhythm of inward thrusts and retreats. In and out. My inner walls rippled around him when he plunged deep, and each time, my temperature notched up another degree or two. "Damn it, you're killing me," he grumbled.

For some reason, that made me feel empowered, extremely satisfied. Not only was he torturing me, it was going both ways. Having some notion of its effect, I concentrated on those inner muscles, deep inside. I tightened them, like a fist, around his cock. He growled. Halted.

Then he licked his index finger, set it on my clit, and began drawing those magical circles again. 'Round and 'round, while his cock slid in and out. Oh, what a delicious combination.

Within seconds, I was writhing beneath him, huge waves of erotic heat crashing over me.

"You're going to come for me. You're going to come now, before I lose control." His voice was husky, ragged.

As if my body couldn't resist his command, it began trembling. A flash of searing pleasure blazed through me, and my pussy spasmed. I heard myself cry out as intense, heart-shattering pleasure zinged up and down my nerves, from the soles of my feet to the roots of my hair.

His thrusts became rougher, but I didn't care. I was being tossed around in a sea of pleasure-pain, lost in sensation and completely surrendering to it. But when I heard him cry out my name, felt that final deep thrust, I opened my eyes, flung my arms around his neck, and pulled him against me. He shook. He huffed. He whispered sweet words in my ear. And when his climax eased, he wrapped his strong arms around me and held me tenderly as he caught his breath.

Kissing my hair, he said, "My little Alice. Sweet Alice." His weight pressed into me, making me sink into his luxuriously soft bed. I felt at complete peace, comfortable, safe, sleepy.

Sadly, he stood. Grimaced as he slowly pulled out. My skin burned. I must have winced. His gaze sharpened. "I was too rough."

"I'm okay."

He pulled off the condom, went to the bathroom. I listened to the sound of running water as I pushed myself back so my legs weren't hanging over the edge of the bed anymore. He returned within seconds, a washcloth in his hands. "Open." His hand rested on one of my knees.

I drew them apart slightly.

"Wider."

A little quiver of sensual heat rippled through me. Did I really want to go again? So soon? Did he?

"It's cold. It'll help ease the pain."

I lifted my knees and slid my feet apart, and he pressed the cloth to my tender tissues. At first, the cold was shocking. Too cold. I jumped. But he pushed it more firmly against me.

"Don't move."

I stilled. Already, I could feel the pain easing as the cold seeped in.

"Yes, that's it." Leaving the cloth in place, he climbed up on the bed, lying next to me. "Leave it there for about twenty minutes. It'll ease the swelling."

I didn't want to talk about swelling. I wanted to talk about what had just happened, about what it meant to Tristan, what would come next. Was he disappointed? Did he want to see me again? I knew he'd orgasmed. But that didn't mean anything, did it?

"Tristan?"

He was lying next to me, on his back. He pulled on my arm, coaxing me onto my side so that I was resting against him. "Hmmm?"

"Do you still want to . . . Did you still want me to become your submissive?"

He stroked my hair. "I don't want to talk about that now. If you're worried you failed in some way, you didn't."

I was glad to hear that. "O-okay."

"Rest. It's late." He gently ran his hand over my eyelids, so they closed. "Sleep."

In the darkness, I focused on the sound of his breathing. I fell asleep, cocooned in his arms.

The next morning the sound of birdsong woke me. I was vaguely aware that I was alone. I confirmed that fact when I opened my eyes. Tristan was gone.

I headed into the bathroom, took care of the necessities, including brushing my teeth with my finger and taking a long, hot shower. The shower was nothing like the one at home. It had jets shooting at me from every which way, and one of those soothing rain heads too. I stayed in there until I was all pruny and, thanks to Tristan's scrumptious-smelling shower gel, I came out smelling just like him. I wrapped myself in a fluffy towel that felt like heaven and barefooted out to the bedroom, in search of my clothes. I found them folded neatly on top of the dresser, along with my purse. Opting to go without panties, rather than wear my dirty ones, I wadded up the scrap of lace and shoved it into my handbag, then dressed and headed downstairs, following the scent of coffee like a hound trailing a rabbit. Coffee. Caffeine. That was the first order of business.

It felt like I hadn't slept. And I was sore all over, but especially between my legs. I hadn't been awake for long, and already I was looking forward to a nap.

I located the coffeepot, discovered a cup and saucer sitting next to it, along with a tray of baked goods. But Tristan was nowhere to be seen. After draining half my coffee and refilling my cup, I took my bagel and coffee and headed toward the back deck, thinking some fresh air and sunshine would help wake me up.

Juggling my breakfast in one hand, I pulled open the French door and stepped out onto the deck. As I was padding across to the table, I saw him, on the grass not far away. He was dressed in a pair of sweatpants, no shirt, and he was stretching. At least, that's what it looked like. I settled into a chair, making sure I had a good view of him. It was quite a sight, him reaching and bending and flexing like that. Could there be a more beautiful man on the earth?

I watched him for a few minutes before he realized I was there. His lips curled up into a ghost of a smile when our gazes met. I thought he'd come over to join me, but he didn't. He carried on with his workout, the movements become more strenuous, more complicated. I began to wonder if it wasn't some form of martial arts. By the time he did finally come to join me, my cup was empty, so was my plate. And his skin was coated in a sheen of sweat. I glanced at the lake behind him, thinking it might be fun to jump in.

He bent over me, cupped my chin, and lifted it. "Good morning. You're up earlier than I expected." Before I could respond, his lips were grazing mine in a kiss so soft I barely felt it. That didn't stop my heart from doing a flip-flop, though.

Even hot and sweaty, he looked good, he smelled good, and, when my tongue skimmed my bottom lip, I discovered he tasted good too. "Good morning to you too," I said, grinning up at him like a goon. "I don't sleep deeply when I'm away from home. What time is it?"

"A little after six."

No wonder I was so sleepy. "I didn't realize it was so early."

"That's okay. It gives us a little time to be together before we have to head back."

Back. Did he have to mention that? My mood soured a smidge. Only a little, though. This place was so peaceful and quiet. I didn't want to leave. "Do you have a busy day planned?"

"Work. It can't be helped."

"I understand."

"We have a couple of hours before I have to get you back home. Is there anything in particular you'd like to do?"

My gaze flicked to the lake.

"A swim?" he guessed.

"But I don't have a bathing suit."

"You don't need one." He took my hands in his, coaxed me to my feet. "My property is completely private. No one will see us." He grasped the bottom of my shirt and, not waiting for me to object, lifted it over my head. Within seconds, I was standing there completely nude. Outside. In broad daylight. I started to cross my arms over myself, but he stopped me with a soft touch and a shake of the head.

"How long will it take you to see what I see? A beautiful body that shouldn't be hidden?"

"I don't know." I was blushing. I could feel it.

He untied his pants and shucked them. "There, now we're both naked." He took my hand in his and led me down the path to the edge of the lake. "Do you swim?"

"No."

"Not at all?"

"I sink."

Hand in hand, we descended into the water. It wasn't so cold it shocked me too bad. Tristan released my hand when we stopped. The water was mid-chest depth. Not too deep that I'd drown, but deep enough for me to paddle around a little. He dove under the surface, swam away, flipped around at the floating dock bobbing on the surface not too far away, and headed back to me. I watched his sleek body glide through the water as he approached. He skimmed his hands up my legs before surfacing right in front of me. His hands continued up, over my hips to my waist. He pulled me flush to him, stared into my eyes.

"I want you. I want you like I've never wanted another woman. I don't know what it is . . ."

I liked the way he was looking at me, and how he'd said those words. Inside, my nerves were buzzing and zapping. My heart was galloping in my chest. I looped my arms around his neck. And then, just because it felt so damn good, I wrapped my legs around his waist. The friction between his hard body and my pussy just about made me melt. It did, in fact, have me seeing stars, and wishing I could slide a little lower and get that thick, hard cock of his buried deep inside me. When he cupped my ass, I thought maybe, just maybe, that would happen right there.

No such luck.

He did, however, smash his mouth against mine and kiss me like he meant it. His tongue didn't just slip inside my mouth, it shoved its way in. And it didn't merely tease me, it plundered, it tamed. The kiss was feral, out of control, and I loved every heart-slamming second of it. As soon as it ended, I was wishing for another.

He walked me toward the shore, fingers kneading my ass. "I wasn't going to do this. I shouldn't."

"Shouldn't do what?"

"How sore are you?"

"Not sore enough to stop you, if that's what you mean."

His smile turned evil. Good evil. The kind that made my insides warm up even more. "That's exactly what I meant. Okay, Alice. Let's go play."

6

My head was a little spinny when we stepped into Tristan's playroom. My palms were sweaty too. And I wasn't sure whether I'd just made the biggest mistake of my life. Would I hate this? Would it be too much? Too painful? Too intense?

I wanted, oh how I wanted, to enjoy this experience, to be whatever it was Tristan wanted me to be. Was I crazy for wanting that?

My gaze jerked from one piece of equipment to another as Tristan led me deeper into the room. We passed the kneeling thingy. And a bench thingy. And a swing thingy. We stopped at a chair. Just a plain old chair. The back was wood, carved in an intricate pattern of swirls and curves. The seat cushion was covered with black leather. It looked like an antique kitchen chair—except for the leather seat. And of all the pieces of furniture in the room, it was probably the least intimidating.

"We haven't gone through the rules yet, so I am not going to get into anything too intense. We're just going to play a little. My focus is going to be only on you, your pleasure, your needs."

That sounded good to me.

"Nervous?" He was smiling at me. It was a kind expression, not at all wicked or naughty.

"Yes, a little."

"You'll learn to trust me." He patted the seat. "Sit."

I sat, crossed one knee over the other.

He raised one brow. His lips sort of curled up on that side a bit too.

I uncrossed my legs.

"Better." Sporting a hard-on that made my mouth water, he motioned toward the armoire. "I'll be right back."

"Okay." I watched him walk across the room. The view was lovely. Firm butt, broad shoulders, narrow waist. Did they come any more perfect that that? Once again, I wondered, *Why me?* Why was I the one here with him now? I'd had a few boyfriends. They'd been attractive, sure. But nothing like Tristan. Not traffic-stopping, model-perfect gorgeous. Nor had they been as successful as Tristan. Or as powerful. Outside of the bondage thing, Tristan was my secret fantasy man, and this was as close as I'd imagined I'd ever come to having my childhood wish of being swept away by Prince Charming realized.

It was almost too good to be true.

He returned within moments. In his hands he held rubbers and lube, a wrapped oblong package, and several lengths of two-inch black satin ribbon.

Nothing looked particularly intimidating, outside of that package. It wasn't large—a little bigger than a box for a bracelet, maybe. But there was no telling what might be in it.

"First, let's get you positioned properly." He reached under the chair and something went *click*. Next thing I knew, part of the bottom opened. Now I was sitting on a chair with a big hole in the center, almost like a toilet. "Scoot a little forward." I scooted. "That's it. Now, your hands. Put them down at your sides."

I let them hang on either side of my hips and watched as Tristan tied a pretty bow around my wrists, fixing them to the rails of the chair. I admit, as I watched him, my pussy pulsed. Heat throbbed through my body. Once he finished, I tested the restraints to see how well they would hold. For not being too terribly tight, they sure did the job.

He checked each one before kneeling in front of the chair. "Now your ankles. Spread your legs."

A bigger wave of heat crashed through me. I was nervous, yes. But also breathless and tense all over, and anxious to see what would happen next. I parted my knees so that my lower legs were on the outside of the chair's front legs.

Tristan's gaze followed one leg up from the floor, halting at the juncture of my thighs, which was now fully exposed, thanks to the trapdoor underneath. "Mmmm. Perfect." Deft fingers tied pretty bows around each of my ankles. Then, he trailed a fingertip up one of my legs, following the straight line of my shin, up over my knee and around to my inner thigh. By the time it was inching closer to my pussy, I was breathing really hard. I was also shaking a little, all over.

"You are so unbelievably responsive," he murmured as he tickled that sensitive spot between my inner thigh and pussy. My back arched, tipping my pelvis up, giving him better access to the parts of me that were aching for his touch. "I can smell your need." He inhaled deeply. I did too. My breath came out in a rough huff, though. His didn't.

Wouldn't he just get this over with? Please? Finger me. Fuck me. Do something so I wouldn't be burning anymore, breathless and on the verge of begging for relief.

My thigh muscles tightened. I stretched them as wide apart as I could. "Please, Tristan."

"Please? You beg so pretty. So sweet." He grazed my nether lips with a fingernail then lifted his hand to my mouth. "Speaking of sweet. Taste." He pushed his finger into my mouth, and I flicked my tongue over it, tasting myself and him. The blended flavors were delicious. I swirled my tongue 'round and 'round, pretending it was his cock. Wishing it was his cock.

He made a growling sound.

With lips pursed around his invading finger, I giggled.

"You're good at that."

I'd had plenty of practice. If a girl wanted to keep her virginity, she had to be creative. Before last night, I'd never had sex, but I'd done other things.

He stood, pulled his finger out of my mouth, and instead fondled my breasts, caressing them, weighing them, pinching and tugging on my nipples. Little blades of carnal heat pricked me as he pinched harder. My pussy burned hotter. All I could think about was having Tristan's hard cock crammed inside of me, stroking away this terrible, glorious need.

He stepped closer, legs straddling my hips. His cock was at roughly face level. The chair I suddenly realized, sat lower to the ground than normal. A droplet of precome shimmered on the very tip. "Suck me." Without waiting for me to respond, he fisted the base of his penis and thrust his hips forward. The tip of him shoved into my mouth. I tightened my lips, forming a ring around the swollen head, and flicked my tongue up and down, up and down. "Oh yes." He grabbed hold of my hair, using it to anchor my head in place. Slowly, he moved, forcing his cock deeper into my mouth. I flattened my tongue, a cushion for his cock as it filled more and more of my mouth.

"Damn, how much can you take?" he asked, pulling his hips back until the head popped out of my mouth.

"All of it."

"All?" His eyes narrowed for a moment. Then that wicked smile I'd come to like so much returned. "Let's just see about that." Once again, he thrust forward, fucking my mouth slowly, inch by delicious inch. As he moved into my upper throat, I relaxed it. Deeper, deeper he went, until my lips were circling the base of his cock.

"Good girl. My sweet, good girl. You will get a reward for this," he growled, his voice husky. "To hell with the training." He pulled back then surged forward again, testing my control over my throat. I took him all the way, again and again. When he pulled out at last, I was so wet and ready for him my outer pussy lips were slick and the air smelled sweet with my musk. He bent down, kissed me fiercely, tongue dancing in my mouth. Before I'd caught my breath, he was on his knees and had my ankles untied, held high up and wide out, and was shoving his condom-covered cock into me.

Oh, to be full at last.

I moaned. I writhed. I thanked him over and over as he fucked me. His cock stretched me as it slammed in and out, over and over. With each stroke, my body became tighter, hotter, until the pleasure was overwhelming and I thought I might die from it.

"Come for me," Tristan demanded. "Come now." He released one ankle to stroke my clit. That was all it took, a couple of soft touches with the pad of his thumb, and over I tumbled, into a morass of swirling, throbbing ecstasy. I felt him still for a brief moment, and then he groaned as he too found release. As he pounded into my spasming pussy, his movements were jerky, abrupt, rough, just shy of too rough, and yet my body responded. I was swept up in another climax, taken by complete surprise. I trembled and shook, my nerves zinging, my muscles clenching. I don't know how long it lasted, but ohmygod, it was insane.

This was what I'd waited for. Was it ever worth it.

Tristan kissed the top of my head. He was still breathing heavily as he pulled out of me. He discarded the condom and left, promising to return in a minute. True to his word, he came back almost immediately, a damp washcloth in his hands. With my arms still restrained, I sat and watched him gently clean me. Only when he was finished, did he untie me.

"You . . . are doing something to me," he said as he helped me stand on legs that felt like molten cheese.

"You're doing something to me too."

"No. I mean, yes, you do that too. But . . ." He studied me for a moment, peering deeply into my eyes. "I don't know what it is about you. I have to go. I don't want to. But I need to get to work."

"It's okay. I understand."

"You'll come back. Next weekend."

"Is that an invitation? Or a command?"

His lips quirked. "Both? I want you, Alice. I want you to be mine. For one weekend. The whole weekend."

"What does that involve, exactly?" I glanced nervously around the room.

"It involves spending forty-eight hours with me, exploring, experimenting, learning what your limits are and how far you'll let me push them."

"Sounds intense."

"It will be."

"I'm not sure I completely understand."

"Come with me." He offered a hand, and I accepted it. We went back to his bedroom. He went to the nightstand, opened the drawer, and a second later, he handed me a book. "Read this. Then decide."

I ran my hand over the cover. "Can I ask you something?"

"Sure."

"Why do you do this? You've shown me you can enjoy regular sex. What is it about the toys and equipment, that you don't want to have sex without them?"

He didn't answer right away, and I wondered why. Was he afraid I was judging him? Did he not know how to answer?

"For me, it takes sex to a level far beyond physical. When I am dominating a submissive, we aren't just connected on a physical level. I am reading his or her reactions, using my mind, I am keying in to his or her emotions too. It's not only a sensual experience but an emotional one as well. It's the only way I know how to connect with people."

I felt a little sorry for him then, at that admission. It was the only way he knew how to connect? Could I help him learn how to connect emotionally to people without the use of chains and manacles? I wanted to.

He pointed at the book, still in my hands. "Read the book. Maybe you'll better understand then."

"Okay, I'll read it."

He nodded. "Now, get dressed. The plane's ready. We'll be leaving in ten minutes."

Such an abrupt shift. I almost got whiplash. I scurried around, gathering my clothes and redressing. In exactly ten minutes, we were out the door. And within the hour we were back in the air. While Tristan worked on his laptop, his leg leaning against mine—an intimacy I appreciated—I started reading the book he'd given me.

One chapter in, I wondered whether I could handle Tristan Stark and his domination games.

He'd said only one weekend.

But I knew that would be only the beginning.

7

By the following Saturday night at 5:45 P.M., I was still unsure what I would say tonight. A part of me was curious about this domination and submission stuff. It intrigued me. But a bigger part of me was absolutely terrified.

The whips, the clamps, the canes.

I didn't like pain. Pain didn't excite me. It made my eyes water. I avoided pain. I'd gotten my ears pierced. A long time ago. But that was the only time I'd ever willfully subjected myself to pain. Well, except for dancing. There was plenty of pain in dancing. Muscles burning, stretching, straining. Feet. Oh yes, the foot pain. But that was different. It was dance. It was art. Expression.

Then again, was it so different?

A knock at the door sent my heart rate into the stratosphere. I checked my watch. Six o'clock. On the dot. It was him. It was time to face him, make a decision.

Oh God.

Please, please make the right choice.

Knowing I couldn't hide my anxiety, I opened the door.

Tristan was waiting patiently, a gorgeous bouquet of flowers in his hands. Orchids, I recognized. Some of the other flowers I couldn't name. He smiled as he handed them to me. "You look beautiful."

"Thanks. The flowers are gorgeous. I'll put them in water before we go." I back-stepped, almost bumping into the box mountain.

His hand shot out, catching my arm, halting me. "No need. They're packaged in a vessel."

I unwrapped the paper. The arrangement was even more breathtaking without the wrapping. "Wow. I've never seen flowers like these." I brought them to my nose and inhaled deeply. They smelled like I would expect a lush tropical forest to smell.

"I have a friend who cultivates rare plant species. These are from his private collection."

"Please pass along my gratitude." I placed the flowers on my desk.

"Will do. Ready?" he asked, his gaze wandering around our tiny space.

"Please, excuse the mess. We're getting ready to move." I repositioned my purse strap, which had slipped off my shoulder. "I'm ready to go if you are."

"Let's go." He motioned for me to head out first. As I passed him, he placed a hand on the small of my back. The touch sent little jitters up and down my spine and made my heart do a few flip-flops.

Why was it that I reacted so intensely to this man? Why not someone else, someone safer? Someone who didn't want to chain me up and whip me?

Why?

Could it be because he was a little intimidating, dangerous?

More like *very* intimidating and dangerous.

With Tristan by my side, I *click-clacked* down three flights of stairs, through the lobby, and down the front walk to the waiting limo. I climbed aboard and settled in for the ride. Tristan sat beside me. He placed one hand on my knee. The other arm draped across the seat behind me. His thumb stroked my skin, back and forth, back and forth. I couldn't help focusing on that soft touch.

"You're very quiet tonight. Nervous?" he asked.

"Yes."

"Why?" His thumb kept moving, back and forth, back and forth.

"This whole thing is scary," I said, staring down at his hand.

With a fingertip under my chin, he coaxed me to look at him. "Tell me, what are you thinking?"

"I'm thinking it might be too much for me, too intense."

He nodded but said nothing.

"I read the book . . . most of it. I kind of understand where the submissive is coming from."

"Could you relate to her?" he asked.

"Sure. But does that mean I want what she has? That I want it all? The whole master-slave thing? That, I'm not sure about."

"Hmmm."

"Can we take this thing in stages?" I asked, feeling as conflicted as ever. Sitting here, close to Tristan, I craved his touch, his kiss. But did all those scary things have to come with that? Wasn't there some compromise we could reach? "Is it all or nothing? Or is there such a thing as Bondage for Beginners?"

"I assumed we wouldn't dive in to the intense submission, sure. We would take it slowly, test your limits, see what you like, what you don't like. What I wanted you to understand by reading that book is the overall nature of the relationship. If you decide to move forward with our arrangement, I will be your master for the weekend. I will determine what you eat, when you sleep, what you wear, what you will do and won't do, and what your punishment will be for making a mistake.

Me. Only me. You will have to abide by my decisions and rules."

My insides knotted at the first sentence, about what I'd eat. Those knots got tighter with every word he said after that. "The same rules as in the book?"

"Yes."

I recalled a few. Not looking the master in the eye was one. Another was only speaking when asked a direct question. Setting aside the question of wanting this, could I do this? I'd been on my own for a long time. When someone, besides Jenn, tried to tell me what to do, I tended to dig in my heels. "Aren't those rules a little . . . extreme?"

"The rules exist for a reason. If you would like to experiment, then you must follow them. Without them, the experience won't be the same."

"And why would I want to have this experience?" I challenged.

"Because it will change your life."

He was too certain of that. How could he know for sure? He cupped my cheek. "I have been living this lifestyle for a long time. I can recognize a submissive from across a room. You want this. Don't let fear stop you."

"I don't know . . ."

"Have I given you any reason to distrust me?"

"No, but—"

"When I took you into my dungeon, did I push you too hard?"

"No."

"I will push you. I will force you to stretch your limits and try things you might not want to try. But I will only do so to increase your own pleasure and understanding of yourself."

When he said it that way, I kind of felt better about it. But . . . "If you are only doing this for me, then what do you get out of it?"

"The pleasure of watching you find ecstasy."

Did I believe that? I wanted to. Because the alternative, that he got off watching me suffer, was horrifying.

"What if I want you to stop?" I asked.

"Say the word *Red,* and I will stop immediately. But trust me, you won't have to say it. I watch, I read your body. I can tell when you can't take anymore."

"What if I disagree?"

"Say the word. I won't gag you." His thumb caressed my lip. His gaze flicked to my mouth. "Say yes, Alice. Say you'll be mine until tomorrow night." He leaned in, brushing his lips against mine. So soft, like a feather. It tickled. Teasing. Tempting. Heat pulsed to my center, between my legs.

"You're not playing fair here." My eyelids were getting heavy. And my nerves were zinging and zapping. I wanted him to kiss me hard, not tease me. I reached for him, but he snapped his hands around my wrists and shoved them out to the sides.

"I always play fair. You'll see," he murmured.

Once again, he was mighty confident. His assumption that I would say yes grated a little. "Don't you think you're jumping the gun?" I hiked up my chin in a show of defiance. My breathless, I'm-about-to-melt voice, however, was working against me.

"Am I 'jumping the gun'? I apologize." He released my hands and leaned back, tossing an arm over the back of the seat and regarding me with a cool, composed mien that had my teeth gritting. Here I was, practically panting, my panties sodden, and he was looking calm, cool, and utterly collected. Bastard.

I wanted him to be as desperate with wanting as I was.

The challenge of getting him to that point made the whole arrangement a lot more palatable. "What if I decided I'm more comfortable dominating my partner than submitting to him?" I asked.

"Then I'll help you find a partner who is looking for a domme."

Could he really do that? Shuffle me off to someone else? Without a second thought? His voice said he could. His words said he could too. But the dark shadow in his eyes . . . that said something else. I liked what his eyes said much better than the rest of him.

The car rolled to a stop, and I glanced out the window. We were parked outside of a hotel. A fancy one. I gave him a raised brow look.

"Dinner. The cook here is amazing. And we can have some privacy. I reserved a suite."

A suite. "Okay." We exited the car, and Tristan escorted me inside. We went straight to the elevators, stopping in front of the one car that went to the top floors. Tristan poked the button, and a little chime signaled the arrival of the car. I stepped in. Tristan followed. The doors slid shut.

"This is a nice place. I've never been here before," I said, filling the tense silence.

"I've never stayed here, but I have dined in the restaurant. Quite a few times."

I couldn't imagine a life where I could afford to eat at fancy places like this whenever I felt like it. Having spent the last few years scraping together pennies to buy schoolbooks, I considered a cheap pizza to be a splurge.

Once again, my heart sank. We were from such very different worlds, Tristan and I. How could we ever find common ground? How could I expect this . . . arrangement . . . to lead to something stable, long-term? After all, that was what I wanted. Now that I was finished with school, I was ready to start looking for Mr. Right. I wanted to enjoy a few years of marriage before having kids.

What am I doing here?

I was a planner. That was how I lived my life. Tristan Stark wasn't a part of the plan. Not him. Not his kinky sex games. None of it.

Tristan led me to a closed door at the end of the hall. He pulled a key card from his jacket pocket, slid it in the slot, and opened the door.

I stepped into the fanciest hotel suite I had ever set eyes upon. Absolutely unreal. And huge. We were standing in the living area, a wide open space with contemporary furnishings and a wall of windows overlooking the city. "Wow, this is some place."

"I was hoping you'd like it, that it might set you at ease."

It didn't exactly do that, but it did distract me a little. "I like it, though it wasn't necessary."

"I'd rather have privacy during our meal, so we can talk freely." He collected me from in front of the windows by sliding a hand across my back and around my side. "This way. Our dinner will get cold."

I let him lead me to the table situated at one end of the room. The lights were low, and soft classical music was playing from hidden speakers. The table was draped in a snow-white tablecloth and set with china. In the center sat yet another beautiful flower bouquet, flanked by lit candles. "I have to give it to you, Tristan Stark. You do nothing halfway."

Tristan pushed in my chair, then circled around to his own seat. He sat, smiled. "That's a truer statement than you could ever know. Now, eat. I won't be responsible for your collapsing from low blood sugar."

"My blood sugar's fine right now."

"We're not talking now." His devilish smile returned.

I had a feeling I had to go through with this or I'd regret it. I would call Tristan Master for the next thirty-six hours or so. But I was enjoying this little game of temptation Tristan was playing. No need to put an end to that yet.

8

Dinner was delicious. At least, that was what I assumed. I couldn't be sure. I'd been too distracted to taste anything.

Tristan was an evil man.

Which was why I'd decided to put my safety, and my pleasure, into his hands. From what I knew of him, I was absolutely certain he was capable. He was also meticulous, attentive, cautious, and wicked.

I didn't know exactly what to expect, but I had no doubt I was in for an intense weekend. Intensely erotic. Intensely mind-blowing, probably.

During the meal, Tristan did everything in his power to convince me to say yes to his proposition. He charmed me with his smile and easygoing disposition. He impressed me with interesting conversation. Yes, both of those. But it was how he seduced me that made me throw caution to the wind and finally say, "Tristan, I've made my decision."

He looked a little anxious as he asked, "What have you decided, Alice?"

"I want to do this."

His smile was so bright, I could have used Ray-Bans to cut the glare. "Let's go." He stood, pulled my chair, lead me out of the suite—good-bye, luxurious hotel—and back down to the lobby. The limo was waiting for us outside, and we were whisked away.

"Will we be flying to your property?" I asked.

"No, not this time. Although I enjoy the privacy of that home, I'd rather not waste any time traveling."

Clearly, he was anxious to get things going.

He closed the screen, shutting us off from the driver. "Come here." He pulled me toward him by my wrists. I leaned but he shook his head. "Straddle my legs."

I was wearing a skirt, a pretty one made out of tiers of intricate lace. Straddling his legs meant my delicate skirt was going to either be torn or get scrunched up around my hips. I eased the lace tiers up my thighs, over my hips. Underneath, I was wearing a tiny thong. A triangle of lace, basically.

His eyes locked on that triangle. "Hmmm. I like that." He hooked his finger in the top and pulled slightly. His fingernail grazed my lower stomach, just above my pubic bone. I hadn't realized how sensitive that skin was until then. I sucked in a little gasp.

He tipped his head, and the corners of his mouth curled up. "Is there something wrong?"

"No, nothing." I let him pull my hips forward. Then, at his direction, I eased down onto his lap, knees bent, resting on the seat on either side of his hips.

"Now, this is better." His fingers kneaded my flesh. Just the right amount of pressure, making me dizzy. "Kiss me."

I cupped his face in my palms and lowered my mouth to his. His tongue traced the seam of my lips, and I parted them on a sigh. He'd barely kissed me and already I was burning up. How would I handle all the torment of the next thirty-something hours? How?

His tongue dipped into my mouth again and again, spreading his sweet, intoxicating flavor everywhere. A deep, throbbing ache started pounding in my center, ripples of wanting pulsing out from there. He was still holding my hips, grasping them firmly enough to keep me from rocking them back and forth. How I wanted to rub away the ache between my legs.

"Tristan," I murmured between mind-numbing kisses.

"Hmmm." Moving one hand, he slipped it under my buttock. A fingertip grazed my labia, and I shuddered. "You're wet for me. Wet and ready."

"Yes, ready."

"Patience, Alice."

Patience wasn't a word I associated with want, with need. No, not at all. Particularly when that hand inched lower, and that finger dipped deeper, sliding into my tight canal.

"Ohhh," I moaned. I arched my back, desperate to have that finger deeper. A burning pleasure was building inside me, and I knew for a fact that he could make it that much better with just a few strokes.

"One of the first lessons a new submissive must learn is how to set aside her own pleasure to serve her master's needs."

I wasn't liking the sound of that. After all, it wasn't my fault I was trembling and tight and desperate for his next touch. It was his. And if my response didn't give him pleasure, what did?

"Lift your bottom," he commanded.

Shifting sideways so my body angled to one side, and straightened at the hips, I lifted my ass off his thighs. His hand glided over the globes of my buttocks. "Soft and firm, exactly how I like them." He audibly inhaled. "And your pussy smells so damn good." He pulled the scrap of lace out of the way and added a second finger to the first, pushing them in and out, fingertips grazing that spot inside that made me shiver all over. "I like you like this, bare, smooth. Wet, hot."

I liked it, myself. On hands and knees, I closed my eyes,

concentrating on the glorious sensation he was stirring in me. Now that he was fucking me with two fingers, I was eager to have more. Three. Or his wide cock. Fucking me hard. Pounding in and out. "How much longer?" I whispered. "When will we be there?"

"When I say we're there. Patience. You're going to learn patience."

I didn't want to learn patience. Wasn't there something to be said for an eager lover? A lover who fucked willingly, who participated wholeheartedly? Who enjoyed her lover's every touch, every kiss, every stroke? That was me.

And, was that ever.

He added a third finger. I was so full. I loved it. And ohmygod, he was stroking my clit. With every stroke, every thrust, I felt my body getting tighter. I was going to come. I was going to . . . I shuddered as a flash of heat zipped through my body.

"Don't you dare," he snapped. His voice was sharp. "Don't you come. Not until I tell you." My pussy clamped tight. Another wave crashed over me. I tried to fight it. I did.

I held my breath.

Stop. Please stop.

I curled my hands into fists.

My foot cramped.

I slackened my inner muscles, but then they clamped tighter, completely out of my control. And, oh yes, that felt sooooo good.

"You will be punished. Do not come, Alice."

"Stop," I said. "Stop."

He shoved his fingers deeper inside. His fingertip flicked over my clit, once, twice.

"Stop, please." I couldn't breathe. Every muscle in my body was tied into a knot, even the ones clamping my eyelids shut.

He didn't stop. He added a fourth. A fourth! I was stretched to the limit. The heat grew, blossomed, exploded through me, and my pussy spasmed around those four fingers. Ah, the ecstasy. The relief. Endorphins charged through my system, making me feel high. I laughed and cried, begged for forgiveness.

"You failed, Alice." His voice was menacing. "Now, we're there. Now, you'll learn what happens when I am displeased. Get down, on the floor, on your knees."

Still dizzy and giddy, I slid to the floor, kneeling so I faced him.

"Clothes off."

I struggled in the tight space to remove my clothes, my skin burning as his sharp gaze studied me. My pussy was dripping, slick heat dampening my inner thighs. Once I was completely nude, I knelt with my knees tight together. "I tried. You won't hurt me too badly, right? I couldn't help it. Not with what you were doing."

His eyes showed no mercy. But the corners of his mouth twitched ever so slightly.

"We'll continue this inside. Follow me."

When I'd taken the job, modeling for Estefan, I'd never stood in front of another human being completely nude before. Since then, I'd modeled for him twice more. And Tristan had made me undress in his backyard during our first date. I'd grown semi-comfortable with being naked in privacy. A good thing, since I was about to step out of a car completely unclothed, naked from the top of my head to the tips of my toes.

But this time I would be seen by someone else.

The car swung open. The driver, I assumed, had opened it for us. He was about to get an eyeful.

Would he be the only one?

I shot a glance out the window, opposite the open door. We were parked in a U-shaped driveway, in front of a large home. I couldn't see the street from where we sat now. Thank God. Hopefully no neighbors would see me. This was the ultimate walk of shame.

"Out, Alice." Tristan sounded slightly impatient. Ironic, since I was being punished for the very same sin.

I stared down at the ground as I reluctantly exited the vehicle. With my arms wrapped protectively around myself, I passed a pair of shiny black shoes on the way to the sidewalk. I said nothing as I padded up to the front door and waited for it to be opened. Tristan was next to me.

"Drop your hands," he demanded.

I didn't want to. A breeze blew over me, and goose bumps erupted over my shoulders, down my arms.

"Drop them, or you won't go inside."

This man was cruel. If it weren't for the fact that my pussy was throbbing with sensual heat, I would have told him what he could do with this domination and submission stuff. But dammit, I felt so alive and alert and excited. Maybe he was right. Maybe this stuff was for me.

With great reluctance, I unclenched my hands and eased them down to my sides. As I did it, I stared straight ahead, at the door in front of us. The closed door that I prayed would be opened soon.

"Better." Tristan cupped my ass cheek, the touch startling me slightly. It also made a fresh wave of heat simmer across my face. If anyone was watching this . . . oh God.

The door opened. At last! I wasted no time stepping inside. The floor under my feet was cold. Slick polished stone. Marble. I was standing in a grand entryway, with massively high ceilings and a stairway arching around in a soft curve.

"We'll head upstairs," Tristan instructed.

I set my hand on the railing. It was smooth to the touch too, and cool. As I ascended the stairs, I couldn't help thinking about how all the slick, hard surfaces in the house reminded me of Tristan. This home was incredibly gorgeous. Immaculate. Just as he was. And there were a lot of hard edges, sculpted lines, just like his personality. But, as I looked down at the foyer below, catching little surprises here and there—the colorful flower arrangement on the table, the fascinating artwork— again, I felt like I was looking at an expression of the man who owned the home.

I wanted to say something, to compliment the décor, the choices of flooring, the beautiful painting at the top of the staircase, but I remembered what he'd said. I couldn't speak without being spoken to first. That rule was going to be a rough one to follow. Not as difficult as the no-orgasm-until-I-say one, though. That one was impossible.

I waited for Tristan to tell me where to go next. He stepped up very close to me, so close I felt the heat of his body. The goose bumps came back.

"The last room on the right," he said softly, his mouth mere inches from my ear.

I nodded and kept going. Up here, a thick, plush carpet padded my footsteps. I'd never felt such soft carpet. It was heavenly.

The last door on the right was closed. I stopped, waited for him to open it. He reached around me, and all my nerve endings tingled. It still shocked me, how strongly I reacted to Tristan. He didn't even have to touch me. All he had to do was be near.

The door slowly swung open.

Another dungeon.

This dungeon was a little different from the first. It was smaller. And a little less scary. The décor was chic. The walls were painted a soft gray. And charcoal draperies flanked two wide windows. The wall-to-wall carpet was the same shade as the walls. But, like in the first, in the center of the ceiling hung a crystal chandelier dripping with sparkling crystals.

The hugest bed I'd ever seen sat beneath the chandelier. Four massive, towering posts reached up at least ten feet at all four corners. Centered against one wall was a wide dresser. On the dresser's top was an arrangement of candles. They were lit. Someone had come in and prepared the room for us.

"Kneel there." Tristan pointed at a spot next to the bed. I did as he told me to, watching as he left the room through a door to my right. He returned a few minutes later, carrying a few things in his hands. He was still mostly dressed—his unknotted tie hung around his neck, the top button of his crisp white shirt undone. He set down his load on the dresser and turned to me. "Now, what to do with you?"

You could start by fucking me until I can't see straight.

"You have some problems being unclothed in public, I see. That's an issue we'll have to address . . ." My heart stopped. "Someday," he added. "Not this weekend. I need to focus on the basics, first."

Relief.

I sucked in a deep breath, held it for a second, then slowly let it out. Wow, was I tense. Not knowing what would happen next was killing me.

Tristan picked up a long, thin stick with little leather straps on one end. I didn't know the name for it, but it looked kind of like the things horse jockeys used to make their horses run faster. Riding crop. That was what it was called. He strolled closer. My heart rate jumped a few hundred beats per minute. And a warm rush of wet heat pulsed between my legs.

He placed the top of the stick under my chin and forced it up until my neck was bent back and I was looking up at the ceiling. "Up, off your heels."

I straightened my thighs, kneeling upright, my hands hanging at my sides.

"Better. Now, those hands. Behind your back."

I clasped them together behind my butt.

"Shoulders relaxed. Chest up. Buttocks tucked in."

I made the corrections, flashing back to ballet class. Yes, this was very much like ballet. And I wouldn't be surprised to learn my teacher did a little domination on the side.

"Much better. Very pretty, Alice." Circling around to my back, Tristan let the tip of that whip thing tickle me, dragging lightly across my skin. He stopped directly behind me, placed the little straps on my shoulder and slowly teased me with them. The touch was soft. Barely perceptible. But what it did to my body.

Within minutes, I was trembling. I was hot. I was tense. And I wanted Tristan to touch me for real.

Actually, what I wanted was for Tristan to say to hell with all this teasing and throw me down, climb on top of me, and shove his big cock into my pussy.

Why couldn't he do that? Why?

"This is the way I want you to present yourself to me whenever we come into this room. Tomorrow morning, when you are woken, you are to eat first then shower and prepare yourself for me. You will be in this room, in this position, no later than eight o'clock."

"Okay," I said.

The little whip thing smacked me on the top of my ass, and I jerked. It didn't hurt; it startled me.

"The proper response is 'Yes, Sir.' "

"Yes, Sir," I echoed as a little wave of nervous energy buzzed through me. I'd been corrected, and it hadn't been too bad. No, in fact, it made this whole experience that much more thrilling. Anticipation was a powerful aphrodisiac. Who would have thought?

He continued, "You will do as I say at all times. Both when we are in this room and when we are not. You will eat when I tell you to. Sleep when I tell you to."

"Yes, Sir."

Coming around to stop in front of me, he dragged the whip down the center of my chest. I sucked in a little gasp.

He said, "You are not permitted at any time to masturbate. Your orgasms are mine."

"Yes, Sir."

"And I repeat, if I push too hard or do something you cannot handle, you will say the word *Red*."

"Red," I echoed.

"Do you have any questions?"

I knew I should, but my brain wasn't working very well at the moment. I was kneeling in front of a man who made my blood burn, and I didn't know what to expect. It was a lot to take in.

"No?" he asked.

I shook my head. "Not right now, I guess."

"All right." He motioned me up with the whip. "Stand."

I stood.

"The bed. Lie on your back."

At last, we were getting to the fun stuff. Yay! I climbed up on the bed, crawled to roughly the center, my head at pillow level. I eased down onto my back and watched as he grabbed some leather cuffs from the stash he'd carried in and joined me.

My heart banged against my breastbone as I watched him buckle the cuffs around my wrists. Then he pulled some chains from somewhere and snapped them on the cuffs so my arms were spread in a wide vee, up and out to the sides.

"Legs." He made a parting motion with his hands.

Leaving them flat on the bed, I slid them apart.

I felt so helpless, powerless. I loved it already.

I was ready. Ready to face whatever my master would do to me next.

9

I hadn't spent very much time in Tristan Stark's adult play-room, and already I knew he was the master of erotic torture.

I wanted him so badly, my teeth ached. So did every other part of my body. Since he'd told me to lie down, he'd used that little whip to make me sweat and squirm and beg for mercy. He'd tapped me here and smacked me there, and ohmygod, I hadn't known that pain could amplify erotic need so much.

I had no idea how much time had passed since we'd come in here. But all I could focus on, as he ran the tip of that whip over my labia, was the almost unbearable need slamming through me with every heartbeat. I wanted relief. I wanted to come. But he would not let me.

I blinked back tears.

"You're doing much better, Alice. Good girl."

Much better, maybe. But I was dying. I lifted my hips off the bed. I couldn't control my body anymore. My muscles were spasming. Tears were streaming from my eyes. But I hadn't come. I was close. So close. I gritted my teeth harder, determined to earn the reward I knew would be mine if I could just hold out a little longer.

One more minute. Only one.

"If you keep this up, you'll have your reward."

He'd said that before. I wanted my reward now, dammit. Hadn't he tormented me enough? Who would've thought pleasure could be a punishment? And pain a reward?

"Yes, you've pleased me. I have something for you."

I waited, my eyelids clamped tightly, arms and legs trembling. I heard the crinkle of plastic. Then fingers parted my labia. My heart slammed against my breastbone. Yes, oh yes. At last, he would caress away this horrible ache.

Something hard probed me, pushing past my outer lips, dipping into my tight channel. My inner muscles clamped around it as I tried to hold it in place. The skin on my chest warmed. Sweat trickled from my brow, down my temple. The hard thing—a toy?—eased deeper. During its plunge, it stroked that spot deep inside, and I jerked.

Can't come. Do not come!

"Control, Alice. Look at you. My beautiful girl. Fighting the pleasure. When you come, you are going to fly high. Just a little longer." He pushed the toy deep inside me.

Full. At last.

My body held on to that invading toy as if my life depended upon it. It felt so good. I nearly cried when it slid back out. And I did cry when it slammed back in.

The toy was fucking me hard. And my legs were tight. My feet were cramping. My stomach was burning.

I couldn't take another second. Not one more thrust.

"Please," I begged. "Let me come."

The toy stopped.

I gasped.

I whimpered.

I writhed.

The cuffs were biting into my wrists. But the pain only made my need that much worse.

"Alice." His voice was sharp.

I forced my eyes open. His face was impassive. There was no playful twinkle in his eyes. No hint of a smile on his lips. He was unhappy with me? For what? For begging for something he'd promised me over and over? For buckling under the weight of his torture?

"Are you angry?" I asked.

"No. But I'm displeased. Our session is over."

Over?

Over!

My pussy was still throbbing. My body was one huge knot of need. And he was finished? No!

"I'm sorry," I said. And did I ever mean it. But I tried. I really did.

"No need to apologize." Reaching up, he smoothed my hair. "My beautiful Alice. You're learning so quickly. I hadn't expected you to last as long as you did."

He'd planned to tease me like this? To torment me and then to leave me?

I hated this game. Despised it.

Through gritted teeth, I grumbled, "You are so—"

He lifted his brows.

I clamped my lips tight. A word was trying to slip out. A not nice word. And I knew if it did then my punishment would be even worse.

He unbuckled my wrists and helped me sit. "You need to rest. Tomorrow, we'll start early. It's going to be a long day."

I wanted to pull away from his strong hands as I stood. But the problem was, I was way too shaky to stand on my own. He'd reduced me to a quivering mess.

Supporting me with an arm around my waist, he escorted

me out of the room, down the hall, and into a lovely guest room.

"You'll sleep here. The bathroom is there." He pointed at a closed door. "You'll find everything you need to prepare for me in there." Once he had me safely on the bed, he smiled. The expression took my breath away. "Thank you, Alice. Thank you for trusting me."

Thank you for torturing me and then leaving me hanging. Meanie.

He leaned over me, eyes delving deep into mine. His lips settled over mine, pressing softly. The tip of his tongue flicked, but when I parted, welcoming him to deepen the kiss, he pulled back, cupped my cheek. "Sweet dreams, Alice."

After checking my wrists—for sores?—he left.

Sweet dreams? How could I possibly fall asleep? I was away from home, in a strange bed, and burning up with need.

If I were home right now, I'd finish things off myself. But no, I couldn't do that. It was against *the rules*.

Stupid rules.

Stupid, *unfair* rules.

Luckily, this little experiment would end in just over twenty-four hours. I could not live like this permanently. No way. More importantly, I didn't want to.

But if I had learned one thing tonight, it was that I didn't want to be on the receiving end of Tristan Stark's brand of discipline ever again. It might not leave any cuts or bruises but I sure as hell hurt.

I woke to the sound of Tchaikovsky. "Dance of the Swans." I stretched—oh, was I sore—blinked a few times, and focused on the man standing at the door.

"Good morning, Alice. It's seven o'clock. Will you join me for breakfast?"

He was wearing old jeans and a snow-white T-shirt. Never

had I seen jeans and a plain shirt look so good. His hair was a little messy, like he'd just rolled out of bed. And dark stubble shaded his chin and jaw.

Gorgeous. Absolutely gorgeous. Insanely gorgeous.

Remember, he's a merciless, torturing jerk.

I yawned, stretched. Blinked bleary eyes. "Breakfast. Sure. But it'll have to be quick. I have an appointment at eight."

He beamed like a boy who'd learned he was getting a new bicycle and I edited that last comment. He was still merciless and torturing. But maybe not such a jerk. "I promise I won't keep you long."

As I hurried into the bathroom to take care of a few essentials, I couldn't help thinking about how odd Tristan Stark was. One side of him was a hard, demanding man. The entrepreneur. The dominant. The cruel bastard who'd teased me to tears. But somewhere inside was the boy I saw every now and then, who still loved to play and laugh. Oddly, I didn't think I could appreciate one side without the other. Like my favorite Thai dish, sweet and spicy, it was the combination of two very different aspects that made the overall effect so intoxicating.

I just hoped I wouldn't fall for this man too hard too fast. The boy inside Tristan might look for more—a girlfriend, a wife—but the businessman, the Dom, ran the show. And all he wanted was a submissive.

My heart sank.

A submissive. Would that be all I'd ever be to him? Someone to play with? When he became bored, would he toss me aside and find someone new? After last night, I didn't even like his torture games.

This was probably the one and only weekend I'd ever spend with Tristan Stark.

My gut twisted.

Stop thinking about this stuff. It's pointless to be worrying about tomorrow, next week, next month.

After freshening up and making use of the brand-new, wrapped toothbrush I found sitting on the smooth stone counter, I wandered back out.

Tristan was standing at the door, waiting. His smile brightened when he saw me. "Did you sleep well?"

"Surprisingly, yes." Nude—and assuming that was the way he wanted me to remain—I met him at the door. When his gaze wandered down my body, I felt myself blushing. "Did you want me to get dressed?"

"No. No clothes. You're lovely, just as you are."

Today, I would eat breakfast in the nude. Another first. But, I supposed, not my last—if Tristan were to offer to make this arrangement a more permanent thing. If. And if I were to accept. A bigger if. "Okay."

Both barefoot, we descended the curved staircase. I followed him to the kitchen. It was a kitchen out of a magazine. I swear. All polished chrome and stone and glass tile. He motioned for me to sit at the breakfast table at the far end of the room. After pushing my chair in for me, he left to prepare our breakfast. I watched. Thoughts buzzed around in my head. Questions.

So far, this experience hadn't been as horrible as I'd imagined. In fact, at times it had been good. Although Tristan acted the part of a dominant for much of the time, he'd switched out of Dom mode this morning, enough to allow me to relax, to develop something of a connection with him. It wasn't all, yes, Sir; no, Sir. Nor was it all pain and no pleasure.

Risking the rules, I thanked him when he brought me a cup of hot coffee. That deserved a heartfelt thanks.

He reacted with another brilliant smile. "You're welcome, Alice." After going to the counter for two plates, he returned, placed one in front of me, one opposite, and took his seat. While I checked out the contents of my plate—fruit, cottage cheese, some kind of funky-looking scrambled egg concoction—he sipped from a tall glass. In it was a thick green liquid. Didn't look consumable. I felt my lip curling.

He must have seen it because he lifted the glass. "Seaweed smoothie. Would you care to try it?"

"No. Slimy and green don't do it for me, thanks. I'm assuming you drink it because of its health benefits?"

"I do. But I won't bore you with the details."

"I'd prefer to stick with land-grown veggies, thanks." I poked at the eggs—which I guessed weren't eggs, after all—and reluctantly brought the fork to my mouth.

"It's an egg substitute. I found it to be acceptable."

I nibbled. Not bad. Tolerable. I took another bite. And another. I wasn't big on experimenting with food, but this morning I was really hungry. Who knew, if he'd set a glass of the seaweed goo in front of me first, I might've tried it. Might've gagged, or worse.

"May I speak freely now?" I asked between forkfuls of faux eggs. "Or are we still in game mode?"

His chuckle vibrated through me. "You may speak freely. What do you wish to tell me?"

I briefly considered telling him off for what he'd done last night. But I decided to let that go for now. "Nothing in particular. I just wanted to know if I could talk."

"You may." He set down his glass and we ate for a moment in silence.

"This stuff isn't half-bad," I said. "What's it called? I may buy some the next time I go shopping."

"I buy it from a food wholesaler. It isn't available to retail consumers. I'll have some delivered to you."

"That's not necessary—"

He cut me off. "It's my pleasure."

"Thanks." It seemed he did get pleasure from small acts of

kindness. And larger ones, I reminded myself, thinking of Estefan. "Speaking of kindnesses, you've been very good to Estefan. I respect that."

He tensed up, his jaw visibly tightening. "I didn't do it to gain anyone's respect."

"Of course you didn't. I didn't mean to imply you had."

"Of course you didn't." His smile returned. It was a weird, sudden shift from happy-go-lucky to defensive and back to happy again. This man rode an emotional roller coaster that made Space Mountain look like a kiddie ride. *Don't get too close. You'll regret it.* "I'm sorry. I've been attacked in the past for supposedly using my money to buy friends."

"Who would say such a thing?"

"No one important."

I didn't buy that.

"Who?" I pushed.

"My brother." Tristan placed his fork and knife on his plate.

"He's jealous."

"He shouldn't be. He says he has everything he wants. A beautiful wife. A good job. A nice home. Two great kids."

"He's lying."

"Maybe. We don't talk much."

"I can tell that bothers you."

He didn't respond right away, and I wondered if I'd crossed a line. Sure, Tristan had brought up the topic, but I wasn't letting it rest. Maybe he'd rather I did.

"We used to be extremely close. We're twins. According to our mother, I spent nine months with Troy's foot in my face." He chuckled. It was a wry, mirthless laugh. "Then Troy spent the next thirty years with his foot in his own mouth."

"I'm sorry. Sometimes siblings are our best friends, and sometimes they are our worst enemies."

"So true. I'd say Troy is more friend than enemy."

I didn't respond to that statement. Anyone who put Tristan

down that bad wasn't a friend of his in my book. The fact that a man who had so much going for him, had such tight control of all other aspects of his life, including his lovers, would struggle so much with this one issue made Tristan seem... more human. And infinitely more relatable.

"I have an older sister I haven't spoken to in years," I confessed. "She thinks I was spoiled by our parents."

"Were you?"

"I don't believe I was. I am the baby of the family. There's just the two of us. But Mary is ten years older than me. I guess our parents were very different when they raised her. Stricter. And more demanding. By the time they had me, they'd relaxed a little. I had more freedom. But I still had to earn everything I got, including the private high school I wanted so badly. I went, and they paid, but they told me they would pull me the minute my grades dropped. Same with dance. I didn't exactly tell you the whole story last week, about why I quit. My parents paid for my classes. But I had to 'earn' the opportunity to go every year by meeting their expectations. The summer before my senior year in high school, I failed. I never went back because I knew I wasn't capable of what they expected, and because I was tired of the pressure of holding the four point grade average and dancing six hours every night."

He reached a hand to me, across the table. I accepted. He said, "I'm no expert, but to me you seem to have a gift for dance. Have you thought of returning to it now?"

"I have. But for what purpose? It's not a career option. I don't have the commitment. And I'm out of shape. Ballet is extremely hard on the body."

"I imagine."

"But I do miss it. If I could find a place to dance just to keep in shape, to keep up my flexibility and maybe perform a little, that would be nice."

"Hmmm..."

"What are you thinking?"

He gave me an "I'm innocent" look.

I wasn't buying it. "Don't give me that 'who me?' look. I haven't known you for long, but I know you well enough to know when you're pulling my leg."

His expression changed. He glanced at the clock as he stood, circling the table. "Would you look at that? It's after eight. You're late for your appointment."

"Oh no." I feigned panic. "I am in so much trouble." I started to stand, but he stopped me, holding me in place with a hand on my shoulder.

"I can put in a good word for you."

"That's very kind, but I wouldn't dream of asking you to do that. I've always had to solve my own problems. Better not to let someone else start doing that for me now, right?"

He shrugged. "I don't mind."

I wanted to wrap my arms around him and hug him right there. That boy inside Tristan was a sweet little thing. And I hoped I'd get to know him better, to understand where the harder, colder Tristan had come from. After this conversation, I had a sneaking suspicion what had happened.

"I'd better go."

Tristan nodded, watched me leave.

I heard him following me as I headed for the playroom. I pushed open the door, went to the spot where he'd had me kneel last night, and took my position.

At this point, I wasn't so wound up, scared, intimidated. I was fairly relaxed.

Tristan strolled in after I'd been kneeling for a few minutes. I glanced at him, noted he was carrying some things. He set them down on the bed, circled me, then squatted directly in front of me.

He cupped my cheeks. "Before we begin, I just want to—" He smashed his mouth against mine, and the air left my lungs in a rough huff. The kiss softened almost instantly, going from a rough claiming to a gentle seduction. His tongue slipped inside my mouth, stroked mine. The kiss was intoxicating. It made my head spin and my body tremble. And I was devastated when it ended.

My eyelids lifted, and I looked him in the eye.

He appeared as breathless as me. "I . . . enjoyed breakfast this morning."

"Thank you. So did I."

"I haven't spoken to anyone about my brother in a long time."

And yet, he'd trusted me. This was significant. I could tell. I wasn't just a plaything to him. I was more. "I'm glad you felt you could trust me."

"I do." His voice rose, as if he was surprised. He nodded, gave me a little kiss on the lips, then stood. I checked his face. He didn't have his Dom face on yet. Was he struggling with this?

"Is something wrong?" I asked.

"No." He stepped back. He turned toward the door, turned back around again, came closer. "I need a few minutes."

"Okay." I remained exactly where I was.

He left the room but returned almost immediately. This time, when I checked, I saw his game face was in place. He was ready now. "I'm guessing you didn't enjoy last night's punishment?" he said as he sauntered closer, that little crop thing in his hand, swinging softly next to his thigh.

"No, Sir."

He dragged the tip of the crop over my shoulder. "Last night you pleased me, Alice. Very much. Today, you will learn how it feels to receive a well-earned reward."

10

A reward.

I was finally going to receive a reward.

I just knew it was going to be wonderful. My whole body shuddered, anticipation dancing up and down my spine. What would he do next? Would he lick and nip me from head to toe until I begged him to stop? Or would he just go for the big event, shove that big cock into my pussy and pound away the ache throbbing deep inside me?

I was good either way.

"Come with me, Alice," Tristan said, offering a hand. I took it, marveling at the happy tingles that swept through my body at the simple touch. He led me to an apparatus that looked a little like one of those swings for grown-ups. But this one had just a couple of little straps for a seat and back.

With gentle hands, he helped me get into the contraption. Butt resting on one strap, reclined way back, feet in the loops. He stood between my feet, pulled them apart, so my pussy was exposed.

"Pretty, Alice. I'm going to enjoy this."

So was I.

He scraped a fingernail down my slit, and quite a few parts of me quivered. "I'm going to get some things. Be right back."

I hung there, literally, and waited as he gathered up some toys, lube, condoms (yay!), and returned. He unbuttoned the top button of his jeans, unzipped his fly, revealing a vee of tanned skin covered in crisp curls to my hungry eyes. I drank in the sight of him, arm muscles bunching and flexing as he pulled the ropes holding me, easing me closer.

I still couldn't believe I was here with him. Me. He was just too freaking beautiful to be real.

"Hmmm. What shall I do with you first?" he asked, playing with the ropes and making me swing gently back and forth.

Fuck me until I was brain-dead?

"Whatever you wish, Sir," I said, thinking that might inspire him to do something extra-special.

What it got me was an evil smile that was hotter than the core of a nuclear reactor. "You're learning quickly, Alice."

"I've always been a quick study." I pulled my legs wider apart for him, stretching my muscles. I liked this swing. Being suspended like this felt sexy, and I felt beautiful, like I was dancing in midair. Strange, that my dance background would come in handy for something like this. I'd never considered the possibility.

"Quick study. So I'm coming to find out." His eyes were dark. His gaze focused. On me. He wanted me. Badly. I felt so powerful, and yet vulnerable too. He eased down onto his knees, which put him at just the right height to eat my pussy. I couldn't hold back the quake that rocked through me.

He parted my swollen pussy lips. "You're so wet already." He audibly inhaled. "I love that smell. The scent of need. In-toxicating."

Intoxicating? So was his deep, rumbly voice. I clenched the

muscles inside, wishing he would shove something in there, fill me, stretch me.

Patience, I told myself. Relax and enjoy.

He leaned closer, blew a cool stream across my burning flesh, and I shivered. My heart started galloping, the beat thumping against my breastbone. I reached up, grasping the straps suspending me, and closed my eyes.

Relax.

He unwrapped something, and within seconds, that something was pushing its way between my pussy lips, circling my entrance, teasing me, and making me whimper and clench.

"Are you enjoying your reward, Alice?" His voice was smooth and silky, as seductive as his words.

"Yes, Sir." Mine was breathless and rough.

"Good." He pushed the toy deep inside, and I clamped my pussy tight, holding it in. Ahhhh, I was so full.

He parted my lower lips, and something warm and wet (his tongue?) flicked up and down over my clit. In response, my pussy tightened, which amplified the sensation of fullness and the burn of need simmering in my veins. When his lips circled my burning clit and he suckled on it, a wave of heat crashed through me. I fought against the rising tide of pleasure, struggling to stay afloat. I wouldn't last long. I couldn't hold out.

"Are you losing control, Alice?"

"Yes, Sir."

His tongue circled over my clit now, and he added the decadent pleasure of the toy plunging in and out of my hot pussy, in and out, in and out, hard, fast.

"Please, Sir."

"Please, what?" He placed a sweet kiss on my pearl.

"May I come?"

"This is your reward, Alice. You may come whenever you wish. But . . ." He stopped shoving the toy deep inside. "I have bigger and better things in store for you—if you can hold on. Your reward is finished once you come."

Did this man know how to torment a girl, or what?

My body went into a full, head-to-toe shiver. I could come. Right now. This second. And it would be beyond words.

But I wanted to know what else he had up his sleeve, my master of torment.

Hold on.

I tightened my grasp on the straps and focused on not coming. As Tristan licked my clit and fucked my pussy with the toy, I fought to think about mundane things. What I needed at the grocery store. What I needed to pack up yet for the move. That worked for a short time.

But then he murmured, "Look at me, Alice."

I looked.

He was pushing those jeans down, over his hips. His cock was hard, ruddy, and a droplet of precome glistened on the tip. He curled a fist around the base, gave it a couple of pumps to the end and back, then tore open a condom wrapper.

Within seconds, the sheathed tip of his cock was easing into me, and I just about cried, I was so happy. Yes, yes. More. He was entering me a fraction of an inch at a time. It was sweet torment. He was holding the straps too, using them to pull me closer, controlling the depth of his thrust.

That was it; I was buying one of these swings. Ohmygod.

I tensed inside, clamping my muscles around him as he slowly invaded me, pushing deeper, deeper until his cock nudged my cervix.

"Ohhhh," I heard myself say.

Tristan eased out of me, just as slowly as he'd entered, and I relished the intimate stroke as the flared ridge circling his cock scraped against my inner walls. So good. A huge wave of heat slammed me, and I bit my lip. A couple more slow thrusts like this and I was done. My stomach clenched. My thighs quivered.

"You are so tight. Damn." I felt his cock swell even more. Another wave of heat blasted me. "Can't hold out," he muttered.

He couldn't hold out?

He pulled out, then slammed deep. A hard, sharp thrust. And another. And another. Yes, at last. He was fucking me hard and fast, and oh yes, oh yes, oh yes, this was what I needed. My body responded within minutes. Every muscle spasmed as I was overcome by a powerful orgasm. I felt it everywhere. My chest. My face. My toes. Incredible.

I heard myself scream above the thundering of my heartbeat. I heard him shout my name as he came too. His movements became jerky as he rammed in and out, pounding away his pleasure, and I tumbled head over heels into the maelstrom of a second orgasm. I was a bundle of throbbing, pulsing pleasure, and I didn't want it to end.

But slowly, gradually, it did, and I was gasping for breath, lifting heavy eyelids, my lips curling up.

Now that was one hell of a reward. I was ready to do anything he asked to get some more of those.

Tristan's head was thrown back. He was breathing heavily, his arms tight, skin covered in a sheen of sweat. He lifted his head, looked at me. "I couldn't wait. I'll do better next time."

Better? If he did better, I feared I might die.

"Okay," I said.

He cringed as he pulled out. He removed the full condom and discarded it in a nearby trash can. Then he sauntered over to me, cupped my cheeks, and kissed me until I was seeing stars again.

"I've never done that before," he confessed. "Lost control like that." His thumb grazed my lower lip. "You keep doing that to me. Making me forget what I was doing and why. All I could think about was having you, taking you. Keeping you." Something flashed in his eyes. I couldn't read what he was feeling, thinking, but I could tell it was intense. "Will you come back, Alice? Will you be mine?"

"Be your what?"

"My slave. Every weekend. Two days, two nights."

Slave. Not lover. Not girlfriend.

"I have to think about it. I need to understand what that means."

He nodded. "You can tell me tomorrow."

Tomorrow. No pressure there.

Crossing his arms over himself, he grabbed his T-shirt and pulled it off. "In the meantime, we need to get down to work."

Work?

He lifted my feet out of the loops. "On your knees, Alice. It's time for your next test."

A test? I wasn't physically or mentally prepared for a test. I was sated and sleepy, ready to curl up next to Tristan and take a little nap. This bondage stuff was a lot more taxing than I'd ever imagined.

I wanted to suggest we take a break, maybe go out for some lunch. But I didn't dare speak without permission. I'd had a taste of discipline. I much preferred rewards.

And so, in the name of self-preservation, I knelt at his feet and waited for his next command.

"Have you ever been fucked anally?" Tristan asked.

"No, Sir."

"Have you ever used a toy in your ass?"

"No. Only a finger."

"Okay. Come with me." Once again, he offered a hand up. Instead of the swing—a new personal favorite—he escorted me to a contraption that looked sort of like a church kneeler. My grandma used to take me to church with her when I was little. I started to bend my knees, assuming he wanted me to kneel on the lower pad.

"Good. Closer," he instructed, using his hands to help me

move into position. "Bend at the waist. The pad will support your upper body. Yes." That last word came out almost as a purr. The vibration hummed along my nerves, making me tingle inside.

Maybe I was physically ready for some more fun.

As he ran his hands over the globes of my ass, my insides tensed a little and a fresh wave of sensual heat rippled up and down my body. Yes, it seemed I was ready.

"Such a pretty ass you have, Alice. The next time you come here, I'll expect you to be ready for me."

He could expect all he wanted. That didn't mean I could make it happen. But maybe he knew something I didn't.

My hole was extremely tight. And sensitive. A lubed finger went in with some effort, but it wasn't particularly enjoyable. A penis . . . ? I shuddered, literally, at the thought.

"I'll help you." After giving my ass a little love tap, he left, heading for his stash of torture devices while I tried to decide if I should make a run for it now while I had the chance. Having sex for the first time was a little scary, but it had been more thrilling than terrifying, since I'd been waiting, anticipating it for a long time. This, though. This was different. I wasn't sure I wanted to train my anus to stretch open that big. Would I hurt myself?

Remember, you have a safe word.

My hammering heart slowed slightly. Yes, I had an out clause. If things became too bad, all I had to do was say one simple word and he would stop.

By the time he had returned, I was feeling slightly less panic-stricken. Slightly.

He touched my ass again, and I jumped. Startled. Nerves.

"Relax, Alice. I promise, you will enjoy this."

That was a promise I couldn't see him keeping.

I glanced over my shoulder, to see what he was doing. He *tsked.* "Maybe I should blindfold you."

I jerked my head back around.

"Yes, I think we should."

Seconds later, something soft was tied around my head, shutting me in darkness. A tiny bit of light seeped in where the blindfold was lying across the bridge of my nose, but I couldn't see anything but whatever was directly below me.

Now I was scared and blind. Great way to help a girl relax.

"That's better. One more thing." I heard him walk around me, the soft *clink* of metal down by the floor. He wrapped something around my wrist.

My heart jumped.

Chained too? Chained and blindfolded?

I didn't like this. Not at all. My stomach flip-flopped as panic set in. "Tristan," I said, my voice cracking. "Let me go."

"Easy, Alice," he murmured, his voice low and smooth and reassuring. "I won't hurt you. I promise."

"It's going to hurt."

"All you have to do is say our word and I'll stop. You remember the word?"

"Yes, *Red*."

"Good." Something soft touched my back. His lips. He gave me little kisses all over my shoulders, trailed down my spine to my tailbone. "I always take good care of my girls. You will learn to trust me completely." A fingertip delved into my crack, not deeply, just enough to make me tense up. "Relax, Alice." One of his hands reached around, cupping my sex. The pressure made my clit throb. Now that felt good.

I rocked my hips forward, pushing against his hand, enjoying the pressure. Then he ruined it by moving that finger deeper, skimming around my anus. I stilled, my body taut. My breath caught in my throat.

His hands left me. Relief. I pulled in a quick breath, knowing we were far from finished. I heard the sound of lube being squeezed from a tube. Nope, this wasn't over. Not by a long shot.

Fingers pulled my ass cheeks apart, and my butt tensed. My arms tensed. My whole body tightened. Even my face.

Something slick circled my anus, cool lube chilling the sensitive skin there. I felt my spine arching, tipping my hips forward, a failing attempt at escape.

"Easy, Alice." Tristan kissed the small of my back, and goose bumps prickled my skin. "Look at that. So damn pretty."

Something pressed at my opening, and I clamped tight, fighting the invasion.

He sighed. "I need another set of hands."

Oh God, no. He wouldn't bring someone else in to do this to me. Mortified at the thought of a stranger watching him shove something into my ass, I concentrated on relaxing. Using a technique I'd used to relax at night when I had insomnia, I first clenched the muscles down there then relaxed them.

"Better. Good girl." The thing, whatever it was, pushed harder at my opening, and I struggled to resist the urge to push it out. It took every ounce of my willpower and a little more. But finally the small thing slipped inside. *Pop.* It wasn't so big. It didn't hurt. A nervous giggle bubbled up my throat.

As I chuckled, a second thing pushed inside me, this one a little bigger. *Pop.* And before I could react, a third and fourth. After each invasion, the ring of muscles clamped tight, holding it in. It had to be some kind of stringed beads.

"Very good, Alice. Just wait until I get the last one in."

I liked the sound of that. Feeling a lot less terrified, and a little silly for being so petrified in the first place, I waited for the next one to push inside. *Pop,* in it went. And another. That one burned a little more as it went in, my body's resistance much greater. How many more were there? How much bigger would they get?

"Stop thinking," Tristan said. "I can see what you're doing, thinking yourself into a panic. Don't do that." He pushed another bead against my opening. My skin burned. I trembled as a rush of heat blazed to my pussy. He reached under me, stroked my clit, and *pop,* that bead went in. Now, I was feeling full and warm, and the strokes to my clit were sending waves of need blazing through my body, one after another after another. Growing more breathless and dizzy with each second, I squirmed, I gasped, I fought the restraints. And when the first wave of my orgasm rolled over me, I groaned. My empty pussy spasmed. My ass spasmed around the toy shoved deep inside. It was intense, almost too intense. I shook and shivered while he cupped my pussy, pressing against my burning tissues.

Ahhh.

"Yes," he whispered in my ear. "Good girl, Alice. You're doing so well." Not waiting for all the twitches and tingles to end, he pulled the toy from my ass. *Pop, pop, pop.* Out it came. And I was empty but thoroughly satisfied. Sleepy.

He took off the wrist cuffs first then the blindfold. He was smiling. How I loved that smile. "You deserve a reward. But first, a small gift." He led me out of the dungeon, through the house, to the living room. "Wait here." He left, returning a few minutes later with a gift bag. "It's something to help you prepare for next week."

I accepted, narrowing my eyes. "You're making an assumption, aren't you? That I will be back next week."

Some dark emotion played over his face for a brief moment before vanishing. "If not, it's yours to keep anyway." He jerked his head toward the bag. "Open it."

I reached inside, finding a wrapped package of pink graduated beads with a *T*-shaped handle on one end. I imagined they were identical to what he'd used today. "Um, thanks."

I liked beads. And, as it turned out, I didn't dislike this variety. But it was slightly embarrassing that he'd given me a set as a gift.

"There's more."

I dug deeper, fishing through the wadded tissue paper in the bottom of the bag. I found a small-ish box in the very bottom of the bag. It felt like a jewelry box.

Oh God.

I pulled it out.

There was a scrolling name on the outside of the box. I lifted the lid, finding a necklace made of gorgeous silver-gray pearls. I'd never seen pearls that color. They were cool and smooth to the touch. Shocked, and unsure how to respond, I trailed an index finger over their surface.

"They're black Tahitian pearls. Do you like them?" Reaching around me, he took them out of the box, carefully lifting them up for me to take a closer look.

"I've never seen black pearls."

"Do you like them?" he repeated, placing them at my throat.

I reached up with a hand, touching them while he fastened the clasp. "I do. I'm just . . . overwhelmed."

"Overwhelmed is good. Now, let's go get some lunch somewhere. And then shopping. I want to buy a dress to match these."

"Shopping?"

"You didn't expect to spend the whole day in here, did you?"

"Well . . . sort of. You don't have to buy me anything."

Using hands on my shoulders, he steered me around until I faced him. "I know I don't *have* to. I want to. Now, get dressed. Where we're heading, you have to have clothes on." He kissed me softly.

For the first time since I arrived, I regretted that our time together would be ending soon.

11

Tristan had sent in another dress for me to try on?

How many was that now? My eyes shifted to the loaded hooks on the wall. There were six hanging there, I was wearing one, and the salesclerk had already hauled away at least ten others. They'd all been rejected. Not by me. No, I'd have been happy with any of them. They were all insanely gorgeous.

I'd learned something else about Tristan Stark today. He was a picky shopper with meticulous taste. One little ripple or pucker where it shouldn't be, and the dress was sent back to the rack.

I inched open the door to accept the latest offers, only to have a certain fussy man shove his way into the tight space and shut the door.

"What are you doing?" I asked.

He clapped his hand over my mouth. "Shhh. I'm here to help." Hands on my shoulders, he steered me around. He pulled the zipper down. Then, because he was evil, he trailed his tongue down my spine, from nape to base. I was covered in goose bumps by the time he stopped.

"You're terrible," I whispered, afraid the salesclerk would come back any moment, hear Tristan, and call security. I held the unzipped dress up with a hand on my chest as I turned to face him. "Thank you for the help. Now, you'd better leave."

"I'm not going anywhere yet." He stepped closer, wedging me between the wall and his big, scrumptious body.

"Now, what are you going to do?" I tipped my head to look him in the eye.

"For starters." He stepped back a little, bent down, grasped the dress I was sort of wearing, pulled it up, over my head, and dropped it on the bench next to me. That left me with no bra, just panties. Panties that were getting a little damp. His gaze turned hungry as his eyes devoured my unclothed form. I knew what he was thinking.

"Tristan, we can't—"

He grabbed my face and smashed his lips on mine. The kiss was commanding, tongue and teeth and lips seducing me, tormenting me. His hands quickly traveled south, following the column of my neck, down to my shoulders, then my chest. His palms flattened over my nipples, and I groaned into our joined mouths.

Using all two hundred and some pounds of him, Tristan forced me back until my spine was flat against the wall of the tiny room. He shoved a knee between my legs, and I tightened my thighs on either side of it, tipping my hips back and forth, grinding myself against him.

The sane part of me was screaming at full force to stop. But the insane part of me was in control at the moment, thanks to Tristan's bone-melting kisses. He knew exactly how to touch me. He kneaded my breasts, pulled the nipples until they were painful little peaks. I gasped and writhed and whimpered.

He broke the kiss, only to lick and nip my neck, my earlobe. I was dizzy, shaking, barely able to stand. Thankful the wall was behind me, I steadied myself, bracing my arms against Tristan's shoulders, and closed my eyes, letting the pleasure his deft mouth and hands were stirring inside of me roll over me like a wave. I could hardly believe what was happening. I'd never, not in a million years, imagined myself doing something like this in a public place.

I heard voices, coming closer. I panicked, pushing at Tristan's shoulders. "Tristan!" It was a whisper, but a warning too. "Can't you hear? Someone's coming."

"Shhhh." He kissed me again, trapping my objections. His hands traveled lower, down my stomach. One pushed under my panties, fingertip grazing my labia. I shuddered and swallowed a moan, afraid to make a noise. Outside our door, I heard the salesclerk talking to a customer. A door slammed. Footsteps approached. A soft knock on my door.

Oh God!

Tristan's finger, the one that had been teasing me, plunged inside.

Oh God!

I swallowed a scream.

He added a second, and I almost fell over.

Breaking the kiss, he lifted his other hand to my mouth, brushing his fingers over my lips, his way of telling me to keep quiet. He didn't have to tell me that. If there was one thing I feared in life, it was going to jail.

Another knock. "Miss Barlow? Are you all right?"

The doorknob jiggled.

Oh God, she was going to unlock the door.

"I'm fine!" I squeaked. "Thanks. Just . . . taking my time trying on these dresses."

"Okay, if you need any help, I'll be outside."

Tristan rammed three fingers in my pussy, and I almost lost control.

"Thanks," I shouted, sounding like I was running a marathon.

Tristan growled in my ear. "I want you now." His fingers continued their plunging torment, in and out, fingernails scraping my inner walls and sending shock waves of pleasure through my body. "Unbuckle my belt."

With shaking hands, I did as he said.

"Now, pants."

I unbuttoned the top button, unzipped the fly, and pushed his pants and snug black athletic boxers down his hips. His thick rod sprung free.

"Condoms are in my wallet." Still fucking me with his fingers, he bent down to tease a hard nipple with his tongue. I gasped, fighting to concentrate, barely able to function. I reached for his bunched-up pants, fished around in the folds of fabric. He finally shoved my hand aside with his free one, found the wallet, and handed it to me. Almost blind with need, I unfolded the leather, fumbling for a wrapper. When I found one, the wallet fell from my hands, landing on the floor at our feet.

"I'm going to fuck you so hard, Alice. You've been such a good girl." As if to illustrate, he slammed his fingers home, stroking me hard and deep.

My pussy clenched. A huge wave of carnal need slammed me. Oh God.

I had the condom. All I had to do was tear open the package. But my fingers weren't working. I fought with the damn thing. Wouldn't rip. I whimpered as Tristan pulled hard on my breast, teeth grazing my nipple.

"Alice."

"Wrapper."

He took it from me, grasped it with his teeth, and tore it open, then handed it back. "Put it on."

That I could manage, though it wasn't easy. And then he lifted me up by the hips, back against the wall, and shoved deep inside. His hands slid down, to cup my ass and hold me up.

A full body shiver quaked through me, and a groan slipped from between my lips. I wrapped my legs around him, arms around his neck, and held on as he fucked me hard, just as he promised. It was exquisite. Decadent pleasure.

The salesclerk came back into the fitting room area, checking on the other woman a few rooms down from me. She knocked again on my door.

"I'll be done in a few minutes," I said, trying not to sound like I was being fucked to oblivion.

"All right." Her voice was a little flat. She probably suspected something, but I was full of Tristan, and he was holding me so tightly, and to hell with her or security or anybody else.

"You naughty girl," Tristan murmured. He bit my shoulder. His fingers delved into my crack. "I'll let you come now. Come for me."

His words were like a potent aphrodisiac. One more thrust, and a blaze raged through me. My pussy spasmed around him as the powerful orgasm took hold of me. I heard myself shouting, "Tristan," before I could stop it.

Amplifying my pleasure, Tristan's thrusts came faster, harder, rougher. He was on the verge of climax. As hot as I was, and despite him being nearly fully clothed, I could still feel the heat radiating off him. I dug my fingernails into his cotton-covered shoulders and bounced, body still spasming from my orgasm. He bit me as he came, hard enough to hurt, hard enough to throw me into a second orgasm. I felt as if I had been swept up by a wild, thrashing river of sensation. Overwhelmed. Powerless. It completely took over. And I knew, right there, right then, that Tristan Stark had taken me over, just as that orgasm had.

I couldn't end this today.

I couldn't end this tomorrow.

No, I wanted Tristan in my life and all the pleasure—and

pain—that came along with him. He was my first master, maybe my only master, if that was how it was meant to be.

Still clinging to him, I kissed his neck, nuzzling him, pulling in his scent.

There was more to this than sex. I could tell by the way he looked at me, held me. Tristan needed me too. Possibly more than I needed him.

With his cock still buried deep inside, I whispered, "Tristan, I'm yours."

His hold on me tightened. He kissed me tenderly, and whispered, "Thank you."

He had thanked me.

Yes, I'd most definitely made the right choice. Not because he was rich.

Not because he gave me orgasms that nearly stopped my heart.

But because he appreciated me, cherished me, like no man had ever before.

"Let's go home," he said, playful sparkles gleaming in his eyes. "We have something very special to celebrate today."

That, we did. I'd found the master I hadn't realized I was searching for. And, if my suspicions were correct, he'd found the lover, the partner, and the friend he hadn't known he was looking for either.

Beaming, I placed my hand in his and said, "Yes, Sir."

Ruby's Awakening

ANNE RAINEY

1

_____

"You want the truth?" Ruby shouted into the phone. "Because you have a small dick! There, feel better?"

Ruby cringed at the angry tone on the other end of the line. They'd dated for close to two months and Ruby still wasn't sure why she'd let it go on as long as she had. Bryan, like all the other men before him, just didn't light her fire. She was starting to wonder if there was something seriously wrong with her when she looked forward to having alone time with her vibrator more than she did a flesh-and-blood man.

As Bryan went from angry to downright mean, spewing out nasty things about her body, her job, even her mother, for crying out loud, Ruby pulled the phone away from her ear and clicked the END button. She placed the phone on the railing and let out a sigh of relief.

As she stood on the deck of her two-story home in the burbs and looked out at her freshly cut lawn, Ruby took a mental tally of the number of relationships she'd ended in a similar fashion. Okay, it wasn't a big number, thank God for that. Still, it made her wonder if she'd ever find a man capable of satisfying her. Hell, it wasn't as if her expectations were over the top. A nice guy with a good job would be welcome. A decent-sized cock and a cute smile would be a plus. Preferably someone who wasn't living in his mother's basement. So, why was it so hard to find Mister Satisfaction Guaranteed?

Pondering that ever-present question, Ruby lifted her glass and swirled the dark red liquid before taking a sip. It was good. Slightly pricey, but when she'd purchased it she thought it was going to be worth the money. It was Friday night and Bryan was supposed to be there celebrating with her. She'd finally landed the job as director of operations. It was a big deal, and yet she stood on her deck in the dark, alone. She should've taken her friend Carol up on her offer to hit a few nightclubs. Dancing and loud music would've at least taken her mind off her orgasm-starved body.

The sound of splashing water caught her attention, and Ruby looked to her right. Her neighbor, Drake South, and his latest sex kitten, had apparently decided to go for an evening swim in his pool. She rolled her eyes as the woman's naked breasts bobbed in the water. "Fake," she muttered as she watched the pair of lovers. When Drake caught the woman around the waist and pulled her up against his hard, wet chest, Ruby froze. Whoa, was he naked as well? It was too dark out and the water hindered her view of the lower half of his body.

Ruby had often wondered about the dark-haired hottie with the scruffy facial hair and the lightning bolt tattoo that traveled down his right bicep. He was big and muscular, not an inch of fat on him thanks to his landscaping business. His tanned body could make a nun drool. The harsh features of his face could never be considered handsome, but there was something primitive about Drake. Something rough and wild. It appealed to her on a level she generally chose to keep hidden.

Unfortunately, Drake lived life on the edge, and Ruby had always steered a wide path around him. She'd seen his type.

Her own father had been an adrenaline junky. He'd never taken life seriously. His need for adventure had eventually killed him. Ruby could still remember that moment as if it were yesterday. It'd been a perfect summer day. A nice breeze, warm sun shining down. She'd been twelve years old and already more of an adult that her father. She'd heard her parents arguing that morning right before her dad had stormed out of the house. He'd sworn to be home in time for supper. Only he'd never returned. Ruby had learned later that her father had died in a skydiving accident. Ruby's heart still ached when she thought of the sadness in her mother's eyes. The knowledge that it all could've been prevented had her dad stayed home that day. It still made Ruby angry enough to see red. Her father's drive for that next big thrill had been the only thing on his mind that day.

Ruby was the exact opposite of her dad. She prided herself on her well-ordered life. She had goals and was determined to meet them. She liked men who were responsible and stable. To Ruby, common sense was more attractive than empty promises. The Drake Souths of the world had no place in her world.

So, why was she watching him kiss a petite blonde as if it were his last day on earth?

Just then Drake's gaze lifted, and suddenly Ruby was caught in his snare. All the blood left her face. She froze in place, unable to look away from the heat in his eyes. Unable to do the right thing and go inside, giving the lovers a measure of privacy. Ruby clutched the deck railing and watched the erotic display playing out in the pool next door. When Drake lifted his head and his lips curved upward, Ruby's heart nearly stopped beating. Oh crap, he knew she was watching! Her pussy flooded with liquid warmth and her nipples pebbled. *Go inside. Simply turn around and walk away.*

Ruby didn't move. Could barely think as Drake lifted the woman to the edge of the pool and sat her down on the hard cement. As his head descended between her thighs, Ruby's own clit throbbed and her panties grew damp with arousal. "Ah hell, this is so freaking wrong," she mumbled as she let her hand travel downward to the hem of her black skirt. As she lifted the material and touched the soaked, silk panties beneath, the muscles in Ruby's legs quivered. At that moment, the blonde's legs widened and she let out a loud moan.

"Ah, screw it," Ruby said to herself. It wasn't the celebration she'd anticipated, but a live show was better than her vibrator, any day of the week.

Ruby was clearly out of her mind. "Do the right thing," she quietly scolded her inner bad girl. "Go inside and give the pair of lovers their privacy." The demand didn't do a bit of good, though. Instead, the fire sweeping over her raged wildly out of control. "Oh God, I'm going to hell," she whispered as she watched Drake, her neighbor, use his mouth and hands to pleasure his petite, blonde date.

The woman wrapped herself around Drake's large, muscular frame and moaned.

A niggling of jealousy crept over Ruby as she quickly took a step backward, slipping deeper into the shadows of her deck to keep from being seen. Drake titled his head back, his gaze unerringly seeking hers in the darkness and a forbidden thrill ran through her.

"He can't see me now." Ruby's breath caught in her throat. "Surely, he can't see me."

Ruby cupped her mound through the dampness of her panties and watched as Drake clutched the woman's hip in one hand, holding her firm while he smoothed his other hand up and down her bare, wet back. As his head once again descended between the blond woman's thighs, Ruby massaged and kneaded, running her fingers in little circles over her clit. In her mind, she imagined it was Drake's hands on her body. *His* fingers teasing and playing.

As she slid the silky material aside and touched the slick and swollen folds of her pussy, Ruby heard someone moan. Her eyes shot wide, wondering for a moment if the sound had come from her. When she saw Drake cover the other woman's mouth with a palm, Ruby relaxed once more.

"What the hell am I doing?" she muttered, even as she slipped a finger inside her overheated pussy. Her gaze took in the erotic sight next door and a rush of moisture trickled down her thighs. Drake mumbled something, but Ruby couldn't make out what. The woman spread her legs wider and arched her back. Ruby thrust her middle finger deep and her legs quivered. As the blonde pressed her pelvis into Drake's face, Ruby's heart raced. What would it be like to have Drake's undivided attention like that? To be on the receiving end of all that untamed male hunger? She suspected he would easily have her begging for him with the slightest effort. There was just something about Drake. It was part of the reason Ruby had steered clear of him. From the moment he'd moved in next door earlier last year, Ruby knew she wasn't cut out to handle him. He was too intense, too extreme for her tastes. She preferred a man she could keep at arm's length. Drake struck her as the type who wouldn't be content unless he was snug and warm under a woman's skin.

Suddenly Drake lifted his head, tilting it sideways, and once more Ruby could swear the heat of his gaze was scorching a path over her body. It was impossible, of course, she was too well hidden with her back pressed against the siding. A large walnut tree provided a decent amount of cover too. Between the distance, the tree, and the darkness, she knew he couldn't see her.

When Ruby slipped a single wet finger in and out of her slick opening, teasing gently, she flattened her other hand against the cool wall behind her, desperate for the support. She closed her eyes and an image of Drake filled her mind. Suddenly she pictured him thrusting his long, talented fingers in and out of her, stroking her to a fever pitch. She could almost feel the brush of his body against her sensitive nipples. Each erotic image brought forth a moan and Ruby had to clamp her lips closed tight to contain the eager sounds.

She used her thumb to flick her clit and a cry tore free. Ruby thrust two fingers deep, but it wasn't enough. She needed more. She wiggled a third finger inside her, and the snug fit caused her to widen her stance. She pumped hard and fast. Her husky groans turned sharp with desire. Ruby coasted her other hand down her body and fondled her distended clitoris. At once, Ruby flung her head back and burst wide open. Her juices soaked her fingers and her pussy clenched and unclenched, making her ache to feel the heavy weight of Drake's hard cock. It would feel good; she knew it in her bones. Drake would fill her. He wouldn't be like Bryan, content with a quickie in the dark. Drake would take her all night long. Fuck her until she couldn't stand up.

As her body relaxed, her pussy softening, Ruby pulled free and opened her eyes. The pool was empty, Drake and the woman gone. Ruby sighed and stepped away from the wall, feeling more alone than ever. "I need a man," she muttered. Once more, Drake's sexy smile slid into her mind. The way he'd stared at her just moments ago. Her fingers itched to touch his big, powerful body. Ruby's heartbeat sped up and she cursed. Why had she watched? She'd tortured herself and now she would never get the man out of her head. "It's going to be a long, lonely night." She turned and headed back inside. Another glass of wine, that was what she needed. It'd relax her and maybe, just maybe put her to sleep.

As she tugged on the sliding glass door, a sound from behind her caught her attention and she froze. *Please don't be Drake.* Ruby turned. "Bryan?" She frowned when she saw him stagger.

Was he drunk? Fear skittered up her spine. "What are you doing here?"

"Y-you hung up on me, Ruby."

Oh, he was definitely drunk. And pissed, judging by the ugly glare. His white-knuckled fists weren't giving her a warm cozy feeling either.

Wow, could her evening get any worse?

2

Drake watched Skylar back her little red coupe out of his driveway. After she was gone, he closed and locked his front door and shoved a hand over his face in disgust. "I'm fucking insane," he gritted out. Why else would he tell a hot blonde who was willing to do anything and everything he asked of her to leave before he could even get her to the bedroom? "I'm certifiable." Skylar had been more than willing to play with him the rest of the night. He could be satisfied fifty ways to Sunday instead of standing in the middle of his living room with his dick as hard as granite in a pair of soaking wet swim trunks.

Too worked up to sleep, Drake went upstairs and changed into a pair of old, worn jeans and a black tank. A few minutes later he headed into the kitchen and grabbed a beer from the fridge. That's when he knew the truth. Ruby was to blame for his hard-on. He popped the top and took a long drink, then slammed the longneck bottle onto the countertop. Ruby had been standing on her deck earlier. Watching. Drake had felt those baby blues of hers on him.

He smiled when he thought of how she'd hidden deeper in

the shadows, thinking she couldn't be seen. But Drake had known she was there. He could feel her. Unfortunately, the knowledge that she wasn't the one naked and in the pool with him had put a real crimp in his Friday night plans. It'd taken him all of ten seconds to realize that Skylar was nothing more than a substitute. He even knew why he'd chosen her from all the other women at the club tonight. "She was Ruby's exact opposite," he muttered. Short, petite, and blonde. Skylar had big brown eyes that weren't anything like Ruby's deep blue pools. The two women couldn't be more different. No doubt about it, Skylar was cute and eager, but she wasn't Ruby. Only his red-headed neighbor's voluptuous body would satisfy the ever-present ache that Drake had been living with for the last several months. The problem was, Ruby avoided him like the damn plague, and he was getting good and tired of it.

If he smiled at her, she frowned. If he said hello, she mumbled under her breath and stuck her nose in the air. Like a queen addressing a lowly peasant. Shit. No way in hell was he going to get a wink of sleep tonight.

He'd never get any peace of mind. Not until he had the snooty woman in his bed. Drake crossed the room and opened the back door. He wondered if she was still up. When Drake stepped out onto his deck and looked toward her house, his hopes plummeted. No movement at all.

Their houses were close enough together that if it were daytime he'd be able to see the dirt on Ruby's white siding. He'd noticed the almost totally unobstructed view of her entire backyard the moment he'd moved in. He'd been impressed with her well-groomed lawn and the flower beds she clearly took great pride in. He'd yet to spot a single weed anywhere. Last week she'd purchased a new patio set. When she seemed to have trouble putting it together, Drake had offered to help, seeing it as a chance to get to know her better. Then her asshole boyfriend had shown up and screwed with his plans. The pale little dweeb with his perfectly manicured nails and neatly pressed shirt had struggled for hours putting together the swing, making Drake wonder what the hell she ever saw in the guy.

The woman had the sort of curves a man drooled over, but she wasn't just a pretty face. She was smart and independent and ambitious as hell, judging by her work schedule. So why was she with the dweeb? He'd cursed and gotten nasty with her, and she'd put up with it. Drake groaned and rubbed at the sweat beginning to bead on his forehead. Midnight and still hot as blazes. August in Ohio sucked.

He closed his eyes and thought back over the one time he'd gotten more than a quick glimpse of Ruby's pretty curves. A little over two weeks ago, Drake had been lucky enough to catch the little beauty sunbathing. He'd spotted her through his kitchen window as she'd sprawled out on her lounger wearing the cutest little black bikini he'd ever seen. He'd stood there, unable to move, staring at her. Her round, lush bottom beckoned him to walk right over to her and grab a handful. Hell, even now Drake remembered the little white drops of sunscreen she'd dribbled on her skin. Drake couldn't figure out why she'd bothered to lie out to begin with. Ruby didn't have a tan. Her skin was way too fair, and probably too delicate. She'd burn to a crisp. Still, he'd sure as hell imagined how delicious all that creamy skin of hers would taste against his tongue. He wanted to lick every inch of her body just to find out if she tasted as good as she looked. Drake had enjoyed the view that day, but he'd vowed to stop torturing himself with fantasies of taking her to his bed. Which was why he'd brought Skylar home.

"Great plan, dumbass," he muttered as he stood alone in the dark, aching for a woman who didn't even know he existed.

He needed a cold shower. As he turned to head back in, movement from next door caught his eye. Someone came around the side of Ruby's house and stepped onto the deck. It wasn't Ruby. And judging by the way the person staggered, Drake would bet money that they also weren't sober. Suddenly Ruby came out of the shadows of the deck and Drake wondered if maybe she was meeting a man on the sly. Drake couldn't make out who the person was in the dark, but the larger frame definitely resembled a man.

When the guy stepped onto the deck and grabbed hold of Ruby's arm, Drake stiffened. She jerked away and started for the house, but the guy was faster as he grabbed Ruby around the waist, pulling her to a stop.

"What the fuck?" Drake muttered as he sprinted across his deck and hit the grass running. When Ruby yelped, Drake saw red. He'd break the bastard's hand if he hurt her.

"Bryan, I thought I made myself perfectly clear on the phone," Drake heard Ruby say. "You and I are through. You can't just pop up here in the middle of the night, as if you have the right."

Drake slowed as he reached the steps leading up to the deck, and listened as Bryan tried to talk his way back into Ruby's bed.

"Ah, you don't mean that, sweetie."

"Yes, I do," she bit out. "And don't call me sweetie. I'm not your *sweetie*."

Ruby was clearly pissed, and Bryan was drunk as shit. Drake had just about heard enough. He rushed up the steps as Bryan grabbed Ruby by the arms and tugged her up against him.

"Let go of me!" she yelled as she tried to wrench herself free.

Drake knew she was angry by the tone of voice, but it was the fear in her eyes that spurred him into action. He took hold of Bryan by the back of the collar and yanked him backward. "You heard the lady, Bryan," Drake bit out. "Get lost."

Ruby's gaze widened as she looked over at him. Unless he missed his guess, there was a huge dose of relief in those blue eyes too.

"Who the hell are you?"

Drake about gagged at the amount of alcohol on the guy's breath. "Do us all a favor, buddy, and shut the fuck up." He looked over at Ruby. "Do you want him to stay?"

She rubbed her upper arms and shook her head. "Definitely not."

Drake nodded. "Then you might want to call the law. I'm not sure it's a good idea for Bryan to get behind the wheel right now."

"Oh, of course!" She turned and ran for the back door.

"Fuck you," Bryan spit out. "I'm not going anywhere."

After Ruby was safely inside the house, Drake wrapped a hand around Bryan's wrist and squeezed. "Lay a hand on her again and I'll break it." Drake tightened his grip for emphasis. "We clear?"

"I wasn't going to hurt her," Bryan sputtered as he tried to pull free.

Christ, was he going to start crying? Drake had zero patience for drunks and even less for a man who would hurt a woman.

"You blew it with her. Time to move on." Drake dragged Bryan to the nearest chair and shoved him into it. He heard a siren off in the distance. "And Bryan?"

"Huh?"

"Don't come back," Drake warned.

The next hour was spent talking to the cops. Bryan mostly cried. Ruby barely looked at either of them. The few times that her gaze had strayed his way, a blush stole into her cheeks and she'd quickly glance away. Drake thought he knew why too, but he wanted to hear her say it.

Once they were alone, Ruby escorted him into the kitchen and offered to brew a pot of coffee. It was the olive branch Drake had hoped for, and he wasn't about to turn it down.

Once they were seated at her round, oak table, each of them nursing a hot cup of coffee, Drake found himself at a loss for words. Ruby was so quiet, and Drake was beginning to worry that maybe Bryan had meant more to her than he'd initially realized.

"Did you love him?" Drake asked, needing to know what he was up against before he moved any further on his campaign to get the woman in his bed.

Ruby's gaze shot to his. "Who? Bryan?" Drake nodded. "God, no. I'm not sure why it took me two months to break it off with him, to be honest."

"Then why so quiet?" Drake thought of the way she'd rubbed at her upper arms earlier and he frowned. "Did he hurt you when he grabbed you out on the deck?"

She shrugged and ran her left hand over her right arm. "Not really. I'll have a bruise probably, but I bruise easily."

Drake got up and came around the table. He crouched in front of her and took her arm in his, rubbing over the spot Bryan had grabbed. "That little shit," he ground out. "I should've hit him."

One corner of Ruby's lips kicked up. "No, then Bryan could've said you assaulted him or something. This way he gets to spend the night in a jail cell and you get to sleep in your cozy bed."

He grinned and went back to the chair he'd vacated. "You do have a point there."

"I'm sorry you had to deal with all this." He watched her look toward the other end of the kitchen. "God, it's one in the morning, you must be exhausted."

Drake shrugged. "I couldn't really sleep anyway."

Ruby's cheeks turned red and Drake knew immediately that she was thinking about the little interlude in the pool. "Oh, I, uh, I see."

Drake smiled. "What about you?"

"Me?"

"You're up later than usual, aren't you?"

"Oh, well, sort of. I was celebrating."

"Celebrating?" She'd been alone, hadn't she? What sort of celebration was that?

She nodded. "I got a promotion at work. One I've worked really hard for. It was a big night for me."

And yet she'd spent the evening alone. "Then Bryan had to go and ruin it, huh?"

She swirled a finger around the rim of her cup and Drake wished like hell that finger was playing with his cock instead. He tamped down on his overeager sex drive. A woody wasn't a good way to start off things with a woman as classy as Ruby.

"I was supposed to be celebrating with him actually."

Drake frowned, not liking the idea of her celebrating anything with Bryan. Or any other man, for that matter. "Then why were you home alone tonight?"

Her nose wrinkled. "I said some not-so-nice things to him when I broke it off with him on the phone earlier."

He chuckled and leaned closer. "Now this I've got to hear."

She shook her head. "No, you don't. It was rather crude."

"Now I definitely need to know."

"Well, I sort of told him he had a small—"

Drake held up a hand to stop her, not needing to hear the rest. "Ouch, no wonder the guy was wasted."

She snickered and slapped a hand over her mouth. "Oh God, I'm a horrible person."

"Hell, you ask me, he deserved it."

"No," she rushed to say. "He isn't really that bad. He and I just didn't click, that's all."

"So, you never got to celebrate."

She shook her head. "Not really."

Drake stood and carried his cup to the sink. He poured most of the contents down the drain, having only managed a few drinks. All his concentration had been on Ruby. When Drake turned, he caught her staring at him. She bit her lower lip, and Drake imagined what it'd be like to have the right to tug the plump flesh free of her teeth and lick the little sore she was creating there. *Quit stalling. It's now or never.* "How about you and I celebrate together then?"

Her gaze widened. "Huh?"

"I can pick you up tomorrow around noon. There's a little place that serves the best ice cream known to man." He crossed his arms over his chest and leaned against the counter. "Are you in?"

Ruby was quiet a moment, her gaze eating him up from head to toe. Finally she stood and crossed the room. This close, Drake could see the way her full breasts filled out the flimsy blouse she wore. Drake's mouth watered for a nibble. "Is this a date?" she asked, a frown marring her pretty features.

Damn, the woman was skittish. Drake crossed the little bit of linoleum separating them and cupped her chin in his palm, needing the connection. He was desperate to touch her. Every inch of her. "I'd like it to be, yes," he answered.

She shook her head. "I'm not sure that's a good idea."

Drake shrugged, uncaring if it was the smart thing to do or not. All he could think about was spending more time with her. "What do you have to lose?" he asked, hoping logic would sway her to his way of thinking.

She took a deep breath and let it out slowly before replying, "When you put it like that, how can I say no?"

"Exactly," Drake murmured. He suddenly felt as if he'd won the lottery. He dropped his hand, but before he left there was one other little matter to tend to. He leaned close and whispered against the shell of her ear, "I saw you tonight, by the way." Ruby gasped, telling him in a heartbeat that she knew exactly what he was referring to. Before she could attempt to recover, Drake growled, "It was naughty of you to watch, Ruby." He stepped back and their gazes connected. "Good thing I like naughty."

"Drake, I—"

"I'll pick you up tomorrow at noon," he said, halting her rushed explanation. "It's supposed to be a hot one, so you might want to wear shorts."

She nodded. "Yes," she replied in a shaky, quiet voice. "Okay."

"Sleep tight," he murmured, leaving her standing in the kitchen and staring at him as if she wasn't quite sure what to do with him. On the other hand, Drake knew exactly what he wanted to do to her.

As he reentered his own house, a shot of adrenaline sped through his system. Tomorrow he would take Ruby to lunch, but if the gods were at all kind, it'd be her delectable body he'd get to feast on afterward. "About friggin' time too." He'd ached for the woman long enough. It was high time to bring a few of his X-rated thoughts to life.

3

"Let me get this straight. You watched the two of them having sex in his pool?" Connie asked around a mouthful of chips. "Yet, he asked you out on a date today?"

When her wacky, purple-haired friend had called earlier asking to come over, Ruby hadn't wanted to see her. She was too nervous about her date with Drake. But Connie wasn't one to take no for an answer, so she'd come over anyway.

"Er, is it really a date? It's lunch, not dinner and a movie. Does that still count as a date?"

"It's Saturday and he's a hot guy. Of course it's a date, you skinny fool. He could've had blondie all to himself until the wee hours of the morning, yet he chose to have coffee with you instead. He's obviously into you."

For Connie to call her skinny was just downright hilarious. The woman was so thin she looked anorexic. At six foot one, she towered over most men, not that she could ever really appear intimidating. 'Course, her bold mouth was pretty intimidating. And it wasn't that Connie was really anorexic. Heck, she could out-eat most guys. She was just one of the lucky few who didn't gain an ounce. A trait Ruby had often envied.

"For all I know he did spend the night with blondie. Crap. Another thing to consider here. I mean, what sort of man asks a woman out while he has another in his bed?"

"Uh-uh." Connie pointed a chip in her direction. "Sounds to me like he sent her home. Right after he caught you spying on him." She winked. "You little voyeur, you."

Ruby blushed. "Either way, I'm not calling this a date. Not until I find out more information first."

"Like, is he single? Does he want you as badly as you want him? And is he hung like a horse or did he get the short end of the stick like poor old Bryan?"

Ruby really didn't want to laugh, but she couldn't help it. Connie had a way with words and had since they were in grade school together. The woman was incorrigible. "Terrible way of putting it, but yes, those are all valid questions."

All at once Connie stopped eating and her gaze widened. "Ooh, yummy," she practically purred, the bag of chips forgotten.

Ruby turned in time to see Drake at her back door. He wore a pair of black shorts and a white T-shirt. It appeared as if he'd even tried to tame the wild mane of his hair, not that it had done much good. Dark strands hung over his forehead and he kept pushing them back. God, he looked good enough to lick, to hell with the ice cream.

Ruby strode across the room and slid the door open. "You can use the front door, you know?"

He grinned. "I thought of that about halfway up the steps."

"I'm ready. Just let me grab my purse." Ruby heard someone clear their throat and too late she realized Connie was still there. "Oops, sorry," Ruby muttered. "Connie Rush meet Drake South, my neighbor, and last night my savior." Ruby pointed to her friend and said, "Drake, this is my oldest and dearest friend. She and I go way back."

Drake stepped forward and offered his hand. "I think I've seen you coming and going a few times. Nice to finally meet you, though."

Connie took his hand and shook it. "It's the purple hair," she replied with a grin. "It sort of attracts attention."

Drake laughed. "Yeah, it's memorable." He released her and looked back at Ruby. "Any more problems with Bryan?"

"Nope," Ruby answered, as she tried to surreptitiously look at the lightning bolt tattoo on Drake's arm. Oh yum, the man had great biceps. Thick and strong and she badly wanted to reach out and squeeze, just to see if he was as hard and muscular as he appeared. A byproduct of his landscaping business, no doubt. Ruby about drooled.

"If I had to guess," Drake said, as he leaned against the wall next to the fridge. "I'd say he's probably feeling like an idiot today."

"I hope so," Ruby said, wishing for the thousandth time that she hadn't wasted the last two months on the guy. It was two months she'd never get back. Life was too short to throw away on assholes, she decided.

"Well, if you ask me," Connie said, "drunk or not, Bryan is a fool."

"On that we agree, Connie," Drake said, as he smiled over at her.

A rush of jealousy zipped through Ruby. The ugly emotion surprised her. She didn't have any claims on Drake. He could smile at whomever he chose. "You ready to go?" she asked him, as she grabbed her purse and cell phone off the counter.

Connie picked up her keys from the table. "That's my cue to skedaddle." She headed toward the front door and motioned for Ruby to follow. Out of sight of Drake, Connie whispered, "If you don't want him, I'll take him. Hot damn, he's adorable."

Ruby frowned. "Hey, he's my hot neighbor, go find your own."

"My neighbor is bald, lives off the state, and has about fifteen cats." She shivered. "No thanks."

Ruby grinned, not at all sorry. "That's your sad luck then."

"Okay, okay, retract the claws, woman. I get the hint loud and clear."

Ruby let herself relax a measure. "I'll call you later."

She nodded. "Good, I'm going to want lots of details." She stepped into the summer sun. "Oh, and for the record, he's definitely into you, girlfriend."

"How can you tell from that itty-bitty introduction?"

She rolled her eyes. "It doesn't take a genius. The man kept watching you as if you were a tall, cold glass of ice water and he'd just found his way in from a really long trip in the desert."

The description had Ruby laughing. "You're outrageous, but I love you."

After Connie left, Ruby went back into the kitchen and found Drake sitting at the table. "Sorry about that. She can be a lot to take in upon first meeting."

Drake stood. "I like her," he said as his gaze journeyed over her from head to toe. "I like you a hell of a lot more, though."

Ruby was instantly glad she'd chosen the white tank top and red shorts, considering the heat in Drake's gaze. "Yeah?"

"I wouldn't be here if I didn't," he murmured as he closed the distance between them.

She immediately stepped backward and held a hand up in the air. "There's something I want cleared up before we go any further."

He quirked a brow and shoved his hands in the front pockets of his shorts. "And what might that be?"

Get right to it, Ruby thought. *No sense prolonging the pain.* Like a bandage, Ruby chose to tear away the surface covering the issue that nagged at her the most. "The woman you were with last night, are you and she . . ."

He shook his head. "No. I met her last night and brought her back to my place, but that's all there was to it. We aren't together."

"And you didn't, what I mean is, you and she didn't . . ."

"What you saw us do in the pool was the extent of our involvement. I wouldn't have asked you out to lunch today if there was more to it than that. You have my word."

Relief swept through her at Drake's sincerity. "You don't know how glad I am to hear that."

Drake stepped forward and took her face in his palms. "You have my undivided attention, Ruby. I promise."

She smiled and her heart skipped a beat. "I won't lie, I like knowing that."

"Now, about that ice cream," he murmured as he slung his arm around her shoulder. "I'm hungry, and I'm afraid if we stay here much longer it won't be my stomach I satisfy."

The confession sent a jolt of electric heat through her bloodstream. God, how she wished she were bold enough to tell him what she really wanted. And it didn't have a darn thing to do with pralines.

4

She was killing him. As he sat across from her in the little red booth licking a pralines and cream double scoop cone, Drake groaned. Hell, Ruby had barely finished off the first scoop. She still had another to go. What the hell was wrong with him? He needed to think before his brain blurted out something horny and stupid. When she moaned around a mouthful of the sweet cream, Drake raked a hand through his hair and said, "I take it you agree with me, huh?"

"Hmm?" she mumbled as she licked up another mouthful.

"Is it the best ice cream you've ever had or what?"

"Oh my, yes," she said as she dabbed at her lips with a napkin. "Thanks for bringing me here, Drake."

I'm going to end up with a permanent hard-on. "You're welcome."

Ruby's eyes narrowed. "Why aren't you eating?"

"I'm having too much fun watching you," he admitted.

Her gaze traveled south, not that she could see his crotch with the table between them, but she wasn't naïve. Her cheeks were pink by the time her blue eyes were once more locked with his. "I, uh, feel sort of silly here."

Drake smiled at her predicament. "Don't. Every man in the place is eager for you to lick that cone again."

As if playing a game of hot potato, Ruby immediately dropped the cone onto the napkin in front of her. "If that was supposed to make me feel better, you failed."

He chuckled, reached across the table, and took her hand in his. "Don't feel shy, Ruby, it wouldn't matter what you were eating anyway."

"It wouldn't?"

"Hell, no. Men would still watch you. You're hot no matter what you do."

"Oh," she said, her voice softening. "Thank you."

"I'm just glad that you're with *me*." He wagged his eyebrows at her and rubbed his thumb over the back of her hand. "So, tell me, Ruby, do you have brothers and sisters?"

Drake wasn't turning out to be what Ruby had expected. He was sweet and funny and attentive. She decided there was more than met the eye with him. She picked up the cone and pulled away the bits of the napkin that had stuck to it, then started eating again. Only this time she made sure she gave it a few extra-long licks. She grinned as his gaze watched the action.

"No brothers and sisters," she answered. "I'm an only child. Connie and I are as close as sisters, though. We've known each other since grade school."

"What about your parents?" he asked, as if genuinely interested in her.

"My mom moved to Arizona. Dad died when I was young. Mom loves the weather down there. It's easier on her arthritis. Less humidity, I guess." She shrugged. "I've been out there a few times to visit and she comes here. We make it work."

His gaze darted to her mouth as she licked the cone. "You, uh, don't miss having her around?"

Ruby was having a hard time keeping a straight face. Drake was trying so hard to change the subject, to keep from thinking naughty thoughts, but Ruby didn't think it was working out well for him. "Not really," she said, keeping to the conversation. "I guess I've always been pretty independent."

"Now, why doesn't that surprise me?" he asked with a wink.

She wrinkled her nose. "Mom says when I started kindergarten she had to insist on walking me to the bus. Apparently, I didn't see the need. I knew what I was doing and where I was going, even then."

He chuckled. "You aren't the clingy type, huh?"

She shook her head, then licked the cone again. It was nearly gone when she said, "So watching me eat is turning you on?"

"Hell, woman," Drake groaned. "I'm never going to be able to stand if you keep that up."

Ruby grinned. "Good, I like knowing that." It was bold and she was baiting a tiger, but something about Drake made her act more reckless than she normally would.

Without warning, Drake stood. "Come on, we're leaving." With Ruby's hand still in his, Drake tugged her out of the booth and toward the door.

"Wait, I thought this was a celebration. Where are we going?" As they made their way to the front, a short, pudgy man got out of his booth and smacked up against Ruby. If not for Drake holding on to her, she would've fallen backward. Drake stopped and turned around. The guy held up both hands. "Sorry, I didn't see you there."

"It was my fault," Ruby said.

Drake offered a quick apology as well, then continued outside until he reached his black Blazer. He pushed her up against the passenger side door and thrust his leanly muscled body into hers. "Do you know how badly I want you right now?"

Ruby wanted to reply, but he didn't give her time. His mouth descended on hers, and before she could take a breath, Drake kissed her firm and quick. Ruby only had a few seconds to inhale his warm, masculine scent before he all too quickly lifted his head.

He ground his pelvis into her hips. "Do you feel what you do to me?" he whispered for her ears alone.

"It's the same for me," she answered, giving him her own dose of total honesty.

Drake grasped her around the middle with both hands, spanning her waistline. "Tell me to shove off if this isn't what you want. If I'm moving too fast. Tell me now, Ruby."

He watched her eyes heat up. As she pulled him close, closer still, fitting her lower half to his, and kissed him long and deep, Drake knew he had his answer. "I say we continue celebrating back at my place," he murmured against her open mouth.

"Yes," she replied in a breathless whisper.

In record time Drake drove the short distance back to his house. He was surprised a cop didn't bust him for speeding. Once he had her inside with the front door locked, Drake looked toward the kitchen counter. The sturdy granite top . . . it was only a few feet away.

"I won't last long enough to get you up the stairs," he explained as he walked backward, pulling her along with him, their lips locked together.

When he felt the cold wood of a bar stool nudge the backs of his knees, Drake turned and pushed the stool out of his way. Gently lifting her, Drake sat her down on the cold, smooth surface.

Ruby's startled hiss brought him to a halt. She took her lips from his. "It's cold," she pouted.

"Not for long, I can promise you that."

"Wouldn't we be more comfortable in a bed?" she asked, her hushed whisper turning him on. Everything about her made him ache with hunger and need.

He winked. "Comfort is overrated."

Ruby didn't argue, simply bit her lip and looked away. When Drake began inching up her tank top and he got his first glimpse of her white lace–covered breasts, he let loose a low groan. "Delicious," he praised, as he dipped his head and sucked one already erect nipple into his mouth, lace and all. Ruby moaned and dug her fingers into his hair, holding him tight against her.

God, she was sweet. He tugged the cups of the bra down until they got caught beneath the soft orbs. Ah, hell, she was soft, and so freaking perfect. He could feed on Ruby's luscious tits for hours at a time. The woman was a meal fit for a king.

He flicked his tongue over and around her pink nipple gently at first, then rougher, demanding her flesh to beg for him. He cupped the round globe and pulled it up higher, kneading the supple skin with skilled fingers. He heard her moan of delight and felt her writhing beneath him. Drake took joy in her animated responses to him. He gave in to his primal cravings and bit down. She arched upward, eager and begging for his touch. His hands answered her pleas and tugged her tank over her head and tossed it to the floor. Her bra went next. Once she was sitting atop the counter with her upper half exposed, Drake stood back and drank in the gorgeous sight. Her breasts were full and creamy white with large berry nipples, and freckles the color of cinnamon littered her shoulders and chest. Drake had a need to kiss each one, maybe play connect-the-dots.

He reached down and went to work on her shorts. The instant she was naked, his nostrils flared as he picked up her succulent scent. A fiery spice to match the delicate red curls covering her mound. Drake dipped his finger into the damp heat and found her budding desire. She was swollen and throbbing and sopping wet. For him. Only him. As he fondled and toyed with the little nub, Ruby circled her hips and pleaded with him to fuck her. Her orgasm came out of nowhere as she exploded all around his finger, screaming out his name.

"Jesus, that was fast," he admitted.

"It's been awhile," she admitted in a low, hoarse voice.

More proof that Bryan was an idiot, Drake thought to himself. He leaned forward and licked her clean, needing to taste every inch of her. He'd waited too long for her delicate flavor as it was.

Drake moved away and tore at the fly on his shorts, freeing his erection. In the red haze of his lust, Ruby's pleading barely reached his ears. His gaze connected with her blue pools and he swore he lost a piece of his heart to her in that moment. She stretched her arms out, waiting to embrace him.

But Drake had the intention to enjoy the beautiful seductress. He wouldn't be rushed. Moving behind the counter he grabbed a clean white linen hand towel and brought it to her.

"What is that for?" Her arms fell to her sides as she stared at him in confusion.

He didn't answer, only folded the napkin into a makeshift blindfold and placed it over her eyes, sending her into darkness.

"Uh," she said hesitantly, "I'm seriously not sure about this."

"I am," he whispered against her cheek as he tied the material into a knot at the back of her head.

The quiver in her soft voice gave away the anxiety she was feeling with his erotic game. "You know I would never hurt you, Ruby."

"Do I?" She cocked her head to one side. "We don't really know each other that well, after all."

True, but he felt as if he'd known her forever. He'd sure as hell craved her for the better part of a year. "How about I prove it to you, then?" he asked, giving her the option to back out. She didn't speak and Drake went for broke. "Trust me, baby. I'd never take advantage of you. Only pleasure, and a whole lot of it."

She relaxed and Drake wanted to let loose a predatory roar of triumph over her surrender. "I do trust you, Drake. And . . . I want you so bad."

"Good," he said as he ensured the blindfold was secure. "Is it too tight? Too loose?"

Silence surrounded them as she shook her head. Only her choppy breaths and the thumping of Drake's heartbeat filled the air.

"I want you to do nothing," he explained. "Only feel what I do to you. Give yourself to me. I want you to experience every touch, and every little stroke." An excited little bob of her head and Drake knew beyond a shadow of a doubt that she was more than ready. His hand skated up her thigh, and Ruby jumped. The blindfold made everything more pronounced for her. "Without your eyesight you'll be forced to rely on your other senses. Hearing, touch, taste."

He watched her lick her lips and nod as she attempted to gain her composure. Impossible, considering she was perched atop his kitchen counter, her plump tits bare and her pussy totally exposed for his pleasure.

Drake moved his hand up her thigh as he listened to her heavy breathing. As he reached her sweet center and began to flick his thumb back and forth over her clit, Ruby's voice grew thick as she moaned his name.

"Do you want me?" he whispered into her ear.

She shuddered beneath his hand. "Y-yes. You know I do. Please, Drake . . ." Her voice, now a thready bit of sound in the quiet room, drove every one of Drake's senses wild with need.

He plunged his finger into her pulsing heat, then kissed her gently on the lips. "Mmm, good answer."

Her hips began moving, arching into his hand as he fingered her. Drake continued sliding a single digit in and out of her opening, driving himself mad. Goddamn, he was already so hard he hurt. He wanted to plunge deep, thrust his cock into that honeyed pussy where he knew paradise waited.

"Oh God, Drake, that feels so good. Please don't stop."

"I couldn't if I wanted to, baby," he admitted. "You're so perfect, every inch of you. I want to sip and savor you. I want to take in your scent and enjoy the essence of your sweet femininity. I want you, Ruby. I've wanted you for months, damn it."

"Then quit teasing and take me," she softly ordered.

Drake gave her what she craved. He slipped his finger out and spread her juices over her pouty lips. "This is the spicy taste I want on my tongue, no other could ever compare to your luscious flavor." Then he licked her, slowly, drifting his tongue over her bottom lip. Her body bowed and Drake moved downward, tasting the satiny skin of her neck first, and then the ample softness of her breasts. She fit his mouth, his hands. This woman was made for him and he devoured her.

First he licked and then sucked on her nipple, luxuriating in her gasps and moans. Her hands fisted in his hair, pulling him closer. He toyed with one and then bit down on the other, giving equal attention to both beautiful tits. He could easily spend hours suckling and nibbling her.

"Do you know that you drive me to the very brink of insanity?"

"Then put your cock inside my pussy, Drake. Right now. I see no reason to torture yourself further."

Drake lifted his head and stared at Ruby's widespread thighs. She sat, blinded by the white linen cloth, her sex dripping wet, breasts glistening from the heat of his mouth. He wondered if she realized how open she was to him in that moment. Covering her eyes had unlocked a door for Ruby, and she'd unknowingly dropped the last shreds of her shyness.

"Fuck, you look hot like this, baby."

"That's nice. But can you please put your cock inside me?" she politely asked as she reached between his legs. It took her several tries before she had his dick grasped in her small, soft hand. She squeezed hard, drawing a low, deep groan from him. "Before I'm forced to tie you down and do it myself."

He chuckled. "I don't think you'll ever have to force me." Then, before she could make any more demands, he grasped her hips and pulled her to the very edge of the bar. He dipped his head between her legs and lapped up her sweet flavor. She went pliant when his tongue and lips moved over her. "Your tangy little pussy tastes so good," he murmured against her dewy center. "I want to lick you for breakfast, lunch, and dinner."

He slowly flicked her delightful berry nipples with his thumb, and voraciously sucked each until she was groaning raggedly and arching into him. She clutched at the bar top for support.

Drake lifted his head. "I want your mouth on my cock. Will you lick me the way you did that cone?" Ruby smiled and her eager nod sent his libido into overdrive. "Ah hell, yes."

He grasped her around the waist, pulled her off the bar, and set her back on her feet. She wobbled, but steadied herself quickly. "Bend forward at the waist," he instructed. "I'll guide you."

She did as he asked. Once her mouth was a breath away from the bulbous head, Drake took hold of her hair and stopped her. "Far enough. Now, open wide so you can take all of me." Again, her breathing quickened, but she silently obeyed his gentle demand.

Drake took his cock in his hand and brought the dripping tip to her waiting mouth. She tasted it with her tongue first, then took him all the way in, nearly bringing him to his knees with the wet suction of her lips.

"Jesus, baby," he groaned.

She bobbed her head up and down, sucking and licking several times before she released him. After she placed a teasing kiss to the swollen tip, she stood back up and placed her hands behind her back. "Your cock tastes very good, Drake. Much better than the cone. Did I do well?"

"You know you did," he replied, barely finding his voice. "And such a good little girl should get what she deserves, don't you agree?"

Her lips curved seductively. "I am celebrating, don't forget."

Drake lifted her back to the counter. "Mm, yeah." He lapped at her juicy pussy and sank his tongue between the sensitive folds. He tongue-fucked her and teased her clit. Suddenly another climax tore through her, drenching his fingers and tongue in her liquid heat. Ruby was practically lying on the hard surface by the time he was finished with her. Drake loved the sight of her there. He vowed he would see it again and again. This wouldn't be a one-time thing. No way in hell.

"Hold that thought," he said as he bent and grabbed his wallet out of the back pocket of his shorts. He took out a condom and quickly ripped the foil packet open. After he had it rolled down his dick, he nudged her thighs wide and stepped between them. "Now, Ruby," Drake demanded. Without another word, he plunged into her with a quick kind of force that had them both gasping for air.

He stayed still inside of her for a moment, enjoying the satiny clutch of her. Her inner heat burned him up from the inside out. Slowly, he pumped at her tight sheath, his movements growing fast and furious as need swept through him, heating his blood and making him ache to somehow bind her to him.

She came back at him with her own brand of passion too, scoring his back with her fingernails, marking her territory. He reached a hand between their bodies and touched off the beginning of a third orgasm for her. She screamed and wrapped her long, curvy legs tightly around his waist, squeezing him and sending him over that same blissful cliff with her this time. Drake drove into her one last time and exploded, filling her with hot come, her body contracting and sucking him in farther, milking him dry. They came back down to earth, landing together in each other's arms.

Several seconds passed before Drake pulled away. He stood there a moment, transfixed, staring at her sated body still shuddering from the orgasms he'd coaxed out of her. A pleasant smile lit her face; her hair a mess of red curls, and her eyes, those beautiful expressive blue pools, were still hidden by the makeshift blindfold. Drake thought she looked more beautiful than ever.

"I've never experienced anything like that before, Drake. Never."

He pulled the cloth from her eyes and tossed it away. As she became accustomed to the light, Drake bent and picked her up. Cradling her close to his chest, her head resting against his shoulder, Drake thought she felt perfect there. It felt right to hold her like this.

"Where are you taking me?"

"To a nice hot bath," he answered as he took to the stairs. "Where I plan on taking my time cleaning every inch of your hot body."

She hummed her approval. "You wash mine and I'll wash yours."

For the first time that he could remember, Drake actually trembled.

5

As he stepped into the bathroom and flipped on the light, Drake noticed Ruby's wild-eyed gaze land on his in the mirror. "What's that look for?" he asked, curious what was going through her mind.

She closed her eyes tight and buried her face into his chest. Her body went rigid as he stood her on her feet. "Talk to me, baby," he urged as he went to stand directly behind her and wrapped both arms around her middle to cup the undersides of the creamy swells of her breasts. He nudged her ass with his dick. "Are you regretting what we did?"

"No," she rushed out, "not at all."

"Good, because all I've been able to think about since I saw you spying on me last night was bending you over and pounding into you from behind." He shrugged. "Crude, I know, but I want nothing but total honesty between us, Ruby."

She licked her lips and Drake felt that light stroke clear to his balls. "You've been on my mind constantly. You're all wrong for me, though. Yet, here I am," she said.

"Wrong how?" he asked, not liking where the conversation

was headed. "Because from where I'm standing it feels damn right."

"We lead very different lives. I'm all about saving and planning for the future, while you live life on the edge."

He cupped her chin in his palm and stroked her lower lip with the pad of his thumb, craving the small connection. "If that's what you think, then you don't know me very well, baby."

"I've seen enough and heard a few stories to know that you're an adrenaline junkie." He started to protest, but she rode right over him in that snooty way of hers. "The wildest thing I've ever done is file for an extension on my taxes. Seriously, I lead a pretty sober life."

He *tsked* at her erroneous information. "I do like to let loose sometimes, I won't lie about that. But I'm not as reckless as you think. A little motor-cross racing from time to time, but that's about it. The landscaping keeps my ass too busy for anything more than that, believe me."

She squinted at him in the reflection, clearly not believing a word he was telling her. "What about three months ago when you came home with a cast on your arm?"

She'd seen that? A small thrill ran through him that she'd maybe been watching him as intently as he'd watched her. "That happened on the job," he explained. "I fell when I was unloading mulch and landed the wrong way. Broke my wrist." He tapped her nose and shook his head at her. "You shouldn't be so quick to judge."

"You're right, I shouldn't. But I've seen the proof for myself, Drake. You haven't had a serious relationship since moving here. Why is that?"

He quirked a brow at her. "You can't guess?"

She frowned. "No," she said in a voice so soft Drake had to strain to hear.

"The only woman I was interested in having a relationship with kept shutting me down."

"You're talking about me," she stated, her cheeks turning pink.

"Yeah, I'm talking about you. You wouldn't give me the time of day, woman. Hell, I was beginning to think I had cooties or something."

She shook her head, a slight smile curving her lips. "Not cooties."

"Then why?"

She shrugged and looked down at the counter. "You scare me, I suppose."

"Me?"

"Whenever you came anywhere close to me, I felt . . . out of control. I don't like to be out of control." She held out her arms and said, "I mean, look at me. I've never had sex on the first date, yet here we are."

"Is that why you date guys like Bryan?" he asked, needing to understand her better. "To maintain control?"

She bit her lip and her gaze darted to his in the reflection. "Maybe," she replied. "I don't know."

He loved her honesty. Ruby didn't hold anything back, and that sort of attitude was refreshing as hell. "Then take control now."

She cocked her head to the side. "What do you mean?"

"Allow me to be your servant, Mistress," he murmured against her ear as he gave a woman the lead for the first time ever. "After you're refreshed, I will see to your other needs."

Ruby's eyes grew drowsy with desire and her nipples pebbled. He let his hands drift upward to cup her more firmly, pressing against the aching peaks. She moaned and rested her head against his chest while he worked her upper body. Her responsiveness was a lick of fire down his spine. He wanted to be deep inside her. Feel her closing around his shaft in a way no other woman ever had. Ruby's cunt was a tight fist and he craved it.

First things first, though.

He drew back, steadying her before he went to run her bath. After the temperature was just right, he added a little shampoo to create some bubbles. It wasn't luxurious, but it was the best he could do for now. Once the water was at a decent level, Drake turned the tap off, then held out a hand. "Your bath, Mistress."

Ruby's eyes grew round. "You're really going to let me take control? Seriously?"

As if he were a lowly servant, Drake bowed at the waist. "If it pleases you, yes."

For a second she only stood there, as if unsure what to do with him. Finally she stepped forward and took his hand. Drake helped her into the warm water and waited for her to get comfortable before he knelt beside the tub. He picked up a washcloth from a shelf, got it good and wet, then dribbled the water over her breasts and ribs and stomach. Her full, round tits protruded out of the water, inviting him to kiss each hard nipple. He placed a soft peck to each rosy tip before drifting the cloth over her silky, wet skin. Ruby's eyes closed and she laid her head back against the tub, as if treasuring the moment.

Drake took his time washing her. Each arm and hand got special attention. Her slender neck and then all the parts in between. As he reached her pussy, he dropped the cloth and used his hands to massage and tease. Her eyes shot wide as he dipped his middle finger between her soft, feminine folds.

"You don't have permission to touch me there."

Drake barely contained a grin at Ruby's haughty tone. "Sorry, Mistress."

"You should be punished for such boldness."

The authoritative tone had a surprising effect on his cock. The bossier she sounded, the harder his cock got. "May I continue bathing you?" he asked respectfully.

"Yes, but hurry. The water is getting cold."

Again Drake was a little shocked by how quick she caught on to the game. "Yes, Mistress."

He picked the sponge back up and finished washing her smooth slick front, careful not to stray into forbidden territory again. Once he was finished, he stood and held out a hand. "If you stand, I'll wash your back."

Ruby placed her hand trustingly in his and let him tug her to her feet. When her ass was facing him, Drake was tempted to lean forward and sink his teeth into her sweet flesh. He held himself in check, barely, and picked up the washcloth again. With each inch of her he washed, his cock grew harder. As he reached her ass, Ruby softly ordered, "Use your fingers. Not the cloth."

Drake grinned. "Thought you'd never ask." He dropped the washcloth on the tile floor and clutched her hip in one hand, holding her firm. Drake smoothed his other hand over both ass cheeks, massaging and kneading. When he ran his fingers in little circles, letting them slip into the slick crevice between, Ruby moaned his name.

Drake growled as he encountered her tight, puckered anus. He released her hip and parted her. His eyes took in every inch of her pretty pink softness. Her body belonged to him. No other man had a right to her.

He slipped a wet finger inside her puckered opening, rimming it gently. Her hand shot out and slapped against the wall next to her for support, then she pushed her ass toward him, giving him permission to go further.

Drake obliged and slid his finger out, then stroked her labia, lightly teasing her sensitive skin. Her moans drew him like a moth to a flame. He used his thumb and index finger to pinch her pussy lips together and her moans turned to cries of need. "Do you want to feel my fingers inside this hot cunt, baby?"

"Yes. Oh God, yes!"

Drake released her folds and slid two fingers deep. Ruby cried out his name and bucked against his hand. He watched her flesh closing around his fingers and felt his dick drip with need. He slipped a third finger in. It was a snug fit, but she only widened her stance, giving him better access to her body. He pumped her hard, fast. Her husky groans turned sharp with desire. His other hand snaked around and fondled her distended clitoris. "Come for me. Do it now, Ruby."

As if she'd merely been waiting for permission, Ruby flung her head back and burst wide open. Her pussy clenched and unclenched, making him ache to slide into her. Her shouts were music to his ears as she bathed his fingers in her dewy warmth.

As her body relaxed, her pussy softening, Drake pulled free and sucked her juices off each digit. Her taste fueled his already rampant need. He stood to his full height, then grasped her by the waist and lifted her out of the tub. After he towel dried her, he flung her into his arms and carried her to the bed. He laid her gently on top of the black comforter, then came down beside her. Drake turned her to her side, facing away, and entered her in one smooth stroke from behind. Ruby's inner muscles clamped tight around him and molded to his shape and size. Drake thought he'd go up in flames from the heat of her pussy.

"Fuck me faster, Drake," Ruby whimpered as her need took over, blocking out everything else in that moment in time.

Drake pounded into her, driving his cock deeper. He reached around and cupped her breast and squeezed, as he slid in and out of her tight heat. "Do you feel how well we fit? Just feel, Ruby. For right now, nothing else exists except you and me."

"You make me want to let myself go, Drake."

"Good," he replied. "I won't let anything happen to you, baby."

After that stark confession, the only sounds in the room were of Ruby and Drake touching and playing. Their bodies came together with new purpose.

They made love late into the night, and somewhere along the line, Drake's heart got into the game. That wasn't supposed to happen, and he wasn't at all sure what to do about it.

6

Drake was having a very hard time keeping a straight face. He really didn't want to offend her, especially considering she'd baked him food. God, it was good to see her. Ever since he'd dropped her off at her front door the previous morning, Drake had found one reason or another to call her and text her. He was beginning to think he was becoming a nuisance, coming on too strong, so he'd backed off.

Just as he was about to cave and go over to her house and ask her out on a second date, she showed up at his back door. He'd watched her work up the nerve too. Twice she'd started across their yards, only to turn back both times. Apparently the third time was the charm, and Drake wasn't about to let her escape, not now that she'd finally come to him.

"Well, are you going to stand there all day holding those cookies hostage or what?" he asked around a grin. "Because I have to say, they look delicious and it'd be a shame to let them melt out here in the hot sun."

Several seconds drifted by before Ruby glanced down at the

melting chocolate treats. "Crap," she grumbled. "Sorry. I, uh, baked these a little bit ago. For you," she quietly added.

Drake took in the sight of Ruby in a pair of cutoffs and a black halter top, then whistled low. Oh, he appreciated the cookies she'd baked for him, but her pretty legs kept snagging his attention too. "Sweet Lord, you were blessed with a great pair of legs, woman," he murmured. They were long and shapely, with muscle tone in all the right places. Not pencil thin. Those muscles had already come in real handy, and he hoped like hell they would again.

"Oh, uh, thanks."

Before Ruby had arrived, Drake had been working up a bill for an office complex that he'd done some landscaping for. But how the hell was a man supposed to concentrate when a hot redhead came bearing gifts of food? "Look at me, standing here like a damn fool." He stepped back and let her enter, but his gaze went straight to the sway of her cute ass. Ah, damn, he never should've looked.

"The cookies look tasty," he said, hoping to get his mind off her body for five minutes. "Want to share with me?"

"If you have milk, then I'm in," she answered with a smile.

Ah, to hell with it. A man could only stare into the face of temptation so long before he surrendered. Drake pulled Ruby against his chest, anxious to feel her sweet curves against his body. He tipped her chin up and whispered, "Looks like you were sampling the goods, baby." Drake dipped his head and licked at a spot of chocolate on the corner of her mouth. As his tongue came into contact with her mouth, sweeping back and forth over her soft lips, he heard her whimper and wrap her arms around his neck. God, he loved when she did that, came at him with her own heady dose of hunger. When Ruby parted her lips and teased his tongue with hers, Drake angled his head and pulled her closer, fitted her curves to his. Their bodies aligned so perfectly, and he wished like crazy they were both naked.

As their mouths played, Drake knew he was no longer in control. Around Ruby, control went up in smoke. Her tongue shyly explored his, but it wasn't enough. He coasted his palm down her back, cupped one firm butt cheek in his palm, and squeezed. Ruby gasped and froze a moment, then all but melted into him. With her soft curves pressed so close there was no way she couldn't feel the rigid length of his cock nudging her belly. He took hold of her full, womanly hips and pulled her in tight, needing her to feel what she did to him. Damn, why was it so hard for Drake to relinquish her mouth?

Ruby was effectively knocked off-kilter. A kiss was the very thing she'd longed for, but she hadn't let herself hope. She'd missed him, and it had infuriated her to know how quickly he'd gotten under her skin. It was Monday and she hadn't gotten a damn thing accomplished at work all day because all she could think about was the night she'd shared with Drake. How perfect it'd been. And how badly she wanted a repeat.

And, oh God, he had the most incredible mouth. She heard someone whimper; it could have been her, but she didn't really care. Though she knew without a doubt that if she didn't pull away from him he'd be able to have her right there on the kitchen floor. As much as that prospect tantalized her, she was reminded of Connie's lecture at lunch about men enjoying a challenge. The thrill of the chase. She was not giving Drake much of a challenge or a chase. In fact, she was pretty darned shameless.

Ruby pushed at Drake's broad chest and managed to break the kiss, hopefully saving a little of her dignity in the process. Drake simply stared down at her with brooding eyes. "I missed you," he admitted. He stared at her mouth as if he wanted to devour her one bone-melting kiss at a time.

He shoved a hand through his hair. "I'm pretty sure if you

hadn't stopped me just now, I would have yanked down those sexy little cutoffs you're wearing and taken you right here." He shook his head, took the plate of cookies from her, and placed them on the kitchen counter. "I'm acting like a friggin' deer during rutting season here. Sorry."

Ruby shifted from foot to foot, not sure how to respond to his stark confession. "Not sure if you noticed, but I wasn't exactly protesting."

His eyes darkened. "I noticed." The deep timbre of his low voice sent jolts of electricity through her. He picked up a cookie and popped the whole thing into his mouth. "Mm," he said after finishing it off. "They're good. Thanks."

"You're, uh, welcome." She took a fortifying breath. "And thanks for the text this morning." He'd woken her with the message GOOD MORNING, BEAUTIFUL sent to her cell phone.

Drake grinned, and once again his gaze traveled the length of her. "I would've preferred to wake you with a kiss, though."

Since Ruby was still feeling the effects of his masterful mouth, all the way to her toes, she decided not to respond. Instead, she turned and started for the back door. "Well, I won't keep you."

Drake stopped her when she reached the door with an arm around her waist. "I want to take you out Friday night. Are you free?" At her hesitation, Drake took another step closer. "Didn't you enjoy our first date, baby?"

"You know I did," she said, unable to hide the quiver in her voice. Ruby could feel every hard inch of Drake pressed up against her back, including the impressive bulge beneath his fly. He was aroused. It made her feel ten times better to know she wasn't the only one turned on. Heck, her knees hadn't been steady since he'd taken her on the kitchen counter. The need rushing through her scared her, though. No man should be able to get under her skin so quickly. What was wrong with her?

"Then let me take you out again. Seven o'clock sound good? We could go out to dinner and a movie. Would you like that?"

Drake was still talking in that low, sinful voice of his, and the feel of his breath so close to her had moisture pooling in her most private of parts. Ruby said the first thing that came to mind. "I do want to see you again. It's crazy how much I want to see you." Belatedly she realized that she hadn't merely been thinking those words, she had spoken them aloud.

Drake turned her in his arms and placed a gentle kiss against her forehead. "You'd better get your tail home, baby, before I decide I want to keep you here the rest of the evening."

His words had the desired effect. Ruby quickly opened the slider and stepped out into the late day sun. She couldn't seem to speak around the knot of emotion clogging her throat. When she reached her own yard, Ruby turned and caught Drake quietly watching her. Her blood pounded hot in her veins as Drake's gaze zeroed in on her backside. She watched as he licked his lips and shook his head. To tease him a little, Ruby added an extra twitch to her walk. Drake dragged a hand over his face, and Ruby had to bite back a smile. *Good,* she thought, *he's as hot for me as I am for him.* Only seemed fair really.

7

Ruby looked out at the dance floor and smiled when she saw her friend Connie dancing with her on-again-off-again boyfriend, Jason. When Ruby had told her friend that Drake wanted to take her out again, Connie had suggested a double date. It'd sounded fun so Ruby had agreed, but she secretly thought maybe Connie was attempting to keep an eye on Drake. She didn't trust him. She'd mentioned his off-the-cuff tendencies and risky behavior more than once. Connie was afraid Ruby would get hurt in the cross fire. She'd wanted to listen to her friend's advice, but there was something exciting about Drake that made her a little bit impetuous. It was a side to her personality she hadn't realized she possessed, and she sort of liked it.

"I've missed you this week," Drake said as he leaned close to be heard over the din of the music. "Friday took forever to get here."

"I missed you too." She pointed to the dance floor and said, "I hope you don't mind the change in plans."

He shrugged. "As long as I get to spend time with you, it

makes no difference." His gaze went on a slow, heated journey over her body. "And you look amazing tonight. Every man here is checking you out in that sexy dress."

Ruby smoothed a palm over her midriff. "Thank you." A little trill of excitement raced up her spine at Drake's praise. The dress had been expensive, but worth it, judging by the heat in Drake's dark eyes. It was a little black strapless number put together in the most erotic way with little triangle-shaped cutouts down the front, stopping just below her navel. The triangles were very strategically placed so as to show cleavage, but nothing more. She felt exotic wearing it. Like maybe she wasn't the serious and dull office worker for once in her life.

When Ruby's gaze landed on Drake again, she had to force back a moan. His black jeans molded to his muscular legs and lean hips as if custom-made. God, his ass was so solid a girl could bounce a quarter off it. His simple white T-shirt wasn't anything special, but on Drake it looked better than Armani. His wide, solid chest made Ruby want to reach out and touch. With the easy move of his hips and the smile kicking up the corners of his mouth, Ruby couldn't stop staring.

And why should she?

Earlier, as he'd escorted her to their booth, he'd taken her breath away. Just as the thought flitted through her mind, his brow arched up in inquiry, as if he could read her so easily. As if he knew what she was thinking. Heat crept into her face and Ruby wanted to groan. Great impression.

She breathed deep and resisted the urge to hide, then sat up a little straighter. Her best friend in the world was dancing it up and having a great time. Then again, Connie always appeared so darned confident. If only an ounce of that confidence would rub off on her, Ruby would be a happy camper.

Drake reached out his hand, which effectively stopped her train of thought. "It was my good fortune that I should decide to come here tonight, Ruby."

His voice was deep and rough. She loved listening to him talk. A voice like that could make a woman do all sorts of illegal things. Too late Ruby realized she was clinging to his hand as if it were a lifeline. She released him.

"Hey, you were getting used to my touch. Why shy away?"

She shrugged. "I don't know. This thing between us, it's moving too fast for me."

Drake stared at her a moment, then reached for her hand once more. This time he didn't take it in his own; he only drifted his thumb back and forth over the back of it. The light touch went clear through to her womb.

"I get that, but it feels right to me." Drake smiled slightly. "Are you still scared?"

Ruby's heart fluttered at the sensual tone in his voice. "No," she said, but she knew it was a lie the minute the word was out of her mouth. "Okay, yes. I'm scared."

"Is that why you brought Connie?" He motioned to where Connie and her date were dancing several feet away. "Were you afraid to be alone with me again?"

Ruby followed his line of vision and smiled. "Actually, that was Connie's idea. She knew I was nervous about tonight and offered to double date."

"She might be biting off more than she can chew with that guy she's with, though." Drake motioned to Jason with a tilt of his head. "He's pretty intense."

"I know what you mean, but Connie's a big girl." Ruby frowned as she looked at her friend. "She hardly needs my approval to dance with a good-looking guy."

Drake's gaze shot back to her, only now they weren't filled with easy humor. In fact, he looked annoyed. "You think he's good-looking?"

If she went by the sneer in his tone, Ruby assumed he didn't find that notion pleasant. "Yes, but he's not the man holding my attention lately."

Drake moved toward her and she forced herself to stay still, to not back away. "Yeah?"

Ruby chuckled. "Don't get cocky," she softly warned.

Drake leaned in close. His hot breath caressed her ear, and she wanted to pant like a hungry puppy. "I want to be alone with you."

Her heart sped up. He was so close she could smell his woodsy, masculine scent. God, he was potent. "Drake," she breathed out.

Drake licked her earlobe, then gently bit the sensitive flesh. "I miss you. Your taste on my tongue. Your sweet body pressed to mine."

He kissed his way down her neck and sucked at her pulse. She was surrounded by his large, powerful body and Ruby forgot all about the nightclub; even Connie and her date were temporarily pushed to the back of her mind. Everything vanished as Drake's mouth made an erotic journey over her skin. When he pulled back an inch, she whimpered.

"Come back to my place," he softly urged. "Give yourself over to me tonight, Ruby."

Did she dare? She was sinking deeper and deeper into Drake's web until she wasn't sure which end was up. But as Drake began smoothing a palm over her back, she knew she was helpless to him. In the end, there was never any other choice save for the most obvious one.

"Yes," Ruby blurted out. As the word whispered past her lips, she thought of Connie. She looked out at the dance floor and saw her friend engaged in a conversation with Jason.

Looking at Drake, she saw an answering heat there. They were both about to experience something thrilling. Honesty forced her to admit that he scared her a little. No, that wasn't right. It was the way he affected her. He so easily turned her body to fire and all he had to do was smile. That kind of power was frightening to her. She was a confident woman. She was in control of her own emotions. No one else. And certainly not a man.

Ruby stood and went to Connie. She explained the change in plans. It turned out Connie had made new plans as well, with Jason. Ruby worried, but knew her friend well enough to know that once she had her mind set on something, that was all she wrote.

After getting the go-ahead from her, Ruby went back to where Drake was still sitting. "I'm ready if you are."

His grin was predatory. The juncture between her thighs went liquid as his gaze traveled over her body, then he gave a nod. Without another word, he took her by the hand and led the way out of the nightclub and down the stairs to his SUV. He let go of her while he put her into his Blazer, only to take hold of her again after he was situated behind the wheel and on the road.

It was as if he meant to bind her to him. Odd that she should think that. They'd only just met and he didn't seem any keener on permanent relationships than she. Still, he acted like he was staking a claim.

In the dark, close confines of the Blazer, Ruby swore she saw him smile. It was feral and wicked, and her stomach went all jumpy.

Damn, what had she gotten herself into?

He looked like temptation in the flesh with his sinfully gorgeous hair and intense black eyes. Eyes a woman could drown in. Those eyes had been focused on her as if she'd been the only person in the bar. It was a thrilling notion.

She imagined being alone with him, in a room lit only with candles. She wouldn't be wearing a stitch of clothing, nor would he. But in his strong, callused hands he clutched scarves of every color. He'd approach the bed, where she would be sprawled out for him. He would use the soft, silky scarves to tie her down, making her vulnerable in every way. She wanted this with him. She wanted to completely immerse herself in Drake South. He might not know it, but he was going to give her a night to remember.

Drake expertly steered the big, black Blazer into his garage. His gaze swung her way. "We're here."

"So I see," she said. As he left the car and started around to her side, Ruby opened the door herself.

Drake frowned. "I open my date's door. It's the gentlemanly thing to do."

Words like that could quite easily make her fall head over heels for the big cutie. "Didn't know there were any gentlemen left in the world."

He bent and looked into her eyes. "You've been hanging out with all the wrong men then."

She laughed and reached up to cup his jaw. "We're in agreement there."

He winked and grasped her hand. "Come this way."

It didn't take Drake long to have Ruby inside the house and up the stairs. He barely had Ruby inside his bedroom before he slowly lowered himself to his knees in front of her. Her eyes rounded and there was a fire he hadn't seen in them before. "I need a taste of you, Ruby."

She started to protest, and he could see the way her cheeks bloomed pink at his erotic words.

"You wouldn't deny me, would you, baby?" Drake didn't wait for a reply as he grabbed handfuls of her dress and slowly tugged it upward, tenderly exposing the lower half of her body. The soft down of her pussy was hidden from his view by her panties. He frowned, took hold of them in both hands, and yanked, easily tearing them in two. Drake tossed them aside, pleased now that her glistening mound was visible to him. He was suddenly very hungry. Staring at the beauty of her there, he groaned. "Fuck, I'm becoming obsessed." He should've known once wouldn't be enough. Not with a woman like Ruby. She was more than a pretty face. Everything about her drew him like a bear to honey. He needed more time with her. To know her, inside and out. "Yep, definitely obsessed."

"You won't hear me complaining," she quickly replied, spurring Drake on.

"Put your leg over my shoulder, Ruby." Unsure, but eager, Ruby did as instructed. The position put the apex of her thighs directly into Drake's face. She felt awkward and wobbly in her pumps, but Drake only grasped her hips and pulled her to him. He kissed her, then used his fingers and spread her open, exposing her clitoris.

Ruby couldn't move, and in fact had to force her lungs to take in air. As Drake's mouth closed around her clit, Ruby rocked forward. The physical act of what they were doing mingled with the intensity of her emotions until Ruby felt totally exposed. Drake's tongue moved in and out of her pussy in a rhythm akin to making love. His hands clasped onto her bottom, bringing her closer and delving deeper. Drake seemed to be giving her everything he had to give. A groan tore free of his throat as Ruby raked her fingers through his hair and clutched on to him for dear life.

"More," she shamelessly begged. "I need so much more."

"Fuck, yeah," he whispered against her overheated skin. He flicked his tongue over and around her clit, time after time, until her thighs started to quiver and her body began to spasm out of control. Without warning, Ruby shuddered and screamed as she came into Drake's greedy mouth.

"Christ, you taste sweet, baby. So damn sweet." With a flick, Drake unsnapped the front closure of her bra and walked her backward to the bed. He pushed her gently down and then let her watch him as he undressed.

She felt exposed, emotionally as well as physically. Her first thought was to cover herself from his hungry gaze, but her mind came to a crashing halt when his shirt came off. His chest was beautiful and masculine. His muscles were hewn to perfection by hours of hard work. The sprinkling of dark chest hair all but begged Ruby to reach out and play. She followed the tempting line down over his stomach to the intriguing way it disappeared into the waistband of his pants. Drake took hold of his fly, unsnapping and unzipping. Ruby's mouth watered as she waited, knowing the heavy weight of his cock was so close yet so far out of reach. Within minutes he stood in front of her, naked and hard and ready. Her pussy was already wet with anticipation of the pleasure Drake would give her. Only Drake had the power to make her cry out in ecstasy.

Drake saw the arousal in Ruby's deep blue eyes. She wanted him, but part of her still seemed to be holding something back. Drake reached toward her and took hold of Ruby's hand, then brought it to his cock. "Do you feel the way I need you? I'm like this twenty-four hours a day for you. I can't seem to stop thinking about you."

Her small fingers wrapped around the base of his dick with no hope at all of actually encompassing his entire width. She squeezed, as if familiarizing herself with his weight and size. When she stroked up and down, torturing him with the gentleness of it, Drake cursed.

His voice was thick and unsteady, when he growled, "Enough, baby, I'll never last if you keep that up."

She gave him a startled look, but she saw the pained expression on his face and she smiled wickedly at him then stroked once more.

He pulled her hand away gently. "You little tease, come here." Then he lowered himself on top of her, careful to keep his weight on his arms. "You have beautiful breasts, Ruby." His tongue darted out and brushed the tip of one. "And you taste as sweet as cream." Another lick, then, "Pretty little drops of cherries in a bowl of luscious cream." Then he gave in and sucked, long and hard, biting down just enough to make her squirm and moan.

"God, Drake, it feels so good when you do that."

"You mean this?" And he continued to lick and nibble on the other breast.

"Oh yes, that." She arched her back trying to get yet closer to him, to his clever mouth. She squirmed under him, agitated, needing something just beyond her reach. She began caressing the length of his back, her cool fingers sparking off flames everywhere they touched. It was his turn to moan and she felt heat spiral through every inch of her body. By slow degrees he was turning her inside out. His lips journeyed down her ribs and stomach, his hands wrapped around her hips, massaging little circles. When he slid down further, tonguing her belly button, she felt herself coming apart. She had no idea the belly button could be such a fount of sensation. But then his fingers skimmed over her hips and touched the springy curls between her thighs. She froze, automatically throwing her hand up to stop him.

"Drake, it's never been like this. It's different. You're different."

Her soft voice, so fragile, was his undoing. "Shh, I know, baby. It's the same for me, trust me."

She let up on her hand just slightly and nodded, her heart swelling with emotion. He kept his eyes on hers as his fingers began their erotic discovery. He rubbed his thumb across her swollen clitoris, enjoying the way her eyes slowly drifted closed, and her breaths began to come in tiny gasps. Holding himself back was the hardest thing he'd ever had to do, but he wanted to give her as much pleasure as he could before he took his own.

"Open your eyes for me, Ruby."

She complied and he thrust one finger into her tight opening. Her mouth opened, but no sound came out. Drake began moving in and out; feeling her muscles clench around his finger was a sweet kind of torture. She was warm and wet and inviting. He slipped a second finger in and felt her body stretching to accommodate. She began to protest, but he only stopped her with his thumb to her tiny nub. He rubbed her clit back and forth, pumping her tight passage with his fingers at the same time. She started moving now, caught up in the fires of ecstasy. Undulating against his hand and throwing her head from side to side, pleading with him, begging him as her body flew out of control. She screamed out her orgasm and Drake was lost.

His control snapped.

Yanking his fingers free, impatient for his cock to feel her incredible grip of flesh and muscles, he levered himself on top of her and positioned himself at her opening. Then he thrust forward, penetrating her in one smooth movement. He swallowed her cries with kisses meant to soothe, and held himself still while her body molded around him. The muscles in his neck jumped and quivered with his restraint. But it was the tear that escaped the corner of her eye and made a trail over her temple that had him feeling something real similar to love.

He angled his head and licked it away, then began trailing little kisses everywhere at once. Touching his lips to her temples, her eyelids, and the delicate slope of her chin. He moved his hand between their bodies, and began stoking her passion to new heights. Surprise registered on her face as she felt herself becoming aroused all over again. He trailed his caressing mouth lower, to her clavicle and over the small indent at her throat, and there he lingered. Sucking the velvety soft skin into the dark recesses of his mouth, bathing her with the soft texture of his tongue. She moaned and twisted beneath him. Her quickened breathing amplified his need a thousand times. Immediately Drake began moving inside her. Slowly at first, building the fires deep within her body, allowing her to feel his fullness a measure at a time. Ruby wrapped her arms around his torso, her legs around his waist. He felt her shyly stroke his back, her shaking fingers an indication of her excitement. With her entire body now draped around him, enfolding him in her innocent web of sensuality, he felt something inside him give way—as if a barricade had been torn down. He emitted a low growl of possession and pushed harder, faster, into her inviting wetness, continually toying with her swollen clit. She arched upward, pressing her breasts against him as she soared over the precipice once more. His hunger took over when she screamed out his name. Her smooth vaginal walls contracted and he joined her this time, her body milking him dry. It was as natural as breathing.

Watching the dark fires in her eyes burn bright was as addicting as any drug. When her tongue darted out, licking at his chest, swirling over the dark patch of chest hair, Drake knew a kind of tenderness he had never known with any other woman.

"Stay the night with me," he urged, needing to hold her throughout the night.

"Yes," she whispered, as she kissed the spot directly over his heart.

Drake shoved out of bed. "Be right back," he explained at her frown. He made quick work of disposing the condom and slipped back in beside her. When he pulled her atop him, blanketing his body with her silky curves, she sighed, content and replete.

"I'm considering kidnapping you," he said, as he pressed a kiss to the top of her head.

"Yeah?"

"Yep," he answered. "The way I see it, it's the only way I can be sure you won't slip through my fingers."

"Could be fun," she mumbled.

He chuckled. "I love the way you think."

She grasped his semierect cock in her palm and winked. "Right back atcha."

Drake had the feeling he wasn't going to get a bit of sleep. Not that he cared. Not with Ruby London all naked and willing in his bed. The woman was a thousand times more potent than coffee, and a hell of a lot more addicting.

8

It'd been three weeks since she'd first said yes to a lunch date with Drake. Three weeks of sheer bliss. They'd spent their evenings watching movies together and vegging on his couch. They'd played sexual games in and out of the bed. And they'd talked. A lot. She knew all about his parents, who lived up near Lake Erie. His brother who had moved out to California and gotten married recently. She'd shared parts of herself with him that she hadn't shared with any other man. But she wanted more. More than a single night at a time. She wanted an entire weekend. And one way or the other, Ruby was going to get it.

First, she needed to talk to Connie. Her attitude toward Drake was beginning to wear on her. Her adamant belief that he would hurt her was a subject Ruby could no longer ignore.

It was Friday night, one week since the night at the club. And it was time Connie did some listening instead of lecturing.

Ruby knew her friend wouldn't like the conversation they were about to have, but it simply couldn't be helped. Connie had expressed her concerns that Drake was moving too fast.

And in many ways, Ruby agreed. But the notion that Drake wasn't in it for the long haul needed to be addressed.

She'd never in her life taken a chance, tossed caution to the wind, the way she'd done with Drake. And damn it, she enjoyed it. Enjoyed him. What was wrong with having a little fun for a change?

Ruby would be spending the weekend in Drake's bed, and in Drake's arms. That was all there was to it.

As Ruby put the last dish in the cupboard and dried her hands on the dish towel, she heard a noise coming from the front of the house.

"Ruby?"

"Back here," she called back. When Connie entered the kitchen, Ruby poured a cold glass of iced tea for each of them.

Connie took it and drank a good portion before saying, "It's hot as blazes out there, and my air-conditioning in that piece-of-crap car is on the fritz again."

The mention of Connie's car had Ruby cringing. "You need a new car, girlfriend. That thing has been giving you trouble for years now."

Connie sat at the table and swiped a napkin over her forehead. "Yeah, but I'm too cheap and this one is paid off." She shrugged. "I'm willing to put up with it a little while longer."

"There's something we need to talk about besides your car troubles." Ruby was still standing and began to pace back and forth.

"Fine, but sit down," Connie ordered as she pointed to the chair across from her. "You're making me dizzy."

Ruby took a seat and looked down at the table. "I wanted to talk to you about Drake."

"I'm all ears. You can tell me anything, I'm a vault."

Ruby looked at her friend-slash-sister and smiled. "You are one of the sweetest people I've ever known, and I don't want you to think that I don't value your opinion."

Connie's eyebrows shot upward. "And?"

"I know you think I'm making a huge mistake with Drake. That I'm moving too fast."

"I'm just worried about you, Ruby." She sighed. "You're a long-term gal, but he strikes me as the casual-sex type of guy. I don't want you to get hurt."

Ruby nodded. "I understand the reason for your concern. And I get it, believe me. He's not my usual type, and I'm not acting myself with him." She paused a minute before adding, "But I care about him. I need him, Connie. I can't explain it, but this thing between us is more than sex. It's more than a good time. For both of us. Please tell me you understand and that I'm not making a terrible mistake here."

Connie smiled at her, then took her hands in her own. "I get it, believe me." She patted her hands once and released them before sitting up a little straighter. "I won't lie to you, though. He does strike me as the love-'em-and-leave-'em type, and I think it'd be wise to guard your heart around him, that's all I'm saying."

Ruby crossed her legs, the only outward sign that she was uncomfortable with this part of their talk. "I hear you, I do. And I'd be giving you the same advice if the situation was reversed."

She wrinkled her nose. "Then you don't hate me for being a downer?"

"Not at all. But I was thinking of going to Drake's house tonight and maybe surprising him. If things go as well as I hope, then you shouldn't expect to hear from me until Sunday evening." Ruby bit her lip in worry. Connie would think she'd gone around the bend, for sure. Spontaneity was so out of character for Ruby, and they both knew it.

Connie shrugged. "Oh, what the hell. If it were me, I'd spend the weekend with that cutie too."

Ruby laughed. "You don't think I've lost my mind?"

"I think you're too damn uptight," she replied, with typical Connie honesty. "You work too hard, and you never have any fun. It's about time you do something spontaneous."

Ruby was about to reply, but the moment was broken by the ringing of the doorbell. "Who could that be?"

"Anyone home?" Drake called out from the front room.

"In the kitchen," she answered. He sounded disgruntled and as edgy as she'd ever heard him.

She stood and started across the room. All at once, Drake was there and pulling her into his arms. "I know we didn't have plans, but I missed you," he whispered before kissing her senseless. The world tilted and her feet left the ground, literally. By the time he relinquished her mouth and put her back on her feet, Ruby was panting. "I'm going nuts for you, baby," he said in a low voice against the shell of her ear.

"Me too," she admitted, a little breathlessly. "But I have an idea how to fix that."

He quirked a brow. "Yeah?"

Ruby drew herself up on her tiptoes and whispered, "How would you like for me to spend the weekend with you?"

Her voice was so full of desire and longing that Drake grew hard instantly. But there was also something else he heard in that soft, whispery tone. He thought she sounded scared, maybe even unsure. Did she really think he'd turn her down? Hell, no man in his right mind could deny Ruby London.

With her mass of red hair falling down around her to lie against her breasts, and the pale yellow sundress that hit just above the knees, Ruby looked good enough to eat. His cock sat up and took notice. In fact, whenever the woman was in the vicinity Drake sported a hard-on.

"Hell of an idea," Drake murmured as he swung her into his arms and kissed her. This time his lips pressed harder. He had a powerful need to brand her, mark her in some way that said she was off-limits to anyone else.

As he pried her mouth open with his tongue and slid inside, Drake tasted a hint of chocolate, but beneath that was the wild flavor of Ruby. He could kiss her for hours and never get tired of her soft, full lips. He loved that she rarely wore lipstick too. It'd been one of the first things he'd noticed about her. Ruby didn't need to wear a lot of makeup. He was glad. She was already so pretty it hurt.

When an image of her kneeling in front of him and loving him with her mouth popped into his mind, Drake reluctantly raised his head and tried to get back some of his self-control. "Do you need to pack a bag?"

"Already did it," she answered, as she laid her head against his chest. "It's by the front door."

Drake spotted a small black duffel and leaned down. "Grab it." Ruby did and when he stood back up, Connie was there. Drake hadn't even noticed her. "Sorry, I didn't mean to be rude there."

Connie shrugged. "No worries." She aimed a frown at him and added, "But you'd better take good care of my girl."

"You have my word," Drake murmured as he grinned down at Ruby.

"Lock up for me, will you?" Ruby asked as she looked at Connie. The pair exchanged a look and Connie nodded.

"Sure," she answered. "And you'd better call me."

Ruby winked. "Of course."

They said their good-byes and Drake was out the door. When they were alone, he growled, "I can't wait to get you all to myself."

Her eyes turned drowsy with desire and she whispered, "Ditto."

When he stepped off the porch, Ruby stiffened. "Uh, the entire neighborhood will probably see you carrying me to your house."

"Good," he growled, as he strode across their yards. "Then all the single men will know you're taken."

"What if I don't want to be taken?" She stuck her chin in the air. "Ever consider that?"

"Too bad," Drake growled as he stepped onto his front porch and placed her back on her feet. "Because you're definitely all mine."

Ruby cocked her head to one side. "Think you're man enough to satisfy me, do you?"

He took her hand and placed it against the fly of his jeans. "What do you think?"

Her fingers curled around him and she hummed her approval. Drake watched the play of emotions run across her face, changing from teasing to desire in a heartbeat. "You're a wicked woman, Ruby London." When she began stroking, Drake removed her hand. "Hold that thought until we get this party indoors."

Within minutes he had her inside. He wanted her in his bed. It was all he'd thought about. And the state he was in, it was either get up the stairs and try for some refinement or push her against the door and pull a clumsy caveman thing on her right where they stood.

He figured she would want the refinement and the bed. More than that, though, was the powerful need to see her in *his* bed. Seeing her completely bare and spread out like a delightful feast being served up was what he craved. He was like a man who'd been on bread and water for a year. He needed to get out of the jeans and into her as soon as possible. And he wanted her out of the dress and kept naked for the next two days. He'd never quite thought of her as a sex slave, but now that he had her all to himself he wouldn't mind playing the role of master.

Ruby as a submissive, her shiny red curls flowing all around her like fire and begging him to take her, wasn't an altogether bad idea.

The weekend was looking damn appealing.

Drake steered her toward the steps, but he only managed to get about halfway there when he stopped her and groaned, "God, you're sexy as hell, woman."

Ruby was still in a dreamy sort of daze from his mouth doing wonderfully sinful things to hers. But as she looked down at him and heard the words he spoke, she began to feel an odd sort of triumph. She felt a womanly sort of power for the first time in her life and it felt good. Knowing that she could elicit such strong feelings in a man as powerfully masculine as Drake was amazing to her. It gave her the bravado she needed to take back the reins and give Drake a sample of what he would be getting tonight.

Her voice was a husky whisper when she said, "Would you like to see what I'm wearing under this sundress, Drake?"

Drake tried not to swallow his tongue when her question reached his brain. And the most articulate thing he could think to say to her was, "Uh-huh." He stood rock-still on the steps watching her peel the sundress up her body.

Inch by inch she gave him a glimpse of her shapely thighs as she did a sort of slow striptease. Once she was about to reveal her panties, she stopped. Drake wanted to reach out and tear the dress away from her body. But it was her show, so he waited.

"Are you *sure* you want to see?"

He was strung so tight he did just about rip the dress off, but he maintained control—by a hair. "Yes." That was all he could manage without sounding like an idiot.

Finally, she was finishing what she had started. Drake cursed when he saw what she *didn't* have on underneath the dress. She wasn't wearing any panties! And as she pulled the dress off and threw it on the steps below, he watched her smile with feline cunning. He looked her over from head to toe. She still had a white tank on but that was all, and she looked like every horny teenage boy's wet dream. Her nipples were hard and poking at the material of her top, and she stood with her legs together, making her look sexy and prim all at the same time.

He reached out and touched one hardened nipple with his thumb and she practically jumped off the step she was standing on. She was as wound up as he was, and Drake knew just the thing to take the edge off.

He went down another step until he was lower than her, and gently ordered, "Sit down." He stood there until she obeyed him. She looked hesitant, but she did sit, and it thrilled him that she was so willing to do what he asked. In fact, unless he was way off base, he thought Ruby liked it when he gave her orders. Maybe it was because she was so self-sufficient, handling every other aspect of her life without an ounce of help from anyone. Surrendering in the bedroom seemed to turn her on.

Drake lowered himself until he was eye level with her legs. He looked into her blue eyes and kept her snared in his sights while he used his hands to pull her legs apart. When he had them as far as they would go, his eyes left hers and rested on her mound. Her neatly trimmed red curls were shining in the little bit of light created by the lamp downstairs, and he could just barely make out her tiny pink clitoris. She was all soft and swollen. Suddenly, as if he was willing it to happen, she dampened and a tiny drop of moisture trickled out.

His head lowered of its own accord without thinking beyond licking that one drop of dew. He touched her opening with his tongue, and she threw her head back and moaned his name. He felt her legs starting to come together as if to stop the sensations she was feeling, but he captured both thighs in his callused hands and pulled them apart again. He held them firm while he stroked her clit and sucked at her like she was a ripe fruit.

He would never be able to get enough.

Ruby had never done anything exciting or wild until Drake.

Bryan had always made love to her in the dark. He'd surely never given her oral sex on the staircase. It aroused her, and the feel of Drake's sensual mouth scattered her inhibitions. He licked and sucked in all the right spots. Just when Ruby thought it couldn't get any better, Drake's tongue probed between the folds of her opening. He fucked her in and out with his tongue, flicking and playing with her clit. From out of nowhere, Ruby came undone, screaming his name and wrapping her legs tight around Drake.

Drake held her open for another minute and kept his tongue inside of her while her spasms bayed, sucking in the last of her juices. He licked her one last, teasing time, then rose up to look at her. Her head was thrown back and her body was arched upward. The position put her breasts high in the air and she looked completely and thoroughly sated. But Drake was far from finished with his feast.

He had only just begun.

Ruby had never felt so deliciously sleepy in all her life. She loved the way Drake used his tongue, she loved how he got that fierce look in his eyes when he saw what he wanted, and he wanted her. She loved the way he could be so utterly gentle and yet so demanding at the same time. And she loved . . . him. Oh God, that couldn't be right, could it? Could she really have fallen in love with her next door neighbor? Before she had time to consider all the ramifications of that thought, he was pulling her to her feet. She allowed him to turn her around and lead her up the stairs. She would walk through fire if he asked her, and that thought didn't sit right with Ruby. She had wanted casual sex, a lover, not someone to give her heart to. Connie's warning to guard her heart sprang to mind. Yes, Ruby would need to give that advice some serious thought later, when she didn't have Drake's strong fingers caressing her backside. Such wonderful strength and yet so sweetly gentle. Ruby felt herself sway, and just that quick she was cradled in Drake's strong arms. He pressed her against his chest and carried her up the remaining steps.

Once they reached the top of the stairs, it was a simple matter of stepping into the first room they came upon. It was dark inside, but still light enough from the open window and doorway to see his big wrought-iron bed. He took her to it and laid her down on top of the black comforter. Her bare skin slid sinuously against the soft material.

Drake left Ruby and walked to the window. He didn't dare look at her for fear of losing the tenuous control he had over his libido. And he vowed that nothing would ruin the magic of the night.

He closed the blinds and turned back to the woman who had his insides tied up in knots. Her curvy figure stood out against the dark color of the bedspread.

He walked back over to her and sat down on the edge, then flicked on the dim lamp sitting on his nightstand. Now he could look his fill, and he did. He'd know how beautiful she would appear lying on his bed. With her pale ivory skin and sweep of red hair, she looked like a blazing diamond resting against the black-as-night spread.

Though while he looked down at her, watching her expression change from blissful contentment to one of a shy butterfly, he realized what he felt for her went far beyond the lust and obsessive need that he had felt for her from the start. He had wanted her body since he'd moved to the neighborhood, but now he wanted more, and he wouldn't give her up until he got what he wanted. Drake knew he acted like a spoiled child who wouldn't give up his precious toy, but he'd never before felt such an overpowering need to treasure and possess. He had always kept women at arm's length, enjoying them, yes, but never giving too much of himself. Ruby had stolen into his heart like a thief in the night.

He wondered what that meant exactly, but he didn't want to

take the time to think about it. Not now with her looking all loose-limbed and sexy. Now he only wanted to see her face change back to that satisfied expression again. Only this time he'd be embedded deep inside her tight body while he sailed over the edge with her.

Drake leaned down and placed a loving kiss to Ruby's cheek. Then he spread kisses over her entire face, enjoying the feel of her soft skin under his lips. He took it further by trailing little touches of his lips along her jawline and down her throat. She instinctively arched, giving him access to the vein that pulsed erratically in her neck.

And he took what she freely offered.

Taking his time, he kissed his way down until he found just the right spot. Then, without warning, he bit her. It was the light scraping of teeth against soft womanly flesh that sent him into overdrive. When he felt her shiver and whimper for more, he reveled in his own success. His tongue flicked out of its own volition, licking the spot he'd just bitten. Then he sucked on her, enjoying the catlike sounds she made and feeling the vibrations of her body under his mouth.

Drake kissed his way down to the edge of her tank top and stopped. He raised up only long enough to yank the scrap of cotton over her head and throw it to the floor, before tasting the sweetness of one nipple. Licking it into a hard bead and sucking as much of her breast into his mouth as he could. But when he spread his work-hardened hand over the other breast and pressed down, massaging in little circles, it drew incoherent moans from Ruby.

He immediately stopped what he was doing and stood up. With his chest heaving and fists clenched, Drake waited.

Ruby blinked her eyes open, staring at Drake in uncertainty.

"Undress me," he gently ordered.

Ruby trembled slightly, but she managed to sit up and move her legs over the side of the bed. Drake stepped between them.

He was so close that she could smell the clean scent of his soap and the musky heat of his skin. His stance put her at eye level with his groin, and she was suddenly nervous. Her hands shook as she reached for the button of his jeans. Slowly, she popped it out of its hole, then looked up at him for reassurance. She found none. Drake watched her with such single-minded focus that she felt her every nerve ending tingle.

Sensing her hesitation, he thrust his hips forward. "Continue," he demanded in a low voice.

She pulled his T-shirt out from the waistband of his jeans and dragged it upward, revealing tanned, flat abdominal muscles. Drake quickly grabbed the shirt away from her and pulled it up over his head. He threw it carelessly to the floor and waited. Ruby's gaze shifted to his chest. His dark chest hair took her eyes on a sexy journey downward, only to have it end when she reached his unbuttoned pants. She frowned, then eagerly grasped his hips with one hand and carefully lowered the zipper with the other. All the nervousness was gone, replaced by a fervent need to see this man in all his glory. She pushed at his jeans until they were wrapped around his ankles. He stood like that, unmoving, his hands fisted at his sides, staring at her.

The only thing keeping Ruby from sweet delight was a pair of black briefs. His manhood swelled and strained against the fabric. She hooked her fingers inside the waistband and carefully lowered them. His cock sprang free and she found herself gasping for air. He was so large, so full, and Ruby's hands had a mind of their own as they took hold of him and squeezed. She was helpless to stop her head from descending; she would die if she didn't taste him. So, she didn't waste a second as she sucked the entire length of him into her mouth. She heard him groan.

"Enough," he murmured, tugging her off him.

Drake quickly took off his shoes, then stepped out of his jeans and underwear. He straddled Ruby on the bed and said, "Playtime's over, baby."

Then his mouth was swooping down on hers in a bruising kiss. Ruby melted, wrapped her arms around his neck, and kissed him back with just as much passion and heat. It was almost scary how hungry they were for each other. She ached all over as she felt her desire start to mount all over again.

He deliberately pried open her mouth and delved inside, plundering her. He took little nibbles and tastes of her lower lip like she was a noontime snack. He tasted her cherry lip gloss and licked what was left of it off her mouth, then there was nothing left but the sweet taste of woman. His woman.

Drake raised his head at last and looked down at her. With her eyes closed and her lips parted and swollen, she looked like . . . sex. She was vibrant and lush and all that a woman should be. Her hair was all mussed and her face was flushed from the fire that was burning inside of her. Her breasts were full and rose to tight peaks. But there was something else he saw. His mark. He stared at a spot on her neck and saw the bruising, biting kiss that had left a smudged purplish bruise behind, and something inside of him snapped. He felt a primal need to mate, to take his woman with force and fiery heat.

"Ruby." His voice was a scrape of gravel in his throat. He sat motionless and waited till her eyes fluttered open. "Turn over."

He rose up on his knees and moved back, allowing her enough space to do as he bid. When she was finally lying on her stomach, he simply grabbed her waist with both hands and raised her up on her knees. Once she was on all fours, he had a perfect view of her round bottom, but her legs were shyly pressed together. Drake forced one hand between them and spread her knees apart. She was completely open to him now, and he groaned like an animal in pain. She was all pink and swollen and ready for him. Her pretty red pubic hair covered her protectively.

God, she was magnificent.

Drake reached out and covered her mound with his hand,

cupping her. "Mine," he said an instant before plunging one finger inside of her. Ruby's back arched and she fairly purred for him. He stroked her inner muscles and felt them tighten around his finger. She was all slippery heat and Drake couldn't wait another second. He felt an urgency he'd never felt before, and he knew that only with Ruby would he feel such an intense burning pain.

Drake reached over, opened the drawer to his nightstand, and drew out a condom. He ripped open the foil wrapper and rolled on the protection. Then he covered her with his body, anchoring his arms on either side of her and willing himself to wait. "Ruby, look at me."

When she looked back over her shoulder at him, her eyes were all dreamy and half-closed. He reached one hand between their bodies and positioned himself. Then, while their eyes held each other captive, he plunged into her. She threw her head back and moaned long and deep. She screamed his name over and over again, begging for him.

It was his defeat.

He rose up, grasped her hips, and held her still for his invasion, then drove into her hard and fast. He was buried so deep. So damn deep. He cursed at the delicious squeeze. It was nothing like the slow, easy loving he'd wanted to give her. It was always the same with Ruby. Hot and hard. Neither of them willing to take it easy. She matched him perfectly. It was basic and animalistic, and Drake nearly howled at the moon.

He pushed at her, forcing her further over the edge. Wanting more from her. He suspected he would always push Ruby to her limits. He bucked and thrust into her, and she went wild beneath him. She threw her head from side to side, screaming his name. All at once, Drake felt her muscles clench him like a lover's fist. In a perfect kind of rhythm, they both flew up and over, disintegrating into a thousand tiny shards of glass.

He stayed inside of her for another minute, not willing to let her go. He could never get enough of this woman, and somehow he doubted that even a lifetime would be enough. He would always be insatiable where Ruby was concerned.

Finally, reluctantly, he pulled out of her. She collapsed onto the bed, looking as if she'd run a marathon. Drake smiled and kissed her cheek. "Be right back," he whispered as he got up and went to the bathroom to dispose of the condom and clean up. When he was through, he came back to the bed and lay down next to her. She didn't move a muscle, just whined like a petulant child. He scooted her over and curled his body protectively around hers. Drake reached down to the foot of the bed and covered them both with the extra blanket that lay there.

For a long while, Drake simply lay there watching her while she peacefully slept in the cradle of his arms. He gently moved her hair away from her face and ran his fingers through it, loving the silky curls against his skin. He wondered what she was dreaming, and if she ever dreamed of him. He hoped so, because he sure as hell dreamed of her. She was in his head whether he was sleeping, eating, working, or showering. She was everywhere all the time. And he knew why: Drake cared about her. In such a short space of time, she'd tiptoed into his heart and held on tight. The crazy part was, he sort of liked her there. But how did she feel about him? Was Drake more than a passing fancy for Ruby? Or was she merely taking a walk on the wild side? He'd find out soon, because the not knowing was killing him.

9

The morning sun filled the room, effectively tearing Ruby out of her dream. She'd been having the most amazing dream about Drake too. The two of them were on vacation together in Hawaii. Drake was being so sweet and romantic, and Ruby wished she could fall back asleep and see where the dream would lead. But that wasn't going to happen. She sat up and looked around the room, but came up empty. "Drake?" she called out, to no avail.

Ruby got out of the bed and grabbed a white T-shirt hanging off the end of the bed, then headed to the adjacent bathroom. By the time she was presentable, a half hour had passed and there was still no sign of Drake. She went searching and found him coming up from the basement. He was sweaty and only had on a pair of gray workout shorts. Ruby wanted to reach out and caress his glistening pecs, but thought better of it when she saw his angry expression.

"What were you doing?"

"Working out," he said, as he leaned down and kissed her. "Morning, beautiful."

The words and the kiss sent butterflies fluttering around inside her stomach. "Good morning."

His expression hardened. "I would've woken you properly, but I needed to work off some aggression."

She frowned. "Why? What's wrong?"

"A client I did some work for is refusing to pay for a job. Nothing gets under my skin more than being ripped off."

"I can understand that," she admitted, getting angry on his behalf. "Did the workout help?"

He shook his head. "Not so much, but seeing your pretty face is doing wonders for my mood." He motioned her back up the stairs and Ruby went willingly.

Drake could easily get used to seeing Ruby in his home every morning. Wearing his T-shirt and looking all sleep-rumpled and sexy. Damn, he wanted her again. He had thought to make her breakfast. Maybe try to impress her with his culinary skills, but that wasn't about to happen if he kept watching her ass twitch back and forth in the shirt. Great, now he was hard as iron. So much for feeding the woman.

"Drake?"

His voice was hoarse when he answered, "Yeah?"

"We need to talk . . . about us."

Ah hell, that didn't sound good. "Let me get washed up first, okay?"

"Of course. I can make breakfast if you want." She went straight to the bed and sat down.

"First things first," he replied as he started stripping out of his shorts. He held back a grin when he caught Ruby staring at his cock. "Hold that thought, I'll be right back."

Drake went to the bathroom and turned on the shower. The hot water felt good on his overworked muscles. He thought of what she'd said about wanting to talk and a knot formed in his stomach. Was she getting bored with him? What would he do if she wanted to call it quits? She was so different from the other women he'd dated. Ruby was kind and compassionate, sensual and loving, and so damn filled with life. The thought of never making love to her again, never hearing her laughter, her cries of passion, sent fear rushing through his system.

Jesus, he loved her. When had that happened? She'd snuck into his heart and had cozied up in a nice warm spot there. It shook him for a minute, but he couldn't stop the smile that crossed his face either. He quickly finished his shower and turned the water off. After he dried off, Drake tied the towel around his waist, then went back into the bedroom where Ruby still waited in silence.

He walked over and sat down beside her. "You wanted to talk?" Drake asked.

Ruby bit her lip and looked down at the floor. "Connie thinks you're a love-'em-and-leave-'em type of guy."

The little meddler. He'd thought Ruby's friend liked him. "Connie doesn't know me as well as she thinks."

Ruby's gaze shot to his. "What are you saying?"

"This isn't a fling to me," he told her, as he ran a palm down her hair, loving the soft texture against his skin. "It's not like I'm just killing time with you until something better comes along. You mean more to me than that. I care about you, Ruby."

She let out a breath and closed her eyes tight. "I care about you too." She opened them again, and if anything, she looked even more concerned. "I'm acting totally out of character getting so involved so quickly. Spending a weekend with a man I only just met . . . that's not my usual MO, Drake."

"I hear you, but we aren't strangers," he explained, as he let his hand drift down her back, soothing the tight muscles. "We've known each other for a year now, Ruby. It just took us a little while to go from point A to point B."

She snorted. "We barely talked, though, until that night you showed up on my deck."

"Luckiest night of my life," he murmured, as he leaned close and kissed her lips.

She slapped his chest. "You had another woman that night, remember?"

"I remember sending her home because my head was all clouded with thoughts of a beautiful redheaded voyeur."

She laughed and scooted away. "Hey, it's not my fault you brought the party out in the open where anyone could see."

"One thing's for sure," he whispered as he moved closer and caged her in with his arms around her body. "I'll never bring you out in the open."

She swallowed a few times. "Oh?" she asked, her voice a little wobbly.

"Your lovely body is strictly for my viewing pleasure, baby."

"Drake," she breathed out, then in another heartbeat, Ruby found herself flat on her back, with Drake sprawled out on the bed beside her. She reached for him, pleased when her fingers connected with the warmth of his chest.

"I love your soft touches," he groaned.

"It's been too long since I've had you inside of me," she complained. "Please hurry."

"Impatient little thing," he crooned as he reached between her legs and stroked her clit with tender care. Ruby was always amazed that a man so big and strong could be so utterly gentle.

"Get up on your hands and knees for me, baby," Drake quietly ordered.

Ruby obeyed, her blood racing, her body on fire with anticipation. Moving behind her, now on his knees, Drake stroked the seam between her buttocks with his index finger. A moan erupted from deep within and he let his finger drift back and forth over her puckered opening.

He leaned over her and kissed the base of her spine. "I want to fuck your ass, Ruby. Do you know how sweet and tight it'll feel?"

"Yes," she answered. "Oh, please, I want you there so badly." Her voice had gone hoarse with need long ago.

Drake reached out and grabbed a tube of lubricant off the bedside table. After spreading a small amount on his finger, he penetrated her, little by little, until the digit was buried deep inside her anus. She shuddered and pushed against him. His finger moved in and out, fucking her with slow precision.

Just as Ruby started to think she could take no more of his teasing, one of Drake's big, warm hands clutched her hips. He told her to hold still, but Ruby couldn't do as he bid this time. She was too eager for his strokes. When he squeezed her bottom, Ruby fairly shook with need.

"I thought I told you to hold still," he growled. Suddenly and without even a hint of warning, he spanked her. The sting sent her into another realm. Ruby couldn't concentrate on Drake's words. Only the way he made her feel. So alive. So filled with heat and passion. Thankfully he didn't wait for a reply, only swatted her four more times.

"Fuck, you make me crazy," he bit out.

Ruby moaned and wriggled, her breasts swelled and her sex grew damp. His finger pumped her ass, while he spanked her over and over. Her pussy juices soaked her inner thighs and her bottom stung.

"Mm, you're all pink, baby." He smoothed a palm over her hot flesh. "And so damn pretty."

When he slid his finger back and forth over her swollen nub, Ruby felt every heated touch. He was slow at first, then faster. Soon a second finger joined the first and Ruby went wild. She gyrated against Drake, while he tormented her clit. When he leaned down and bit her hip she lost it.

Her climax came from somehwere deep inside. Ruby screamed hard and loud, her back arching as her body flew apart. Everything she thought she knew about sexual pleasure seemed to pale in the wake of what she'd just experienced.

Drake's rough voice just barely broke through the quagmire of her mind.

"Son of a bitch, you're gorgeous when you come," Drake murmured as he moved his fingers out of her and cupped her dripping mound. "Look at me, baby."

She turned her head, already limp and sweating from her orgasm, but when she saw the intensity, the insane yearning etched into his not-so-perfect features, her body went from sated to hungry all over again.

"You are mine. From this moment forward, you belong to me."

Ruby didn't know what to say or how to respond. She wanted to be Drake's woman. And she wanted to lay claim to him. But when the heavy weight of his cock entered her bottom, Ruby's thoughts scattered.

He leaned down and kissed her shoulder. "Easy now," he whispered. Ruby rocked against him when his tongue flicked over the sensitive spot behind her ear. "You'll enjoy this, baby, trust me."

"Drake," she warned.

"I'm not the wild card you think I am. Let me have your trust, Ruby, and I swear you will never regret it."

As if unwilling to wait for a reply, Drake began to stroke her hair and smoothed a palm down her arm to her hip, where he cupped her bottom and kneaded the plump flesh. She melted. Drake must have felt her surrender as he slowly glided his cock deep inside her ass until he filled her completely.

His engorged length stretched the tight passage, but not so much that it hurt. It was like nothing Ruby had ever experienced. When Drake thrust two fingers inside her pussy, caressing the silky inner walls of her vagina, tears sprang to Ruby's eyes. The beauty of what they were doing sent a rush of rapture through her.

With each inward stroke from Drake, he pulled his fingers

outward. Her muscles held them both tight. She squeezed her buttocks and Drake cursed.

"Ah God, Ruby," he muttered. Suddenly he shoved forward once more, driving her into the mattress and spilling his hot come deep. The jets of hot come fueled her own orgasm. She came all around his fingers, shouting his name.

Drake stayed still inside her until the last shudder, then he tugged his fingers and cock free. Ruby collapsed onto the bed. He brushed her damp hair from her face and kissed her cheek.

Their weekend together had gone so well, and Ruby knew it was time to take things to the next level with Drake. She loved him. It was time to get the words out in the open and see where it would lead. It was Tuesday evening and they were scheduled to go out to dinner in an hour. Plenty of time to drop the L-bomb and wait for the fallout.

As Ruby knocked on Drake's front door, though, the roar of an engine from behind snagged her attention. She turned in time to see Drake getting out of his SUV. He was limping and he looked as if he'd just gone a few rounds with a raging bull. Her heart slammed against the wall of her chest at the sight of him. He had scrapes and cuts along his cheekbones and dirt stuck to his hair.

"Oh my God, what happened to you?" She rushed to his side and wrapped an arm around his middle, offering support.

"Took a spill," he bit out, as if it hurt to talk. "It's no big deal."

Ruby froze. "Wait, a what?"

He shoved a hand through his hair and spoke so softly she very nearly missed his words. "I had a race today. Sorry, I meant to tell you about it, but I sort of forgot until the last minute. A friend had to remind me." He smiled down at her, but Ruby could tell it pained him to do so. "I've been a bit pre-occupied lately."

Oh God. "You wrecked your motorcycle?"

"Dirt bike, and yeah. But it wasn't bad." He wiggled his fingers. "See? Nothing broken."

They slowly and carefully made their way to the house, and Ruby waited for him to unlock the front door and enter. When he bent to take off his shoes and slip out of his knee and elbow pads, Ruby's stomach did a somersault. He could've been killed. So easily, he could've died. The fact he wasn't taking this seriously scared Ruby more than anything. Suddenly Ruby was thrust back in time to that horrible moment when she and her mother had received the news of her father's accident. He'd been taken from them, and all because of his thrill seeking ways.

Drake gingerly lowered himself to the couch, then looked up at her. "Just give me a minute and I'll be good as new." He reached up and took hold of her hand, then stroked a finger over her knuckles in a tender caress. When he turned it over and placed several small kisses in her palm, Ruby's heart melted.

"I-I can't do this," she admitted. "I don't know why I thought I could, but I can't."

She tugged on her hand and Drake released her. "Do what? What did I miss here?"

Ruby stepped away from him, and her legs threatened to give out on her at the confusion in Drake's gaze. "Spontaneity I can handle. But a blatant disregard for your life?" She shook her head as tears threatened to spill down her cheeks. "I can't live like that, Drake."

He stood, suddenly looking a whole lot less injured and seriously pissed. "You're breaking things off because of a little accident?"

Ruby couldn't believe what she was hearing. "A little accident? There is no such thing as little accidents when it comes to motorcycles, Drake." He started to speak, but Ruby was a runaway train. "My father was the same way. Always needing adventure. A thrill seeker, like you. Right up until the day he died. I was twelve years old when I was told about my dad's skydiving accident. Do you know what it's like to watch your mother cry herself to sleep night after night? It's something I'll never forget, Drake. Never."

"God, I'm so sorry, baby, I didn't know," he murmured. "But I told you before, Ruby"—he stepped closer, all but caging her in, between the door and the solid wall of his muscular body—"I'm not the daredevil you think I am. I'm not like your father. I do take precautions. I'm smart about it, I promise you."

"I can't believe you just said that to me. Did you look at yourself? Your precautions need some serious work." How could he not see the dangers in racing? The thought of losing him to one of these "spills" threatened to shatter Ruby. She turned, ready to run before the waterworks began, but Drake halted her with a single powerful arm around her waist.

"Hey, slow down. I'm fine, baby. There's no need to be upset."

She swiveled on her heels, her eyes going wide at his crazy remark. "And what about the next time? Or the time after that? I can live with your love of motor cross, Drake, but I can't live with you taking this"—she indicated the scrapes on his face with a wave of her hand—"so lightly."

"So, that's it?" He released her and pushed a hand through his hair. "You're giving up and walking away?"

Would he care if she did? That question nagged her like no other. "I don't know. I need time to think."

"I won't let you give up on us, Ruby," he growled as he cupped her face in his hands. "I'm not built like the Bryans of the world. I care about you, and I know you care about me."

"Please," she said, just barely holding back the tidal wave of emotion. "I need time to think."

He sighed and released her. "I'll call you later. Okay?"

Ruby nodded, then turned and raced out the door, determined to be out of his sight before the dam broke. She didn't stop until she reached her front porch. It took three tries before she managed to open the door. Once inside she dropped her forehead against the wall and let go completely.

Several minutes later, the ringing of her cell phone pulled her out of her misery. She grabbed it off the coffee table and read the number on the screen. Her boss. She hit SEND, and then her day suddenly got much worse.

10

Ruby felt like she was making her way through a dense fog. She tried opening her eyes, but flinched when a burst of pain shot through her head. Why did her head hurt so badly? With a little effort, she slowly blinked her eyes open. The light still hurt, but it became bearable as she got accustomed to it. A hospital? And Drake sat in a chair next to her bed, his head bent and arms propped on his knees.

She pressed a hand to her forehead and felt a bandage there. "What happened?"

Drake's gaze shot to hers. "Just relax, baby, everything is going to be all right now." He took her hand in his and kissed it tenderly, stroking his thumb over her palm. Her confusion must have come through loud and clear because he asked, "You don't remember what happened?"

Ruby frowned. Thinking made her head hurt worse. "No."

"Last night after you left my place you were called in to work. Some emergency or something. But you didn't make it there. You were in a car accident."

Her eyes grew large as jumbled images zipped through her mind. "Someone ran a red light. I think."

"Yeah. You scared the daylights out of me, baby."

"Me too," a feminine voice said from the doorway.

Ruby looked past Drake to find Connie standing just inside the hospital room. Her eyes were bloodshot and swollen. She'd obviously been crying. "I'm sorry," Ruby muttered, hating that she'd worried everyone.

Drake stood and bent over her. "Hush, it wasn't your fault."

Connie rushed across the room and came to stand on the other side of the bed. "Drake is right. It wasn't your fault that jerk ran a red light." She paused before adding, "And I called your mom. I told her you were in the hospital, but it wasn't critical. She's leaving on the first flight."

"I'll call her." Ruby knew her mom would want to hear her voice. "Thanks for doing that." She closed her eyes briefly, allowing the darkness to soothe her. "I feel like a semi smashed into my face."

"That would be the air bag," Drake explained. "There's a lot of bruising, but it probably saved your life."

She opened her eyes to see Drake's apology shining in his beautiful eyes. It was starting to come back to her, little fragmented pieces at a time. She remembered Drake showing up all banged up. She'd been angry with him. Scared out of her mind because she'd been afraid he'd end up like her father. They'd argued. Oh God, she'd been ready to leave him. How could she ever consider leaving him? She reached up and cupped his face in her palm. "I'm sorry."

"For what?"

"I was so mad at you last night."

He shook his head. "There's plenty of time to talk about all that. First, you need to rest."

"When you didn't wake up right away, we . . ." Connie's voice shook with emotion, and a tear trickled down her cheek.

Ruby tried to smile, but her cheeks hurt too much. She reached over the bed rail and took Connie's hand in her own. "I'm fine, though. Soon, I'll be out of here and you'll be back to raiding my fridge."

Connie's lips quivered. "I love you, but if you ever scare me like that again I swear I'll paddle your butt."

Feeling incredibly weepy, Ruby said, "I love you too."

She nodded. "I'll go get the nurse and tell her you're awake."

After Connie left, Ruby's gaze went back to Drake. He was so quiet, watching her intently. She took his hand in her own and squeezed. "I'm okay now. You don't have to worry."

He winced and closed his eyes tight. Ruby couldn't tell what he was thinking, and that worried her. "This has been the longest twenty-four hours of my life," he muttered.

The doctor came into the room with a nurse in tow, disrupting the moment. As he ordered tests and scans to be scheduled, he also informed her of the dangers of a severe concussion. Lastly, he took her blood pressure and ordered some medication for the throbbing pain behind her eyes. When he asked everyone to leave so Ruby could rest, her hopes plummeted. She'd wanted to talk to Drake. To tell him how she felt. She didn't want to wait another second to tell him that she loved him.

When Drake only stood there with his arms crossed, all but daring the poor man to try and remove him from the room, the doctor just heaved a sigh and accepted the inevitable. Soon, Ruby and Drake were alone. She reached out to him and covered his hand with her own. "We need to talk," she said, remembering the argument they'd had before all this happened.

Drake nodded and sat on the edge of the bed. "I never want to see you like that again. Ever."

Overwhelmed with emotion, Ruby's eyes filled with tears.

Drake leaned over her and kissed them away one by one. When she had herself under control, he lifted away and stared down at her. Ruby could only imagine what she must look like. Oh yeah, she was a real prize.

Drake swiped at the remaining tears and whispered, "What is it, baby?"

She stared at Drake and faced the truth. "I love you, Drake." He opened his mouth to speak but she stopped him. "You don't have to say anything. I know we both started this relationship out of . . . out of mutual desire, so I don't expect any more than that from you." She lowered her head, suddenly exhausted. "I just don't want to go another second without telling you how I feel, that's all."

Before Drake could reply, Ruby's eyes drifted closed and she was asleep within seconds.

A constant beeping sound woke Ruby several hours later. She knew without looking that Drake was gone. She was alone in the cold hospital room, and she had no idea if he'd ever be back, if she'd ever see him again, or if her words meant anything to him at all. She looked at the clock on the wall and saw that it was eleven in the evening. Her head felt better, and she wasn't as groggy either.

She used the button on the bed to raise herself into a seated position. That's when she saw them. Flowers, balloons, get well wishes, they were everywhere. The sight warmed her heart. Connie. The kind gesture had her stamp all over it.

Ruby moved her neck from side to side, but when there was no pain she thought maybe she could try standing. She hated hospitals. Hated the feeling of helplessness that came with them. Besides, surely she was well enough to leave, right? After all, nothing was broken. A headache was no reason for a hospital bed.

Moving the IV out of the way, Ruby lowered the bed rail

and tossed the covers aside. She gently swung her legs over the side of the mattress. No pain. "Okay, so far, so good." But when she scooted to the edge, put her weight on her feet, and started to stand, a shaft of pain shot through her head. It felt like someone was stabbing her temples with a sharp blade. "Ouch, damn it," she cursed.

A strong, muscular arm came around her shoulders. "Uh, what the hell do you think you're doing?"

Ruby looked up to find a very annoyed Drake South scowling down at her. In her ruined pride she snapped at him. "I'm getting up, what does it look like I'm doing?"

She wiggled to get him to release her, but his arm didn't budge. "You little idiot, get back in that bed."

"I'm not an idiot," she bit out. "And I don't want to stay here any longer. I want to go home."

"It's not a hotel, Ruby. You're here because you were hurt, and you aren't leaving until the doc gives the all clear."

His voice was annoyingly calm, which only made Ruby angrier. But her head hurt too bad to fight with him so she allowed him to help her back into the bed. "You're bossy," she muttered when he fluffed her pillow for her.

"Yep." After she was under the covers, he asked, "Now, what's the real reason you're so anxious to escape?"

She turned her head away. "I told you, I hate hospitals. They're depressing."

Drake turned her face back toward his. "And that's all? There isn't anything else bothering you?"

She shrugged, not willing to humiliate herself further by telling him the truth, that she was worried he didn't love her. That he might never love her. Still, he was here, wasn't he? And by all accounts he'd stayed by her side the whole time. Ruby thought of the worry that she'd put him and Connie through. It must have been frightening to wait for her to come out of it. Shame filled her that she'd only been thinking of her own pride. "I'm sorry," she said, meaning it. "When I woke and my head didn't hurt, I just figured I was good to go."

He took her hand in his own and intertwined their fingers. "Don't be sorry, baby. I'm just glad you're all right. Let's wait and see what the doctor says when he sees you tomorrow. Make sure your tests all come back okay. We'll find out when you can go home then. Besides, feeling no pain probably has something to do with the medication they're pumping you full of right now."

Home. Ruby's first thought was of Drake's big bed and his strong arms holding her through the night. She knew her own bed would never feel the same again. Unfortunately, her declaring her love for him probably had him thinking of moving on to greener pastures. She closed her eyes to avoid looking at him. Great, he probably felt sorry for her. That thought so did not improve her mood.

Drake watched Ruby's facial expressions. He knew what she was thinking. She was feeling uncertain for having opened her heart to him. He decided now was as good a time as any to play the sharing game.

"I love you, Ruby."

Her eyes flew open. "What did you say?" She stared at him, as if trying to find the proof of his words.

"I admit, my heart nearly stopped when you said those three little words earlier. For a long while I couldn't move, I just watched you sleep." He reached out and cupped her cheek. "I hadn't realized until you said them aloud how badly I needed to hear them."

"And you love me too?"

He grinned at the shock that was written all over her face. "I think I've loved you from the moment you brought me those cookies. A way to a man's heart *is* through his stomach, you know?" He swallowed around a lump in his throat. "When Connie called to tell me you were in the hospital, and I saw you lying so lifeless in the emergency room . . ." Drake about doubled over seeing it all over again. "You scared us, baby." He leaned down and softly kissed her warm cheek, needing to feel for himself that she was okay. Some of the tension drained out of him when he felt her breath against his mouth.

Her eyes filled with tears. "Oh God, I do love you. I'm sorry for arguing with you about the racing. I don't think you're irresponsible and careless. I was just scared. The idea of losing you . . ."

"Shh, it's okay. You had every right to be upset, considering what you went through with your dad's death. And I promise to cut back on the races. Seeing you so broken in the ER gave me a good idea what you must have felt when you saw me all banged up. But I swear to you, I don't have a death wish, Ruby." Drake brushed her lips with his. "Damn, I never get tired of kissing you."

"I know the feeling," she said against his mouth. "I realized when I woke up in here that life is unpredictable. There are no guarantees. I don't want to miss out on love because I was too afraid to take a risk."

"It's okay, because I wasn't about to let you walk away from me. I told you, I'm not like Bryan. I was ready to play dirty if necessary. Anything and everything to get you back."

Her brow quirked up, clearly intrigued by the notion. "Oh yeah?"

"Yep. And I can do dirty really well, baby," he murmured as he brushed his thumb over her nipple through the hospital gown.

She laughed and swatted at his hand when the caressing became more intense. "Stop that."

"Never," he vowed. "And I think some sort of punishment is in order."

Her eyes darkened with arousal. "Punishment?"

"Definitely," he replied, as he tucked a lock of hair behind her ear. "You scared ten years off my life, woman."

"W-what kind of punishment?"

He winked. "Oh, I'm sure I'll think of something." He leaned down and braced the bulk of his body on either side of her. "First, you need to recover."

Ruby's arms crept around Drake's neck. "Mm, I can't wait."

Their mouths met, and Drake knew he'd been right the night she'd agreed to go to lunch with him. He *had* hit the lottery, because with Ruby in his life, Drake felt like the richest man alive.

Runa's High

VONNA HARPER

1

_____

"Catch your breath. Then ask your question."

That was easy for Coach to say, but he'd never truly understand what drove her. Hands on hips and leaning forward slightly, Runa Mullan sucked in the early morning air. Today was special, damn it. Not only was the first meet a week away, none other than Jeff Tappe had come to the university track. He was here! Wearing running shorts and shoes, looking almost human. Obviously at home in this setting.

Runa shook back her unruly hair and focused on the man who'd taken the silver medal in the 800-meter run at the last Olympics. He was her idol, her goal, everything she strived to be. Somehow she'd pick the man's brain and make him understand her commitment to their common sport.

Jeff was more muscular than most expected of someone who specialized in a middle distance running event, but she understood the need for strength along with expanded lung capacity. Her own long legs were hard as steel and—

Wrapping those legs around the elete athlete and riding him. Feeling his cock buried inside her. Living, damn it, living!

"I'm, ah, delighted to meet you," she wheezed and shook off the crazy thought. At twenty-three she should be beyond hero-worshiping, but she lived to accomplish what the black-haired man had so it was hard not to place him on a pedestal. "My question is—I'm concerned about peaking. I want to keep getting faster." She glanced at Coach, then decided to hell with it, this was her one chance to get the information she needed to reach her personal goal—the university's 800-meter record for women. "Coach says I've pushed myself as far as I can anaerobically, but I know I have more strength, speed, and power in me. However, I can't reach those benchmarks unless I stress my body to the max."

As Jeff smiled, she felt a twitch in a part of her anatomy she hadn't had time to acknowledge in what felt like forever. He was a sexy man all right, over six feet tall with close to zero body fat and the afore acknowledged muscles. His eyes were nearly as dark as his hair and faint freckles dotted his deeply tanned cheeks. Dressed in blue running shorts and a body-hugging white T-shirt, he carried himself the way she suspected a cheetah did—supremely confident in what his body was capable of. "I watched you sprint and now I'm listening to you breathe," he said. "You gave yourself a pretty intense oxygen debt load. What more do you want?"

To be pushed to the edge. To go past that point. Then to fuck you. "Ah, how about a world record?"

His expression told her he knew she wasn't joking. "All things are possible, at least they're within the realm of possibility. Answer me this. What would you believe you'd accomplished if you broke that record?"

"I don't understand."

"Would you be satisfied then, Runa?"

A nod from Coach let her know Coach had told Jeff about her. Well, why not? She was one of the team's fastest female runners. The other day she'd come in first during a *friendly* competition among the university's 800-meter runners of both sexes.

"I'm not sure," she answered honestly. The other team members were continuing their morning workout, which meant she'd spend the rest of the day mentally kicking herself if she didn't get back on the track.

"No," Coach said, "you wouldn't be satisfied. Runa, that's part of why I asked Jeff to return to his alma mater. You're a rare talent. You're also like a thoroughbred eyeing the starting line. Always pushing yourself. That's good, of course, but I don't want you injuring yourself or burning out."

She'd never burned out on anything, starting with when she'd taught herself how to swim at age four. Okay, so she'd yet to find a man who understood her need to be the best she possibly could, but no man would like the miserable creature she'd become if she fought her A-personality nature.

"Runa," Jeff said, "like I said, I watched you run a little while ago. You have one speed, overdrive. In that regard you and I are a lot alike. Never being satisfied is what it takes to compete in the Olympics. But . . ." He watched as a trio of runners went by. "There's a lot of life to be lived once the Olympics are over—or after you've given the valedictorian speech."

He knew that about her too? Darn it, had Coach also told him she'd gotten through her undergraduate work in less than four years and was now a 4.0 grad student majoring in environmental education? Well, hell, that's what she was, a woman on the fast track through life. It suited her.

Except for those rare times when a man's physique and mind rocked her onto her heels and dampened her panties—like now.

"Do you understand what I'm saying?" Jeff asked. So far his gaze had stayed on her eyes. Now he slowly took in her entire body ending with her running shoes. If he was looking for a runner's form, he'd find that all right, but if he was interested in soft curves, he'd have to go elsewhere. "I was on top of the world the day they put that medal around my neck. Then the crowds went away and I deflated. That's because I'd neglected to address the rest of my life."

She wanted running tips from him, darn it, not his life story. "I guess that was bound to happen." Her shorts and top clung to her sweaty body, so she pried them off her. He watched.

"You don't want to hear that, do you?"

Darn him, was he feeling sorry for her? Thanks, but that was the last thing she needed. If he couldn't give her more hours in the day, how about competitive suggestions only he knew about? "Let me get this straight. You don't believe I should aim for any more anaerobic energy expenditure. What kind of interval training program would you design for me?"

He shook his head. "You don't know how to relax, do you? You think you're hardwired to always push yourself."

"What's wrong with that? You wouldn't have gotten where you did otherwise."

"No, I wouldn't, but that's no longer the way I live."

If that's true, I feel sorry for you. "I do."

"So I see. Tell me something, Runa. What if you were no longer that thoroughbred Coach talked about? What if you had to slow down and smell the roses?"

She started jogging in place. "I like roses. I'll smell them tomorrow."

His mouth twitched. Well, hell, it wasn't as if she could stop. If she was awake, she was on the move.

"No, you won't, unless someone forces you," he said. "Where did this need to push yourself come from?"

"What does it matter? Thanks to my track performance, I got a scholarship that pays about half of my bills." She lifted her head. "Academic scholarships cover the rest."

"Which means, as I said, you might never smell the roses."

She bit down a retort and looked around for something to

hang her thoughts on. That was when she realized Coach had returned to the track. Just seeing the oval made her long to be on it. Of course, if Jeff was running with her, not talking, just pitting his body against hers—"Life's short. I learned that in spades when cancer took my mother shortly after I turned twelve."

He touched her shoulder. The contact lasted only a second, but his heat remained. She stopped jogging. "I'm sorry," he said.

"Yeah, well, bad stuff happens in everyone's life."

"Most girls don't lose their mothers at such an early age."

She had and it still hurt. However, she didn't want to talk about that pain. "Coach, he, ah, he said he'd like to see me rein in a bit, that pacing myself might help. I told him I'd never let that happen. We're at a bit of an impasse." She caught her lower lip between her teeth. "I'm who I am and that person has given herself a goal. I want to set a new 800-meter university record." Damn it, her goal was doable. There was no reason to apologize for stating the possible.

He studied her. "I might be able to give you some pointers. I'll look at your training regime to see if it needs tweaking."

"Wonderful. I'd really appreciate—"

"But there's more to breaking records than spending every minute chasing goals. Your body needs time to recover."

Coach had told her that so many times she no longer heard the words. "I do. Don't forget I have classes to go to and studying—"

"No just being?"

"Being?" The word tightened her throat and made her clench her fingers. She was still aware of his rugged, sexy body, but it wasn't enough. "I'm not wired that way."

As Jeff Tappe stepped into what should be her space, she felt his presence throughout her, refused to give way. "Keep that up long enough and you risk burning out on life."

How had thinking suddenly gotten so hard? "What do you suggest then? Meditation?"

As he shook his head, she wondered if he was trying not to smile. "That wouldn't work with you because you can't slow your mind down." He closed his fingers around her left wrist. "You push and push, but eventually you'll hit a wall unless you learn how to relax. The body is nearly as complex as the mind."

"So I've heard." Did he expect her to pull free? Maybe later.

He lifted her arm and pressed her hand against his chest. Just like that she became nothing more than a woman. Horny. "I'm not a shrink, but here's my thinking. You had to watch your mother getting sicker and sicker, right?"

Unable to speak, she nodded. Those nine months had been a form of hell she'd never been able to talk to anyone about.

"Bit by bit your mother lost control over her body and finally her life."

Walk away. Don't risk him seeing into your heart.

"You refuse to let the same happen to you." He spoke softly. "You fill every minute of your life and keep setting new goals for yourself. You have a choke hold on each day. The idea of anything or any person dictating how you spend those days terrifies you."

Stop it! I can't hear this. "For someone who just met me, you think you know a hell of a lot about me."

Before she knew what he intended, he'd turned her so her back was to him and slid an arm around her shoulder. His other arm pressed against her belly. "Right now I'm in control of your body. How does that make you feel?"

Trapped. A wild animal run down by a skilled hunter. Under his control, facing a new existence. Wanting the challenge.

"What is this about?" Why wasn't she struggling, and how dare this feel so good?

"You might say this is my way of getting your attention. I want you to think about your reaction to what's happening."

His warm, moist breath slid into her hair, but that wasn't the only reason she was shivering. She was proud of what her body and mind were capable of. At five foot ten inches tall and in prime physical condition, she figured not many men would try to take her on, but Jeff Tappe was several inches taller with muscles that put hers in their place. They were out in the open. If she called for help—no, she wouldn't. Couldn't. Didn't want to.

A hard run like the one she'd recently completed left her slightly weakened, but the condition didn't last. She'd pretty much recovered while talking to Jeff, so why did she now feel as if she couldn't punch her way out of a paper bag? Not only that, she remained surprisingly aware of herself as a woman.

"You aren't answering me." He drew her back against him so his erection ground into her. "Is that because you don't know how to handle the loss of control?"

If his being aroused embarrassed him, he wouldn't have let her experience his condition, right? Maybe—hell, maybe he was playing some kind of power game, but why should he?

"I don't get the point." For the first time in ages, she was in a man's arms. Trying to make sense of how it made her feel. Asking herself where her fragmented thoughts about having been captured and enjoying it had come from.

"You want to get back on the track. You'd love it if I challenged you to a run so you could let the inner racehorse loose. However, those things aren't going to happen right now." He tightened his hold. "What point do you think I'm making?"

"I don't know."

"Here's a hint. I'm asking you to consider something other than pushing yourself twenty-four/seven." He spread his fingers over her belly. She wasn't sure what she'd do if he tried to go lower. Let him?

"You can't be asking me to change what I am."

"No. Not change. Better understand. For now, how about

you conceding that I'm in control? I design a plan of action or inaction. You follow it."

"What makes you think I'd—"

"This is an experiment based on the vibes you're giving off, vibes you aren't aware of, yet. If you do what I tell you to, I'd be happy to look at your training techniques and give suggestions. That seem like a fair enough trade?"

She stiffened. "What is it you want me to do?"

"It's really quite simple. For starters, I want you to embrace a relaxation technique by getting a specialized massage."

"What do you mean by specialized?"

His chuckle reverberated throughout her, softened her even more. "I can promise it won't stress you in any way. Quite the contrary, you'll come out of it more relaxed than you believe it's possible to be."

Other members of the track team were starting to take notice of the way Jeff was holding her. Feeling a little foolish but still not inclined to move away, she looked down. The arm against her collarbone was a blur, but she clearly saw the one over her middle. Dark, wavy hair shaded his sun-bronzed forearm. His warmth and strength had already slipped past her skin and was entering her bloodstream.

"Will you do that, Runa? Give up control for a little while."

"Yes," she muttered before she could stop herself. "Yes."

"Good." He leaned over her and touched his lips to the back of her head.

2

"Well, what do you know," Ken Paro said in response to the male voice on his cell phone. "You're the last person I expected to hear from today. I thought you were tied up doing—what the hell did you say you were doing?"

"Returning to our alma mater and talking to some members of the track team."

"That's right." Ken looked around at the treatment room he'd moved into about a month ago. He still liked the subtle browns, rusts, and cream colors the designer had suggested. He'd personally selected the various equipment, such as the pulleys, exercise bikes, treadmills, and gravity tables, and had designed the layout. The three section hi-lo treatment table was his favorite because he could adjust it depending on the patient's size and needs. "Did you get as pissed as I did that time the football coach tried to recruit me as a trainer? I could do whatever I wanted as long as it met with his approval."

"No." Jeff sounded a little wistful. "The whole time I was there I kept thinking how much fun I had just running before the pressure started."

"Pressure's pressure. It turned out pretty well for you."

"For you too."

Jeff was right about that. Ken had parlayed his big, hard-as-nails physique, speed, and aggressive nature into a pro football career that had lasted until he'd broken his collarbone. By the time he was cleared to play again, he'd been replaced and no other team wanted him. Fortunately, after feeling sorry for himself for too long, he'd turned his interest in the human body into a second career as a physical therapist specializing in sports recovery.

"The coeds look as good as they ever did," Jeff said, "but they're a lot younger than they used to be."

"We're getting older, that's why. Are they too young for us?"

"Anyone under twenty-one, yes, but there are a lot of grad students."

As he called up mental images of the campus, Ken walked over to the one-way picture window that looked out at the other medical offices within walking distance of the hospital. The buildings had a cookie-cutter appearance fortunately softened via elaborate landscaping. As a result the area looked more like a park than what it was. He'd insisted on the one-way glass because he didn't want his patients' first view of his business to be of intimidating equipment. Besides, this way his patients also didn't have to worry about being seen from the street or sidewalk.

Thanks to the investments he'd made during his playing days, he didn't have to work a forty-hour week. That gave him time to indulge in what he called his *side interest*, something none of his fellow health-care neighbors knew anything about, but Jeff did.

"I'm thinking of becoming a track coach," Jeff said, interrupting his thoughts.

"What for? Haven't you gotten rich from all those endorsements you've been doing?"

"That's working out pretty well, but it doesn't fill all the hours."

"Are you saying you want to get into my *hobby*?"

"Don't tempt me. I'm serious, sometimes I feel at loose ends."

"Hey, they don't call you an overachiever for nothing. You'll figure it out."

"Speaking of overachievers, I met one today."

Ken stopped pacing. Something told him they were about to get to the reason for Jeff's call. "Go on."

"She's built like an antelope but acts like a pit bull."

Jeff expanded on his description of Runa Mullan and what made her tick. By the time he was done, Ken was smiling and had a hard-on. He loved a challenge, especially this kind. "I can see her Friday. You're sure she'll come?"

"She will. Otherwise I won't help her."

"Got her between a rock and a hard place, do you?"

"She thinks that now. I'm trusting you to change her mind. In the long run it'll work out to her benefit."

"The more barriers I have to break down, the better I like it."

The two men talked a little longer, mostly making plans to attend a pro basketball game together. Afterward, Ken started pacing again. More frequently than he liked to think about, he wondered if he'd made the right choice by placing his business here. The rent had been more than agreeable, but he'd prefer to be closer to the university, which was where a large percentage of his business came from.

Catching his reflection in the window, he stopped and struck a weight-lifting pose that threatened to rip the seams on his shirt. Business was great, he liked being independent, and occasionally he got a call like the one from Jeff that made him look forward to Friday.

Unless she turned tail and ran, Runa Mullan's understanding of who she was would soon radically change.

* * *

What she thought of as a medical center was on the opposite side of the city from the university. As she jockeyed into a parking space, Runa felt as if she were in a different world. She liked getting away from the campus, she just seldom had the time. Although she'd been disappointed because she hadn't heard from Jeff, she was glad the former Olympian wasn't around to watch her gnaw on her lower lip.

Why the hell was she nervous, and if what she felt wasn't nerves, what was it?

It was all Jeff Tappe's fault, she decided as she took in the dead end street flanked by oversized flowerpots and shaded by trees. He'd had no right grabbing her the way he had. Okay, so she'd loved being pressed against that particular male body, but it was hardly the way to start a coach-athlete relationship. He was older than her. He should have known better.

I didn't see you putting up a fight.

She needed to get laid. Then she'd have things back in perspective.

When she called the physical therapist to schedule the appointment she'd been backed into, she'd been caught off guard by the man's deep, deep voice. If Ken Paro was as masculine as he sounded, well, she'd have her work cut out for her not sexually responding to him.

He'd be touching her. Massaging her muscles and talking about relaxation techniques while—while what? She wouldn't crawl all over him. Being sexually aggressive had never been her mode of operation. In fact, most of the time she didn't have much of a libido. Between running miles every day and taking a full class load, there wasn't much else left of her.

Maybe she *could* learn to relax a little, she told herself as she wrapped her fingers around the doorknob. As long as she didn't lose her athletic or academic edges, it shouldn't hurt. The business had what she assumed was a large window, but she couldn't see in. She wasn't sure how she felt about that.

As the door opened, she relaxed a little. Thank goodness this Ken Paro guy didn't do the mood thing with elevator music, incense, and candles. The air smelled of leather, rubber, muscle rubs, and a little sweat.

The main room was good-sized. A fancy blue treatment table with a multitude of levers and supports was along one side, while familiar exercise and recovery equipment took up much of the rest of the space. A closed door was across from where she stood. Suddenly nervous, she jammed her hands in her slacks' back pockets. She'd left campus right after a political psychology class, so she wasn't in one of her running outfits. Having her legs and upper arms covered should have helped her confidence level, the operant word being *should*.

Darn it, she was confident when she was in her world. Unfortunately, this was something else.

"Anyone here?" she called out, then winced because Ken Paro wouldn't have left his front door unlocked and walked away. To heck with him. No way would she let him know she was impatient, even if she was. Darn it, she had three chapters to read and a five-page paper to write on politics and the environment before she went to bed.

The door she'd been trying not to stare at opened, and one of the larger men in the Western hemisphere filled the space. She'd seen her share of football players so she knew the breed, but this guy put college jocks to shame.

"Runa Mullan," he said in the bass drum tone she'd heard over the phone. "Sorry. I was placing an order." He killed the space between them with a few long strides and held out his right hand. "I don't know if Jeff told you, but he and I went to college together. We were both gym rats."

This monster-sized man was more than that as witnessed by

how completely his fingers swallowed her hand. She didn't often come across men so much taller than her, men who made her feel slight and feminine.

"No," she said when she'd found her voice and retrieved her hand, "he didn't say anything about that. I take it you weren't on the tennis team."

"Football."

Of course. In addition to shoulders that looked capable of lifting a building off its foundation, his chest called for specially made shirts. He carried more meat on his bones than Jeff did, but he wasn't fat. "Pros?" she belatedly came up with.

"For four years, which isn't bad in that line of work."

Maybe he was trying to put her at ease by making light of his professional sports career, but she knew how rare his achievement was. Surely he'd understand her determination to succeed at running.

"Did Jeff tell you he's practically blackmailing me?"

"He said something to that effect." Jeff often smiled when talking. In contrast, Ken Paro lifted the corners of his mouth while his eyes remained neutral. Even with other businesses all around, she felt isolated. Trapped with this powerful and potent man.

Oh yes, potent. Everything the word *sexy* signified and then some. Moisture dampened her panties.

"So, ah," she stumbled, "what is it we're going to do?"

"Many things. First, you're going to lie there"—he jerked his close-cropped head at the table—"while I work some tension out of you."

Your hands all over me. Touching my flesh.

"Just like that? I thought you'd want to start with a physical exam." *Did I just say that?*

"I'll watch you walk and execute a few moves, but this isn't going to be a regular session."

"Oh?" She was getting used to his size, but the way he commandeered the room not so much. "What do you mean by regular?"

His gaze intensified. "Usually I get a doctor's report with a new patient. We work on a specific issue or injury."

"And the only thing that's wrong with me, at least as far as Jeff Tappe is concerned, is that I don't know how to stop and smell the roses."

"Did Jeff mention I specialize in athletes?"

"If he did I don't remember." The thought of those pancake-sized hands on her had her tempted to cut and run, but she always faced a challenge and would now. Only was Ken Paro a challenge? She didn't know but wanted to find out.

"Two things ninety-nine percent of athletes have in common is a certain pride or perhaps arrogance about their bodies, plus the fear of losing what means so much to them."

She couldn't argue with that because she'd seen it among the school's other jocks. However, she'd never admitted her private concerns that an injury could spell the end to her goals.

"No comment?" Ken tilted his head to the side. "Maybe you think what I just said doesn't pertain to you."

"I'm trying to figure out where this conversation is headed." She glanced at the wall clock. "Our appointment is for an hour."

"And your days are planned down to the minute." The corner of his mouth twitched. "Jeff said you'd be like that. All right, I want to watch you walk across the room and back. Keep your stride natural."

She did as he'd ordered. If her smooth stride impressed him, he gave no sign. He also didn't comment when she stood on one foot followed by the other, bent at the waist, and squatted low without losing her balance. Any moment he'd tell her she was in perfect physical condition and he had no idea what she was doing here.

Not that she wanted to leave.

"Tell me how you feel about what just happened. Does it seem like a waste of time?"

Surely he was waiting for her to agree, but the truth was, knowing he'd watched her every move had kicked up her awareness of herself as a woman.

Maybe he saw more than a jock. Maybe he'd found something she didn't know existed in her.

"I did what you told me to," she said. "I didn't think about motive." She'd stopped with maybe ten feet between them and his steady gaze slicing through her clothes. The room was so silent she swore she heard her heart beating.

"You wouldn't rather be on the track or hitting the books?"

She gave herself a mental shake trying to distance herself from the have-to list, but he was right. There was always something to do.

"Are you giving me my choice? Running always trumps homework."

"You'll get back to that soon enough, Runa. Right now I want you to get on the table and stretch out on your back."

He was going to touch her, run those potent fingers over— over what part of her anatomy?

"Wait a minute," she said. "Did you see something while I was doing my little dance? Some muscle that needs tweaking?"

"Your muscles are perfect."

"Then—"

"Just do it. You'll understand."

Feeling more alive than since the last time she'd been at a track meet, she did as he requested—or had it been an order? No way could she forget that his strength made a mockery of hers. The man exuded power. Sexual power.

Lying with her body in a straight line, her arms at her sides, her feet toeing out, and only the ceiling to look at made her feel incredibly vulnerable. Sensing his presence only a few inches away, she turned her head toward him.

Damn, but he was big. Looming over her.

In charge.

"According to Jeff, you have one speed, full-out." He moved behind her so she had to arch her neck to look back at him. He held up his hands so she could study them. "To state the obvious, these are my primary tools."

His hands disappeared. A second later she felt them on the sides of her neck. "A lot of people have neck problems. Who-ever designed humans to walk upright made a mistake because it puts stress on the spine."

Ken's fingers were gentler than she thought they'd be. As he lightly pressed against her tendons, she let out a long breath. Refilling her lungs didn't seem particularly important.

"From what you've told me," he said, "it's highly unlikely you have time for regular massages, but by the time I'm done with you, you may want to reassess your have-to list. Give pleasure priority."

3

Pleasure. She was already relaxing. All except for one area of her body. Hoping he couldn't see what she was doing, she tightened her pelvic muscles. That did nothing to ease her sexual awareness.

"I used to be like you." He ran his fingers behind her ears and into her hair, pressing here and there as he did. "Maybe I was even more single-minded because football was the only thing that mattered. I didn't give a damn about my classes. I reached the pinnacle, stood on the top of the mountain, and told myself I'd spend the rest of my life there. Then I got hurt."

He spoke so slow and low she had trouble concentrating on what he was saying. She was melting a little, losing touch with her various body parts.

"How long have you been running?"

A question. Something she was supposed to respond to. "Since junior high."

"You've been injured, right? Torn cartilage, pulled hamstring, trochanteric bursitis."

"All three and more."

"What did you do then?"

Exactly what the trainers and coaches told her not to. "I ran through it."

"How did you handle the pain?"

"I lived with it."

Instead of giving her the lecture she expected, he concentrated on her temples. His oversized hands on the sides of her head felt wonderful. It was more than his heat and competence, more than his professional understanding of her body. She'd had a few massages over the years but those had focused on the areas of strain and injury. None had reduced her the way this one was doing. However, in contrast to the rest of her, her pussy remained on alert.

"There was no working through my broken collarbone."

She tilted her head back, but saw nothing in his expression to hint at what that had been like for him. "How long were you laid up?"

"Forever."

Before she could ask for an explanation, the answer came to her. That broken bone had spelled the end to his pro career. He might be a stranger, but she knew he didn't want her sympathy. This hour was about her, which was how she wanted it.

"You might not wind up the way I did," he said. "I hope you don't, but eventually competitive running will end for you."

She clenched her fingers. "I don't want to talk about it."

"You're afraid."

Angry, she tried to sit up but he easily held her down. She gave a brief thought to struggling, only his hands felt so good.

"Right now," he said, "you'd like to kick me where it would do the most good, but my intention isn't to get you on the defensive."

"What is it then?"

Even though she'd relaxed, he continued to hold her against the table. And she let him, said nothing about not wanting to be restrained. "Runa, I went through a damn hell of a rough time when the rug was pulled out from under me. I drank too much and drove too fast."

And you probably bedded every woman who couldn't get away. "But you got past that. Otherwise, you wouldn't now have your own business."

"Yes, I did. I'm not sure it'll be the same for you."

"You don't know me." *Do you?*

"I know what you think you are. Jeff told me about you losing your mother. It's understandable that you want to hold on to your youth. You—"

"I'm not old."

The pressure on her shoulders let up, and he started massaging her upper arms. The man had magic in his fingers. It was impossible to remain upset, to think of anything except simply being. Feeling alive and sexual.

"I'm not talking about physical age," he continued. She wondered if he knew how hard listening was becoming. "Kids believe they're invincible, that they are superhuman. Unlike most children, you learned how wrong that thinking is, but you keep driving your body. You demand to live up to your expectations." He leaned down and exhaled so his breath spread over her throat. Heat settled between her breasts. "You're scared to death of releasing control over it."

The only control she cared about was not pressing her thighs together again. Damn, but the man knew where her turn-on buttons were.

"Aren't you?"

What are you talking about? "I guess." She couldn't think of anything to add because, even though it wasn't happening, she half-believed she felt his hands everywhere. How amazing that would feel! Worth the assault on her nerves.

His low chuckle caught her attention. Determined to bring herself back to reality, she again tried to bring his upside-down features into focus. Just then he reheated her throat with his breath. She barely stifled a gasp. Her pussy hadn't felt this alive since she couldn't remember when.

"You're out of your element," he said. "I understand that can be a little disconcerting. Trust me, you won't have any objections to the end result."

"Oh. Good."

He made a sound somewhere between a chuckle and a grunt. "My immediate plan is to introduce you to aspects of your body and mind I don't believe you're aware of. Your task is to honestly respond and share those responses with me."

Hopefully he wouldn't ask if she knew what he was talking about because she didn't have a clue. What she wanted was for him to continue showing her what his hands were capable of. She'd experience, enjoy.

Wallow in sexual anticipation.

Was he deliberately turning her on? Preparing her for seduction?

She tensed when his fingers left her arms but relaxed as he walked around the table and positioned himself at her feet. Humming, he removed her left sandal. It clattered to the floor. He started in on the right shoe. "Let me guess. You don't ever wear heels because you want to avoid the strain that would put on your calf and thigh muscles."

"High heels are a stupid invention." Usually she had no trouble pontificating on her opinion of heels, but right now she could not care less. He hadn't asked permission to remove her shoes. He'd simply taken charge.

Her other sandal hit the floor. "Why did you wear slacks?"

"What?"

"You thought you were coming here for a massage. Why didn't you wear something that would make things easier for me?"

This hour wasn't about a massage? What then?

Sex maybe. Bonking this big man.

Fighting the images accompanying her thoughts, she told him about having just gotten out of class, but he had a point. She could offer to strip out of her slacks, but that would leave her wearing only her practical underpants from the waist down. Her running shorts weren't much more modest, but she wasn't in the habit of stripping—

What was she thinking about? It wasn't as if she intended to strip herself naked for the physical therapist, and he wouldn't ask.

Would he?

She was still asking herself the question as he went to the front door and locked it. "You're going to want privacy," he said as he returned.

Swallowing took effort. "For—what?"

"That's what you're about to find out."

Oh crap! What have I gotten myself into and when is it going to start?

As he'd done before, he positioned himself at the foot of the table. He picked up her right leg, rested her heel against his shoulder, pushed up her pants leg, and began massaging her calf. The linen over her crotch wasn't enough. She felt exposed there—and increasingly aware that she was a woman in a man's grasp.

Despite the strain in her leg, she closed her eyes so she could concentrate on what he was doing and how it made her feel. The locked door would prevent anyone from bursting in on them, but it would also slow her down if she felt the need to escape.

Later. Maybe.

For now she'd float. Experience and anticipation something she couldn't put a name to.

"A psychiatrist might feel fulfilled psychoanalyzing you." He'd dropped his voice so low she had to concentrate to hear. "You watched your mother lose command of her body. Others dictated what would happen to it and when, and the disease it-self—"

"It was bad," she muttered. Her fingers slowly opened and closed. "Finally Mom said she'd had enough. She wanted to be left alone."

"Good for her."

Her father hadn't wanted to talk about that, and the few times others had broached the subject, she'd closed up, but that was years ago. The pain wasn't as intense, and she had her memories of the good times.

"I was proud of her." In her mind's eye she saw herself placing flowers on her mother's grave and giving thanks because her pain was over. "She controlled the final chapter of her life."

"And you've tried to manage every aspect of your existence since then."

His observation made enough sense that she wasn't angry at him. If she wasn't so interested in his knowing fingers now traveling from her calf toward her thigh, she would have told him he was right.

"I admire you," he said. "Just as I know you admired your mother. But, Runa, she was dying. You aren't."

Believe me, thanks to you, I know. "Your point is?"

"I'd like you to answer that yourself." He pressed and re-leased, stroked and practically tickled. Her earlier massages hadn't felt anything like this or brought her this close to her sexuality. Her leg might never be the same. "Something you should think about, for two people who have just met, we've touched on a pretty serious subject."

She frowned. "I don't know how that happened."

His lack of a response made her wonder if he had the answer that eluded her. A floating sensation overtook her in waves. Much more of this and she might tell him her deepest secrets, whatever they were.

"You have personal and professional goals," he said. "That's good."

"The, ah, personal one has been pretty all-consuming. I'm not sure how I've kept my grades up."

He covered her thigh with both hands until she felt trapped despite the layer of linen. "So blowing away the competition on the track is the only thing that matters to you right now?"

"I guess."

"You're a young woman, Runa. Even in today's liberated world most women your age want a lasting relationship and children."

Don't go there. "My clock isn't ticking yet. When it does— that isn't why I'm here."

"Right you are."

He lowered her leg and planted both hands on her hips. The way he pressed down she knew she couldn't escape.

Escape. Running for freedom.

From what?

A simple shift placed a masculine hand over her belly. The other made short work of her slacks' waist fastening.

"What—"

"What am I doing? I'm showing you there's more to life than what you've experienced so far."

She made a halfhearted attempt to push his hands away. "I'm content with my life, thank you very much."

"No, you aren't. If you were, you wouldn't constantly be looking for another mountain to climb."

She was aiming at an 800-meter school record, not the top of Mount Everest. "Why would you care?"

"Hopefully before today is over, you'll understand. Here's a hint. I'm either what you've long been looking for without knowing it, or someone you never want to see again."

"Is that a challenge?"

"Maybe a promise."

The pressure on her stomach let up. A moment later she heard her zipper let loose. She opened her eyes and discovered a blurry world.

"This is your one chance, Runa. Do you want me to stop?"

"Stop what?"

"Seducing you."

Oh God!

"You haven't answered me." He rested both hands over her hip bones, his fingers toying with the elastic on her newly exposed panties. "Is this the end of it between us?"

"No."

"You're sure?"

4

It took work, but she managed to bring him into focus. Her feet were so close to the end of the table that they pressed against his thighs. Her legs were discreetly together, but she didn't trust them to stay there. Add that to her swelling breasts and hardening nipples, and things were rapidly going out of control.

"I don't know how to answer you. I certainly didn't expect this." She ran her nails over whatever material covered the table.

"I'm sure you didn't, but it didn't take you long to put me in charge."

"You're the physical therapist." Her argument would hold more weight if his hands weren't heating her stomach and much of that warmth hadn't already traveled to her crotch.

"Which you don't need, at least not the way real patients need me."

Usually she enjoyed discussing semantics, but she could not care less today. There was something about him—she couldn't begin to grasp what it was—that made keeping his hands and her opinions to himself impossible. It could be his size, but she suspected it was more than that.

Bottom line, Ken Paro knew how to command.

He also understood her body.

"I need to understand what you have in mind," she said. "How can I say how far I want things to go until I've experienced . . ."

"Point taken. All right, Runa Mullan, I'm going to teach you some new things. The potential already exists in you. It just hasn't been tapped, in part because you won't let it. In part because you haven't known anyone like me."

She needed a simple conversation, not the complex thoughts swirling through her. Her eyes kept wanting to close so she could go somewhere she'd never been before. She also needed him touching her everywhere. Experiencing his hands everywhere.

Turning her inside out.

"You have a beautiful body." He grasped her slacks at the ankles and began tugging. "You see it as a tool, the instrument you must maintain in order to accomplish your goals." He jerked on the right side until it slid under her buttocks. "Too bad you haven't fully acknowledged what else it is, a woman's form."

Using her elbows to brace herself, she lifted her buttocks off the table, and he tugged again. When he stopped, her slacks rested over her thighs so her legs pressed against each other. It was almost as if he'd tied them together.

"At your core you're a sexual creature." He pulled on the waistband as if trying to refasten it. If he succeeded she wouldn't be able to move her lower body. "Keeping busy twenty-four/ seven makes it possible for you to hide from that part of your nature, which is a crime against yourself."

"I don't hide from anything."

"Yes, you do. I just need time to show you how wrong you are."

"You sound awfully sure of yourself."

"Just experienced."

His words sounded vaguely ominous. They also held notes of promise. She didn't know which to believe.

"Ready for the lessons to begin? This is your last chance, Runa. Yes or no?"

Yes or no what, and why am I trembling? "I'm not afraid of a damn thing, not even a man who weighs what, three times more than I do?"

"My physical size has nothing to do with today's lesson. Right now is about introducing you to your submissive nature."

Submissive? Hell, he couldn't be more wrong.

She'd been looking at the ceiling in an attempt to slow her rushing thoughts and reactions so she didn't see what he was doing until his hip pressed against her thigh. He'd moved to her side without her hearing or sensing anything. He continued to hold on to her slacks.

What have I gotten myself into?

"I want you to describe, not just what I'm doing, but how it makes you feel. Your response will let both of us know whether you're being honest with yourself."

There he went with the convoluted sentences again. Thinking to tell him she didn't appreciate it, she turned her head toward him. He truly loomed over her, a tree of a man. Instead of making a fool of herself by trying to push him away, she raked the table with her short nails. Having something to do helped, a little.

If he believed she had a submissive bone in her body, what did that make him? Dominant? Hell, that went without saying, and yet the word stood for more than physical stature.

"Good," he said. "Very good."

"What is?"

"You're losing it, Runa. Letting go of the person you've been until now and becoming what you need to be."

She *had* to keep an eye on him. Otherwise he'd catch her unawares. Spin his strange logic and seductive presence around her. Despite the warning, however, she simply watched as he bent over her and pressed his mouth against the belly he'd recently exposed.

Suddenly her hands were on his forearm closest to her. Out of breath, she dug into his flesh. If she was hurting him, he gave no sign. Instead, he licked and nibbled. Fire danced through her, and she practically drenched her panties' crotch.

"Oh God, oh God."

"Not God, me."

He'd spoken with his lips still on her, so every syllable reverberated. This was crazy! Insane. Her world turned on end.

"I'm a pirate, Runa, maybe a white slaver. I've captured or bought you. You belong to me."

She licked her unexpectedly dry lips. "You, ah, sound sure of yourself."

"I am. Feel the collar around your neck and the cuffs holding your arms together. Even before I put those things on you, you dropped to your knees in surrender. You know your place, slave."

Slave! Yes! Yes.

"What's that?" he challenged. "Why aren't you insisting I'm talking crazy?"

"I—don't know."

He'd kept his mouth close to her belly while he spun out the insane tale. Now he straightened, smiling a cool smile as he did. He ran a slow gaze over her. "You look good in bondage, slave. Leather and metal on your flesh changes you, turns you into something new."

"You can't mean . . ." She'd wanted to tell him he wasn't just crazy, he was certifiably insane, but she couldn't get the words out. The man didn't just dominate the room, his words and touches ruled her.

"That's all right." He sounded as if he felt sorry for her. "You're in uncharted-for-you territory so I understand your inability to fully comprehend the transformation, yet. One thing you must remember. I can and will gag you whenever it pleases me to, so I suggest you speak while you can."

Gagged. Tape or cloth or something else pressing against her lips and forcing her into a silent world. "I don't know what to say."

"Have you ever fantasized about being abducted, taken against your will?"

"No."

"Are you sure?"

I started to a few times, but it scared me. "Why would I?" she demanded. Even as she asked, she knew her words would have more weight if she wasn't stretched out on his table and his hands weren't holding her in place and she hadn't resisted him doing so.

"I'm hearing a lot of protests. That's going to change once I do this."

He moved fast for a big man. One moment he was at her side. The next he'd returned to his place at her feet and was yanking off her slacks. Her fingers clenched as cool air touched her legs. How had he broken free from her grip so easily?

Maybe because she hadn't tried that hard to hold on to him, or maybe because his determination trumped hers.

"Relax, slave," he muttered and trailed her now useless garment over her legs. "As long as you do as I command, you'll find I'm a benevolent master. I demand total obedience but reward it."

His features were darkening, his voice digging deeper into

her. Her body felt so heavy she wasn't sure she could still move.

That strange, incomplete smile returned as he took hold of her ankles and drew her legs apart. Anticipation lanced her and she moaned.

"I'm going to define our relationship so you understand your new role—so you begin to understand yourself." He pressed his knuckles against the insides of her thighs near her knees. "But you can't truly embrace that role until you understand what I mean by reward. Are you ready for that particular lesson to begin?"

How had it suddenly gotten so hot in here, and what had happened to her strength? Her will? "Yes."

His smile evaporated as he reached over her and took hold of her chin. He forced her head back. "I bought you, slave. What does that make me?"

This isn't happening. I'm having a dream. I must—"My master."

"That's right." He held her head in place. "Your change in status took place before you had time to comprehend it, but sometimes the best lessons are the fast and hard ones. The ones you can't and don't want to escape. I repeat, are you ready to embrace what the rest of today is about?"

Only today. Tomorrow she'd go back to being who she'd always been. "Yes."

"Ah, you truly are a worthy subject."

The pressure on her chin let up and then ended. She didn't try to change her head's position. Neither did she attempt to move her weighted arms. Her legs remained splayed.

Vulnerable. Exposed.

"You've long believed you're many things," he continued, "but you were wrong. Do you want to know why?"

He was looking down at her. Maybe that's why her breasts, belly, hips, and legs felt as if he'd run sandpaper over them.

"It's because you've denied what really matters."

Much as she wanted to ask what he was talking about, she didn't know how to form the question. He expected her to call him "master" but the word was new to her, not foreign so much as untested.

"I appreciate silence in a slave. That means she's learning."

For the second time, his knuckles pressed against the insides of her thighs. They traveled higher this time, closer to her crotch. She obediently widened her stance even more. By putting all her strength into it, she managed to curl her fingers into fists but couldn't say why. Maybe this was her way of ensuring she wouldn't touch him unless he gave her permission.

Permission. One of the words a slave lived by.

"Punishment serves its own purpose in teaching a slave her role." He demonstrated by lightly pinching her where his knuckles had been. She gasped but managed not to move.

"Good slave. You're indeed trainable."

Like a dog? No way!

Despite her argument with herself, she started panting as if she were a pet trying to win his approval.

"I don't want to have to cause you any more pain than necessary in order for the lessons to stick." He scratched where he'd pinched her, then when she tried to scoot away, he grasped her panties and lifted her buttocks off the table.

"Easy, easy. If you fight me, you'll wind up regretting it. However, if you do as I command, you'll be rewarded."

5

It felt strange being controlled like this. The truth was, he hadn't really hurt her thighs. If he had, she wouldn't be getting wetter, would she?

As she waited for his next move, she mentally stepped away from what was happening. She looked more than a little foolish dangling in his grip. Perhaps more importantly, she barely recognized herself. This wasn't the woman who continually pushed herself on the track. She'd been replaced by a helpless creature being molded by her master.

"Where did you go?" He reinforced his question by lifting her hips even higher off the table and lightly slapping her breasts.

"Go?" She started to reach for his hand, but his glare and another slap stopped her.

"You know what I'm talking about." He jerked the panties so she bounced a little. "You checked out. Damn it, you know better."

"I'm sorry, Master. I—didn't mean to anger you." *What did you just call him, and why are you letting him do this?*

"I hope you mean it, slave. You're new to this." He slowly let her down but kept his free hand near her breasts. "I'd like to give you pleasure, but in order for it to be most effective, you need to do everything I tell you to, understand?"

"Yes, Master."

She hoped he'd approve of her response, but it didn't seem to matter to him. "This lesson isn't about seduction. I have no interest in a slow build. A slave takes her pleasure when and however she can and makes the most of it. To demonstrate—"

He pulled down on her panties' crotch and made room for his oversized hand. A rough finger slid over her drenched labia.

"Oh." *Oh shit.*

"Yes. As I suspected and intended, you're already wet." His finger retraced its earlier journey over her sex. "Women think they're complex creatures, but they aren't. This serves as proof."

This isn't happening, she tried to tell herself, but she was growing weary of the lie. For reasons she might never comprehend, she was allowing this near stranger to intimately touch her. To treat her like his slave. Her nails dug into her palms, but she couldn't concentrate on what she was doing enough to stop punishing herself.

He repeatedly teased her pussy. With each electric touch, she sank deeper into this *thing* he'd created.

"Running no longer matters," he muttered. "As for your classes, who gives a damn, because I, your master, am putting you in touch with your true reason for being." A finger touched her entrance. Instead of entering her, however, it remained to tease and promise. Maybe to taunt. "A sex slave has one purpose in life and that is to serve her master's sexual needs. This"—he wiggled his finger—"pleases him. Not you, *him.* Right now it entertains me to arouse you so I can see how you react. Because that could end at any moment, I suggest you make the most of it."

Intercourse had been damn good all right, but the men

who'd gone all the way with her had been more interested in themselves than her. As a result, she'd decided she could do as well on her own for the foreseeable future. The problem was, she kept forgetting to buy fresh batteries. Besides, even if she had a supply, she didn't have the time to get into the mood.

Mood? She was there right now all right, and Master Ken's finger was making mockery of her vibrator.

"I was willing to push you into a climax," he said. His finger slid in maybe a half inch. Despite her effort to keep her response from him, she knew her sex juices had given her away. "But I'm reconsidering. You haven't done anything to deserve a reward."

A small voice warned her that he was playing games with her, but as long as his hand cupped her pussy while a finger invaded what cried out to be invaded, she couldn't think what to do. She hadn't fucked in so damn long. It wouldn't take much to shove her off the edge, a little added movement on his finger's part, a little more surrender on hers.

That was what this crazy game of his was about. He wanted his *slave* to beg.

Closing her eyes against a sudden wave of anger, she dove into sensation. Her panties had been stretched so much they might never recover, and the fabric dug into her. In contrast to the small discomfort, the rest of her body stood on the brink of an explosion.

Surrender. Truly turning her sexuality over to him. Did she have the reckless courage?

Did she have a choice?

Without warning, he ran his commanding finger all the way into her. His palm pressed against her pussy, blanketing and trapping it. Her head whipped from side to side and her hands repeatedly opened and closed.

"Not so sure of yourself, are you, slave? Coming apart."

Oh God! "Please, what do you want, Master?"

"Your capitulation. Complete and without reservation." The pressure against her sex increased. "Do you remember what I said about wanting you to describe what I'm doing to you?"

She didn't have a past, just this presence where Master's hand claimed the only part of her anatomy that mattered.

"No more holding back." He sounded angry. "What's happening to you right now?"

Despite her fear of what she might discover about herself, she focused on her sex and the all-encompassing presence both against and inside her. "You—you've turned me on."

"Come on. You can do better than that. You pride yourself on knowing your body, slave. What message is it giving you right now?"

No matter how hard she tried, she couldn't keep her head still. She repeatedly reached for him only to withdraw. "I, ah, don't know what you want me to say."

"It's getting harder for you to concentrate, which is exactly what I intended. All right, let's see if I can keep things simple. When you walked in here, your libido was next to the last thing on your mind, right?"

She nodded.

"And now getting fucked is darn near the only thing you're thinking about."

"Yes. Master."

He curved the finger inside her so his pad pressed against her channel. The contact seemed even more intimate than what he'd done so far. "Was foreplay involved in getting you to this point?"

I can't think. Please, you have to know that. "No. I mean, I don't think so."

"Why do you suspect I took that route?"

Because his question carried a harsh note, she warned herself to pay attention, but his finger promised so much. "I don't know."

"Wrong!"

One moment she stood on the brink of a climax. The next he'd abandoned her pussy. Before she could make sense of what he'd done, he slapped her crotch. Yelping, she struggled to bring her legs together.

"No, slave! Your body belongs to me. Me, not you. If I decide you need to be punished, it will happen."

He again slapped her too-sensitive flesh. Alarmed, she surged into a sitting position and reached for him. He effortlessly pushed her down. That done, he yanked her arms over her head and crossed one wrist over the other. He gripped them in a single paw. She looked back at him as best she could and watched, barely comprehending, while he reached down for something she couldn't see. He held up a slender length of leather.

"A slave often needs to be restrained. It now appears I was remiss in not taking that precaution earlier."

Both because she knew it wouldn't do any good and because she needed to understand what he had in mind, she didn't resist as he wove the leather around her wrists. When he was done, he brought her arms forward so she could see what he'd done. Not only had he forced her wrists into a crude *X,* but the knotted leather ensured they'd remain that way.

"I was hoping you'd put up a fight. In fact, I'd be surprised and disappointed if you didn't." He *gifted* her with another of his unsettling smiles. Then he pulled her arms up and back. She could tell he was fastening the loose leather end to something at the head of the table.

When he was done, he let go of her and patted the cheek closest to him.

"Go on, slave. Test your bounds."

Her heart both raced and skipped beats as she tugged against whatever he'd tethered her to. The leather didn't cut into her wrists but neither could she bring her arms back down. Not only that, her upper arms restricted her vision.

"You look lovely like that, slave. Buying you cost me more than I intended to spend, but I'm glad I did." He placed his hand over her throat. Her heart continued its accelerated pace, yet she wasn't afraid.

Should she be?

"You're a wild horse, a just-caught mustang. Perhaps you'll prove to be the magnificent racehorse I want to possess, but determining that will take time. Now that I have you properly restrained, I can return to today's lesson." He stroked her throat. "Feel your body, slave. Tell me everything you can about it."

His voice held a disembodied note that reminded her of what taking an online course had been like. The professor was real and yet he wasn't three-dimensional. Except for the hand on her throat, that was what Ken Paro, her Master, had become.

"I, ah, you've tied me down. You can do anything you want to me."

"Bad slave! What have you forgotten?"

When he'd slapped her breasts before, it hadn't hurt. This time he put enough force behind the blow that she was grateful for her blouse and bra—not that he couldn't get rid of them whenever he wanted to.

"Master." She belatedly remembered what to call him. "I'm sorry."

"As you should be." He continued to hold on to her throat as he unbuttoned her top blouse button. "So you've determined that we're playing in my ballpark. You are under my command."

Instead of continuing to undress her as she believed he'd do, he slipped several fingers under her blouse and rested them against her upper left breast.

She waited. Wanted.

"One thing I want to make perfectly clear," he said, "is that I will not hurt you."

It wouldn't take much effort on his part to cut off her ability to breathe, but even as she acknowledged the reality behind the weight against her throat, she nodded as best she could. "I know, Master."

"And why are you saying that?"

Because I told a couple of people where I was going today. If something happens to me, you'll be their first suspect. "That isn't your intention, Master."

"What is, then?"

Was he ever going to do something with the fingers teasing her breast? Darn him, making her wait for something she wasn't sure she'd ever fully grasp wasn't fair!

"Lessons," she said. "You want to teach me some things about myself."

"Yes. What have you learned so far? Let's go back to the subject of your body. What is it experiencing?"

Frustration. "My arms are useless. I, ah, I can't touch myself."

"Go on."

"I feel—I've never experienced something like this, so I'm not sure I have the words, Master. My body no longer belongs to me. I can't make it do what I want it to."

"However, I can. I also know the essentials of what you need. Do you want my finger back inside you?"

Just the thought of that delicious sensation had her tightening her inner muscles. At the same time, years of self-determination made her rebel. She didn't have to lie here like some dumb animal while he played out whatever crazy game he had in mind. Her hands were tethered, but the rest of her was free—not that thrashing about would do any good.

"I asked you a question, slave. You are aware that I can further restrain you. If it entertains me to do so, I'll securely rope you to this table with your legs stretched wide. Maybe I'll walk away leaving you wishing to hell you'd taken me up on my offer. Maybe . . ."

He lifted his hand from her throat and brushed her hair from her cheek. The intimate gesture knocked her almost as much off balance as his sudden command of her pussy had. Did she want this gentle side to him? Maybe she preferred more of the treatment that had robbed her of the use of her hands?

A true and total slave. Tied down for her Master's pleasure. Robbed of speech. Perhaps blindfolded. No longer an elite runner but a helpless sexual object. Living for those moments when Master's attention was on her alone.

"What was I saying?" he went on. Alarmed by her thoughts, she struggled to concentrate. "Oh yes, my options when it comes to training my newest slave. As I believe I've adequately pointed out, I don't have the patience or inclination for a slow buildup. Also, our time today is limited and we both need to make the most of it."

When the hour was over, he'd unlock the door and send her on her way? Maybe they'd never see each other again and in time her memory of what had taken place between them would fade. Wishing she understood how she felt about that, she lifted her head.

"Down, slave." He worked a finger under her bra. "I haven't given you permission to indulge your curiosity."

She might not know anything else, but she had no doubt she wanted to please him so she sank back onto the table. Every time she thought she understood him, he did or said something new that kept her off balance. Undoubtedly that was deliberate on his part, a vital element in his slave-training regime.

Caged and waiting for her master. Heart pounding and palms sweating, not in fear but anticipation. Pussy sticky with longing and nipples hard. Gripping the bars. Listening intently for the sound of Master's footsteps.

6

"Back to the subject under discussion." Ken chuckled. "It really isn't a discussion, is it, because I'm the one directing the conversation." Another finger joined the one already under her bra and he pressed against her breast, flattening it a little. A river of heat flowed over her. She whined and tossed her head.

"What's that, slave? Something you want to tell me?"

"I—I don't know, Master."

His expression was somewhere between compassion and impatience. "You really are raw material. I need to remember that. So, are you ready for me to continue?"

Continue. Sinking deeper into submission and surrender. Trusting him to—"Yes, Master."

"Good. Let's see if we can pick up the threads of the conversation, shall we?"

What were we talking about? "Yes, Master."

"During my recent examination of your vagina, my suspicion that you were already sexually aroused was confirmed. Why are you?"

"Ah, a certain amount of moisture is normal."

He shifted his attention from her face to her still-splayed crotch. "That was and still is more than normal."

Maybe she'd feel more of an equal in this discussion if he didn't have so much to stare at, but she was afraid to close her legs for fear moving would ignite her even more.

And displease him.

"We're all primal creatures," he said. "Some more than others. And each of us goes through periods when our ties to the civilized world become fragile. Let me demonstrate."

He could have easily ripped her blouse apart. Instead, he took his time unbuttoning it the rest of the way. As she waited for him to complete his task, she mourned the loss of his fingers on her breast. Maybe, hopefully, he'd return them to where she needed them to be when he was done.

Master unlocks the cage door and jerks his head at her. Knowing what he wants, she places her hands behind her and walks toward him. He fastens a leash to her collar and uses it to draw her out of where she spends so much of her time. When she stands looking up at him, he again jerks his head, and she turns so her back is to him. Metal cuffs close around her wrists.

Caught. Ready for him.

Sudden air on Runa's breasts stopped the mental images. Master Ken had pushed her bra up, exposing her breasts. The fabric pressed on her sensitive flesh in near duplication of how her panties clung to her thighs. She felt foolish.

Excited.

"Because this is your first session, I've decided to help you more than I have been, at least for a while."

Trembling, she waited as he studied her. What was he looking for, and what would he do with his knowledge when he found it? Maybe he already had what he needed.

"Your breasts are interesting. They're larger than I expected for someone with so little body fat. I'm guessing they jiggle when you're running and that becomes uncomfortable. What do you do, bind them?"

Not long ago she hadn't known he existed. Now he was asking intimate questions and demanding honest answers.

"I wear a snug sports bra." Despite her desire to see what her breasts looked like, the need to keep her attention on Master was stronger. "It holds them pretty well."

"Interesting." He held up his hands and flexed his fingers. "Always something new for a man to learn about a woman, or in this case, for me to educate myself about my newest slave."

Slave. Head down in submission as Master runs his hands over every inch of her naked and helpless body. He has also hooked her manacled wrists to an overhead chain and tightened the chain, lifting her arms and forcing her forward. She waits for him.

Ken's arms dropped to his sides and she'd been certain he was about to touch her in some way or place. So much so that when he turned his back to her and walked out of sight, it took several moments for her to comprehend what had happened. Would he leave her if he'd strung her up the way she'd imagined? Hopefully not.

"Ken? Master, I mean. What—"

"You do not have permission to question anything I do." The direction his voice came from led her to believe he was on the opposite side of the room. "We're going to return to a particular aspect of today's exercise. I expect you to reveal everything you possibly can about what your body is experiencing. Believe me, I'll know if you leave anything out."

Was this his idea of torture? Just when she desperately craved his hands on her body, he deliberately denied her? But if she said or did something he didn't approve of, he might put her back in her cage.

Cage. The lonely, dark place Master deposits his possession when he has no use of her. Alone with nothing except her body and longing, she passes the time by masturbating. As a result, she always gives him what he wants when he pulls her out of her prison.

"My arms are getting uncomfortable," she admitted. "I'm not wearing my sports bra and this one doesn't have as much elasticity. It presses against my breasts and—"

"Do you want me to take it off?"

Be honest. Remember, he knows. "Only if it pleases you, Master."

His chuckle didn't carry much warmth, yet she was grateful for what little he'd given her. His demeanor hadn't told her anything about whether he was getting turned on. For all she knew he had a clinical detachment when it came to his little sideline hobby of messing with women's minds and bodies.

Not a single atom of her body or brain cell was detached from her *predicament*. She was aware of her every line and curve and ached to see what she looked like.

"I hope I please you, Master," she heard herself say. "It is my greatest wish that you enjoy looking at me."

"Hmm. I'm not sure I believe you. You mentioned that your arms are uncomfortable and the bra is digging into your breasts. You aren't used to being restrained. What can possibly be pleasurable about it?"

The cage door creaks open. Master again fastens a leash to her collar, but instead of cuffing her wrists, this time he wraps rope around her elbows and pulls them close together behind her. Because he's done this to her before, she knows to kneel and turn away from him when he sits in a chair near the cage. Even as her fingers begin to go numb, she unzips him and guides his cock out. Swallowing repeatedly, she begins stroking him.

"I'm not sure, Master. I keep thinking . . ."

"What are you thinking about, slave?"

Did he know about the fantasy that kept her both off balance and excited? She was trying to decide whether she dared tell him about it when he returned to her. He again went to her side. One hand settled between her breasts while the other pulled her panties lower.

"Sports injuries are particularly unnerving for athletes." He sounded like a professor. "They don't know how to handle not being able to depend on their bodies' ability to perform. Some have told me they feel as if they're in jail. All they want is to be let out. Unfortunately, they don't have much control over when, or if, that's going to happen."

Any other time she'd be able to concentrate on what he was telling her, but he made that impossible by lightly running his nails over her labia. She shuddered repeatedly. Her legs trembled, tried to close.

Shaking his head, he settled his hand against her pussy. Master had electricity and life in his fingers, hot power that relentlessly and deliciously tore her apart.

"You aren't in jail, slave. There are no bars here. What I'm doing is designed to accomplish two simple things."

His words flitted through her. Desperate to have something other than her out-of-control response to concentrate on, she fought to make sense of them.

"Two things," he repeated. "Can you guess what they are?"

A question. Something for her to respond to. She opened her mouth.

"Let me help. You're already experiencing one. Pay attention."

She hadn't begun to do as he ordered when he caught her pussy flesh between his fingers and tugged. A moment later he lost his hold on her slick labia. Half-crazed, she lifted her buttocks off the table, arching her body as she did. Her breath whistled.

"What's that, slave? You want a repeat of that sensation?"

"Yes, please."

One second followed another until she had no choice but to sink back down onto the table. "Please, Master." She spread her legs as wide as her panties allowed.

"Hmm. Let's see if I'm getting the message."

The hand between her breasts would have been enough to keep her from escaping—not that she wanted to.

"Your message"—he stroked the inside of one thigh and then the other—"appears to be that you're drowning in sexual need."

Help me, please. Let me climax!

"If your imagination was running the show, right now you'd be screaming and jerking about. However, as I don't need to point out, certain nerves need to be stimulated in order for you to climax. I've made studying the female nervous system a priority and believe I can keep you just short of your goal for an indefinite period."

"Why—" She again lifted her ass only to fall back because opening her legs even more had left her without the ability to balance herself. "Damn! Why the hell would you do that? You bastard!"

"Why?" he repeated calmly instead of punishing her as she suddenly feared and hoped he'd do. "Not long ago I explained that today's experience is about imprinting you with two, let's call them lessons. The first is that your body can easily be manipulated into doing something it ordinarily wouldn't. Pay attention now."

She was still trying to wrap her mind about her outburst and its possible consequences so she was slow to realize he was burying not one but two fingers inside her vagina. There was something mechanical about what he was doing, a task he was determined to complete. Before she could climb onboard the sensation and get off on it, his fingers were all the way inside her. No longer moving.

He'd stuffed her with himself. Laid claim to a part of her no man had a right to without her permission.

"I'm disappointed in what you've given me by way of a description so far," he said and drew his hand back from her breasts. He took hold of her bra and used it as a handle to turn her toward him until her tethered arms stopped her. She wasn't sure whether she retained any control over her body.

Or wanted to.

"It's past time to get to the task. What are you feeling now?"

Something about the question compelled her to tighten her channel around his fingers. Even more aroused, she again squeezed. The living invasion didn't move. Frustrated, she repeatedly clenched her sex muscles.

"Can't get off, can you?"

"No," she practically whimpered. Much as she wanted to tighten down again, she'd learned it wouldn't accomplish what she needed.

"To repeat, I expect you to make what you're experiencing as clear and detailed as possible."

If I give him what he wants, he'll reward me. He has to!

"I'm turned on. Incredibly so." She rocked her hips from side to side, licking her dry lips as she did. "I, ah, when I want to masturbate I use a vibrator." She arched her breasts at him. "That always does the trick."

"Why do you think you can't get off the ledge this time?"

Because you're fucking in charge! "My clit—it needs something, a vibrator."

"So this"—he moved the fingers inside her the slightest bit—"gets you to the ledge, but you can't jump."

"Yes."

"Yes what?"

"Master." When had she last called him that?

"What about modesty?" He flicked her right nipple. "I'm

assuming this is the first time something like this has happened to you." He tapped her left nipple.

Sexual energy ran between her breasts and forced a moan from her.

"I usually don't mention this," he said, "but you've come along so quickly that I've decided to. Nothing I do in life gives me more pleasure than teaching a female how to tap in to her true nature. The more you reveal to me, the more you'll get out of our time together. That knowledge will change the rest of your life. Now, slave—" A massive hand settled over her right breast, and he began massaging it. "Reveal."

7

Fiery energy raced through her veins, compelling her to again grip his fingers with her sex muscles. Even when her legs started trembling, she held on. "You—I love it when you call me 'slave.' This—the restraints"—she tugged on the leather—"say my body doesn't belong to me anymore." She turned from him. "It has become yours to do what you want with."

"And what is your desire?"

As he continued kneading her breast, she was hard-pressed to realize that he'd only laid claim to one. Both nipples were so hard they ached. She relaxed her vaginal muscles and concentrated on her stretched flesh there and the fingers responsible for their condition.

"Tie my legs," she blurted. Shocked by how much she'd revealed, she closed her eyes.

"Tie them how?"

She is out of the cage and in Master's bedroom. The last time she'd been in here, he'd secured her arms to two chains hanging from the ceiling and lightly whipped her while she twisted helplessly trying to protect her breasts and buttocks. Today he again catches her wrists over her head, but instead of reaching for his whip, he fastens leather around her ankles and adds a spreader bar so her legs are widely splayed.

"Apart." Hearing her voice threatened to pull her back into reality, so she concentrated on her useless arms, aching breasts, and the fingers stuffing her vagina. "Stand me up. Pull my limbs out from my body and secure them so I can't move and you can beat me."

He was quiet for so long she grew uneasy.

"You like being physically punished?"

She'd said that? Where had the words and more come from?

"No. Who does?" She swallowed. "I don't know, Master." Confused, she turned her head toward him and blinked until he came into focus. "But I've been imagining—"

"I understand."

To her surprise, he leaned over and kissed her on the mouth. Flushed and hungry, she opened hers and pressed her tongue against his teeth. His teeth parted, but instead of letting her in, he pushed her tongue back with his and followed it into her mouth. As his tongue swirled and touched, he flattened her breast against her rib cage.

The masculine fingers fucking her started moving.

In Master's bed. His naked and aroused body wraps around hers. She wears only the slim metal collar around her throat. They are equals here so she feels no hesitancy as she splays her legs under him, draws them high and apart, and guides his head to her pussy. He takes over the task of keeping her available to his warm, wet mouth by pressing down on her thighs. Sobbing in anticipation, she buries her fingers in his hair. His tongue dances at her entrance, then begins a slow, incredible invasion. When he has made her crazy, he withdraws and closes his lips over her hard bud. He suckles. Screaming, she bucks. Comes.

"Where are you, Runa? In the treatment room with me or somewhere else?"

It barely mattered that he'd called her by name. He was no longer kissing her, but his hands still owned her body. Taught it things she'd never known were possible. She tried to pull his fingers even deeper into her sex while rocking her upper body about in an attempt to increase the friction on her breast.

"I don't know where I am."

"What are you seeing?"

"A bed. A man."

"What do you feel?"

"His tongue. On my pussy, my clit. Me climaxing."

"Anything else?"

Master, or should she be thinking of him as Ken Paro, was smiling. His hands held her at the ledge. Knew her better than she did herself.

"There's a collar around my neck."

"Who put it there?"

"My master."

"Is it me?"

"I don't know."

He again leaned low over her. This time he ran his lips over her forehead. He was still kissing her there when he splayed his oversized hand over both breasts.

He straightened. "This is what I've been getting at, Runa. Part of it, anyway. I've asked you to describe what you're feeling so hopefully you'll understand what your body is capable of experiencing. Above everything else, you're a sexual creature. Don't ever deny your capacity for pleasure."

The man who'd turned her world on end studied her for long seconds. Just when she believed she couldn't take any more anticipation, his fingers started thrusting. Something, his thumb maybe, settled over her clit and echoed the same movement.

She stopped breathing, started gasping. A waterfall waited!

The steep, wonderful drop was only inches away, and she charged toward it, limbs flailing, veins threatening to burst.

"You're more than your body, Runa. You're also a brain. Your ability to fantasize brings you great pleasure."

He seemed to be everywhere, looming over her, part of her, holding her so spray from the waterfall drenched her.

"Indulge in that fantasy. Use it to—"

Master. Pinning her to the bed. Keeping a vibrator against her clit.

She climaxed.

When Ken untied her hands and placed them over her still-heaving stomach, Runa debated flexing her shoulders, but the burning sensation would have to wait to be dealt with. She felt as if she'd just run the longest race of her life. She'd won, of course, but instead of slowing so she could catch her breath, she ran another fast lap. Then, because her body still felt wired, she charged up the stadium stairs. Finally she stopped.

She couldn't bring herself to care about Ken until he backed away. Maybe she should feel stronger and more in touch with herself now that his presence wasn't so all-consuming. Instead, she felt a little lost. Abandoned.

Despite the light-headed sensation that accompanied the act, she heaved herself into an upright position. She started to tug her bra back down.

"Leave everything the way it is, slave."

So they'd returned to a master-slave relationship, had they? She had no complaint as long as that meant he intended to give her another climax. She watched as he went over to a shelf with an assortment of equipment and selected a resistance band with handles. He held it at chest level and began pulling. Muscles bulged beneath the tight white shirt. Perhaps he was working off his own sexual frustration.

She leaned forward a little to ensure she wouldn't lose her

balance and turned her attention to what she could see of her wet, reddened sex. Her labia were swollen and so sensitive she hesitated to touch herself. However, after several seconds curiosity overrode caution, and she extended a finger.

"No, don't."

Stupidly eager to obey, she placed her arms behind her to prop herself up and began flexing her legs, bringing them closer together as she did. Her panties looked ridiculous wadded just above her knees, but he was in charge of that as well as everything else about her.

What was she doing here?

When would she be allowed to leave?

"Describe how you're feeling now."

She turned her attention from her panties to the big man. He handled the resistance band as if determined to destroy it. Maybe he was also testing his limits. If he set it down and started toward her—

"Exhausted. Hot and sweaty. Contented." There. She'd said it.

"Not interested in running a race right now?"

He was right. That was the last thing she was up for. In fact, if he had a pillow, she'd be tempted to spend the night there.

But what if he decided to do the same thing?

"What happens now?" The moment she spoke, she knew she'd asked something a slave didn't have a right to.

He glanced at the wall clock showing she'd been there a half hour. "It depends."

On what?

"Usually I find some part of a patient's body that can be worked on, but you've done an admirable job of conditioning yourself. No wonder you're as close to your peak as you are."

Close to but not there, at least that's what he believed.

He dropped the band to the floor and repeatedly twisted at the waist. Then he stopped and looked at her. Started toward her. Her heart threatened to escape her chest, and her pussy heated. He'd taken another step when someone knocked on the locked door.

"Let him in."

"What?" She indicated her exposed breasts and pussy. "I can't like this."

"Yes, you can. And you will. I'm your master. Don't for a minute forget it."

Wondering if she'd lost her mind, she slipped off the table and stood. Her panties slid down her legs and pooled over her feet. Done with the damn garment, she stepped out of it. She'd no sooner done that than she looked around for her slacks. Her less-than-steady fingers reached for her blouse and she started to pull the halves together.

Whoever was out there knocked again.

"Do it, slave. Just the way you are."

Clad in matching silver bands around her throat, wrists, and ankles, she enters the grand room where Master entertains his guests. Male gazes follow her as she walks toward Master holding a large silver plate filled with fruit. She places the plate on the table to his left and kneels before him. Aware of the line of her back and smooth buttocks, she stretches out her arms and lowers her head to the floor. Only pleasing Master matters.

The ever-evolving image had surfaced enough times now that she no longer questioned its existence. She was becoming the slave in her mind, and as such she did what was required of her. Arms swinging at her sides and her blouse barely clinging to her shoulders, she walked over to the door and unlocked it.

8

Jeff Tappe stood outside. He wore a dress shirt and slacks that highlighted his runner's form. Instead of being surprised, she acknowledged she'd known who it would be. Unlike the first time they'd met, she didn't feel in awe of him so much as subservient to the Olympic runner. She laced her fingers together over her belly and stared at the floor.

"Damn, but you work fast," Jeff said. He stepped inside and locked the door behind him.

"It isn't that much work when I'm working with the right subject."

"Hmm." Jeff slid his hand under her blouse and rested his hand on her shoulder. "Please don't tell me I've missed all the fun."

"Hardly. I think you're going to be pleased with what's been accomplished so far. The major shift has been made. She's no longer the same woman she was the day you met her."

"So I see." He tightened his hold, causing her to try to draw back. She couldn't remember how to unlink her fingers. "What's happening, Runa? A little less sure of yourself than you used to be?"

"She answers to 'slave,'" Master Ken said. "Right now I want to keep her focusing on her submissive side."

"As do I, as do I." Still gripping her shoulder, Jeff cupped her chin and tipped her head upward. His stare was as incomprehensible as Master's had been. Master? Did she now have two? "It's quite the transformation, isn't it." Jeff didn't make it a question. "You're a lot more amenable to what my friend or I tell you to do than you used to be. You don't question, you simply obey."

"Do I?"

Jeff looked at Master Ken. "What does she know about you?"

"I decided to wait until you were here. You can do the honors if you want."

"Why not?" He positioned his face inches from hers. "There's more to mammoth man than meets the eyes. I'm not sure how long he's been into the kinky stuff, but—"

"Only a couple of years. Finding a woman who understands my interest in domination and wants to assume the opposite role hasn't been easy."

"I sent you a submissive in the rough today," Jeff said and smiled at her. "That's the vibe I got when we met the other day, at least I was pretty sure that's the message you were giving out. My plan was simple. I'd get Master Ken and you together and let him determine whether I know my vibes."

Master Ken chuckled. "You do. You're better at sniffing out a potential sub than I thought you'd be."

"I'm learning. Anyway—" Jeff turned his attention back to her. "Ever since my buddy told me about his *hobby,* I've wanted to see if it was something I could get into myself. The more I learned about it, the more it appealed to me. Neither of us is particularly interested in classic BDSM. The rough pain element, well—" His gaze narrowed. "Let's say the concept takes us out of our comfort zones. This experiment with you is about a possible basic dom-sub relationship. Who knows? Maybe it'll be mutually beneficial for the three of us."

She couldn't think of anything to say but maybe he didn't care, just that she understood. She'd heard of BDSM, of course, and had been both curious and uneasy about the lifestyle. Mutually beneficial? What was he talking about?

"You get your reward yet?" Master Jeff asked Master Ken.

"No. Like I said, I wanted to put the focus on her."

"In other words she—"

"Climaxed? Yes. But not until I made it happen, right, slave?"

"Yes, Master."

The pressure on her shoulder lessened. Suddenly she was afraid he'd walk away from her, so she stepped closer and arched her back so her breasts grazed his middle. Fear gave way to embarrassment, prompting her to retreat.

Master Jeff grabbed both sides of her blouse and hauled her against him. "Hands behind your back, slave."

She is still in the massive room filled with men but no longer presents herself to Master because he orders her to stand and points toward a man wearing a fur cape and nothing else. Unsteady feet take her to the newcomer. He grips her arms and spins her around. Rope tightens around her wrists, and he cinches her wrists to the rope he'd placed around her bare waist.

"A lovely present," the newcomer says. "Exactly what a man who has been traveling alone needs. I'll use her well."

"Not use," Master says. "Share. Tonight she belongs to both of us."

Master Jeff wasn't as large as Master Ken, but he handled her with equal confidence as he glared at her, silently commanding her to obey. Tears she refused to shed heated her eyes as she positioned her hands as he'd ordered.

Nodding, he let go of her blouse and stepped back. "Turn around, slave. I want to see what you really look like. Keep rotating until I tell you otherwise."

She wasn't totally naked and yet she was in all the ways that counted since the blouse was open revealing her breasts. The bra pressing against the upper mounds gave them an unnatural appearance. She'd been shaving her pubic hair for years because she liked the feel of nylon against flesh.

"That's a body to be proud of," Master Jeff said. "I take it you didn't have any trouble getting her to respond."

Master Ken had remained near the equipment table, but now he joined Master Jeff as she obediently completed one circle after another.

"Even less than I thought I might. She's easy to condition."

Easy? Yes, she was. When her back was to the men she pondered why she'd turned self-determination over to them and why it excited her to know their attention was focused on her.

"She won't remain in this particular sexual space for long," Master Ken said. "After all, you can't take the jock out of a woman."

"Nor would I want to. Face me, slave."

Responding to Jeff's command, she kept her stance wide in attempt to counteract her sudden light-headedness.

"So you've made the transition into sexual slavery," he continued. "For the record, it's a temporary but easy-to-resurrect condition. I wouldn't have turned you over to my experienced friend if I wasn't convinced that today's encounter would change your performance on the track for the better. Also . . ." He looked down, drawing her attention to his erection. "I believe you can figure out the rest of my agenda without my having to spell it out. I'm committed to doing what I can to bettering your running time, but as a man, well—come here."

Feeling as if a sensual magnet had taken over, she closed the gap between them. Jeff Tappe had been her hero, but knowing she'd turned him on left no doubt that he was human. What had it been like for him when all that pressure to excel was heaped on his shoulders? Not only did he have the media and public scrutinizing his every step, but he'd represented the United States in the Olympics. If he earned a medal, he'd become a hero and advertisers would sign him to lucrative contracts, but if he failed, all those years of work and sacrifice would have been for nothing.

"Was it lonely for you?" she asked, unable to do more than whisper. "While you were training for the Olympics, I mean?"

"Sometimes not so much. Sometimes a lot. Why?"

"Because I want to get to know you better."

His eyes widened.

"The ball's in your court, Jeff," Ken said. "Take it from here."

Nodding, Jeff rubbed the heel of his hand over the bulge in his slacks. His other hand went to her shoulder and he drew her blouse off her. He let go of it. "Finish the job, slave. I want you naked."

Even though in essence she already was, she reached behind her and unfastened her bra. The sudden loss of pressure on the tops of her breasts felt wonderful. About to drop the bra on top of her blouse, she handed it to Master Jeff. Nodding, he ran his fingers over it before discarding what she could care less about.

"A question: do you have any objections to what has happened so far?"

Master Jeff had resumed massaging his cock. She placed a hand between her legs and slipped her middle finger inside her. Instead of the relief she was hoping for, she clenched her teeth against sudden hard, wonderful need. Wanting more, she covered her breasts with her free forearm and pressed on the swollen flesh.

"No objections, Master. I, ah, loved every minute of it." *Maybe more than you'll ever know.*

"Especially the kind of climax he led you into, right?"

"I—it didn't call for much work on his part because it's been so long since I've—well, you know what a training schedule is like."

"Yeah."

His one-word reply made her wonder if he regretted admitting anything, but he'd already told her how set apart he'd once felt.

"Look at the current physical difference between us," he said after a short silence. "I can step out and rejoin the world any time I want. In contrast, the only thing you're in any condition to face is me." He again planted the hand not over his cock on her shoulder, his thumb resting near her throat. If he wanted to, he could easily cut off her ability to breathe.

"Think about why that is," he continued. "What happened between my friend and you that made you decide clothes are unimportant and your hand needs to be on your sex?"

"I don't know, Master."

"I think, if you're honest with yourself, you do know."

He was demanding a great deal from her, but despite the danger and her simmering sexual hunger, she wanted to give it to him. Staring at his chest, she filled her lungs. "My mind—I kept imagining I was a slave. Instead of being afraid, the thought excited me." She glanced over at Master Ken, then turned her attention back to Master Jeff. "I imagined that I lived in a cage where—"

"Maybe you're still in there."

Catching her unawares, he gripped her waist with both hands, lifted her off her feet, and placed her over his shoulder. She planted her hands on his back in preparation for lifting her head.

"No!" Master Ken snapped. "He's in charge, not you."

Besides, she loved how helplessness felt as she hung facedown with her fingers brushing Master Jeff's ass and his arm wrapped around her naked body to keep her in place. He started toward the table where earlier Master Ken had both restrained and pleasured her.

Master—a different one from her earlier owner—walks into the opulent room where she'd been brought to wait for him. Even lying down with her arms and legs tied to the edges of the bed, she sees how weary he is. His hair is dirty and tangled, his shirt ripped. A pistol rests on one hip, a knife on another.

"War," he says. "Endless war. And countless battles. This is the only place I can relax. You're the only one who can make me forget the hell."

This man owned her. He'd bought and chained her, and she has no choice but to spend the rest of her slave life with him, but he isn't the beast she'd feared he was.

He places his weapons on a nearby table, then removes his ruined shirt, revealing the four-inch-long cut where a knife had sliced his chest. He touches the dried blood.

"It's all on my shoulders," he says. "The decisions, the danger, the need to lead."

His mouth tight against pain, he stands beside the bed and cups her breasts with his dry, scratched hands.

"You're the one human who will ever see the real me. Do you understand why I must have you?"

Crying, she nods.

Grunting elaborately, Master Jeff eased her onto the table and left her sitting up with her legs dangling over the side. "Interesting tan."

She placed her dark hand over her pale belly. "I don't have the time to do anything about that. No afternoons sunbathing for me."

His smile died, as he clamped his fingers over her throat. "Don't put yourself down."

"I'm not. I—"

"No excuses. Take pride in your body."

She was hesitant to tell him she did, especially since he'd already released her neck and was pushing her knees apart. Much as she longed to place her hands over his to let him know she approved, she hadn't been given permission.

Permission. More proof that she wasn't equal to the men.

Not long ago she would have called them chauvinistic pigs and insist they join the modern world, but she was naked while they remained dressed. Even more telling, Master Ken had sent a climax spiraling through her as proof of his mastery.

They knew her body while she knew nothing about theirs.

Confused, she rested her hands on her thighs and watched, openmouthed, as Master Jeff kicked off his shoes. That done, he unfastened his slacks and stepped out of them. On the opposite side of the room her other master stripped. Naked, Master Ken was all muscle. Power upon power. She couldn't summon enough moisture to swallow. In contrast, her sex juices drenched her labia, undoubtedly staining the table.

"I know Ken has already asked you if this is what you want," Master Jeff said, "but I'm going to repeat it for myself. No objections?"

With her throat still so dry, she didn't trust herself to speak, so she ran her fingers over her pussy and gathered proof of her arousal. Her intention had been to hold up her fingers for him to see. Instead, she touched them to his mouth.

He grabbed her wrist and guided her fingers to her own mouth. Hungry, she opened it and licked.

"Yes," she muttered. "I want."

"Why?"

Because I'm turned on! Only that wasn't the entire story. "He called me 'slave.'" She indicated the naked former football player. "He handled me as if that's what I am. I'm not ready for the experience to end. I need . . ."

"To submit," Master Ken supplied.

In her cage. The room dark. Footsteps coming closer. Trem-

bling in anticipation, she stands and grips the bars. A dim light kills the night, and her masters are standing there. Naked. Aroused.

The metal door swings open, and she steps out. Silver rings dangle from her nipples, connected by a silver chain. She takes hold of the chain and lifts it by turn toward her masters. That done, she lowers herself onto her knees on the cement floor with her back to the two who rule her. She rests her forehead on the cement and spreads her legs to give them an unobstructed view of her sex.

She waits.

9

"Yes, Master, I need to submit. To both of you."

Master Jeff looked over his shoulder at the big man who'd initially turned her world on end. "Do you think she's earned it?"

"It's possible. However, I'm going to reserve judgment until she shows us how she responds to a total loss of control."

Hadn't she already done that? Instead of pointing that out to Master Ken, she struggled to comprehend. His massive muscles seemed to absorb the artificial lighting. Except for his buttocks and erect cock, every inch of his beautiful body was deeply tanned. If she'd been an opposing football player, she would have fled the moment she saw him coming toward her.

"You first," Master Jeff said to his friend. "You've earned it."

"Plus I have a damn good idea how to get to her."

As Master Ken started toward her, Master Jeff walked around the table and stood behind her. His strong hands closed over her shoulders and he drew her back so he supported her.

Master Ken stepped into the recently abandoned space between her legs. Suddenly overwhelmed, she scooted back only to have to stop because Master Jeff wasn't giving way.

The former football player splayed his strong hands over her thighs. "Relax, slave. Remember what has happened so far. It's all been good, right?"

She nodded. Then to her surprise, she placed her hands over his. He nodded at what she'd done. "This is all about trust."

And my bondage fantasy.

He must have taken her silence as acceptance because after briefly stroking her thighs, he slid his fingers down her legs. His superior and all-knowing strength explored her knees, not as a doctor would, but lightly, sensually, possessively. When he reached for her calves, she groaned, bent her legs, and rested her feet on the table.

Here's my surrender, my body, offered to you.

She barely noticed when Master Jeff grasped her wrists and brought them up and back.

Off balance. Her pussy open and vulnerable. Shaking and hungry. Eyes half-closed. Heart hammering.

"Today you're a piece of clay," Master Ken whispered. "Newborn. Sexual."

On a high, hard bed in a dark room. Arms bound behind her and ankles lashed together, she lies on her side with her knees deeply bent, waits.

Rough hands grip her ass cheeks and draw them apart. A man's cock presses against her vaginal opening. That done, he takes hold of her hair and pulls back her head. Something touches her lips, and she tastes precome. Eager, she opens her mouth. An aroused cock slips into the space she'd just created. At the same time, the man behind her claims what belongs to him.

Both of her body's owners taking her at the same time. Thrusting until she feels as if she is being hurtled between them. Tied the way she is, she can't fight even if she wants to.

She doesn't.

"Show her what she's good for," one master gasps. "Teach her the meaning of her existence."

Someone grasps her breasts. She wonders if whoever it is is trying to prevent them from flailing about.

This isn't her body. It hasn't been since the masters bought her. But her existence is good, all good. Wonderful.

Trapped by them. Used by them.

Using them.

"You have a rare gift," Master Ken said as he worked his hands over her legs. "Football was my life for so many years. No matter what I accomplished, there was always a new goal or challenge. Much of what happened was out of my hands."

Leaning forward, he ran his tongue over her thigh. She shuddered and blinked, bringing him into focus. As superb as he'd looked as he was slipping out of his clothes, that was nothing next to having him so close. His body had been carved from equal amounts of genetics and hard work, powerful beyond belief.

"I'm guessing Jeff wants to tell you the same thing." Every word sent warm, moist air over her skin. "Part of why you're here is because our intention is that from now on, you'll see your speed as something to celebrate, the same as everything that happens in here."

"He's right," Master Jeff said while Master Ken again laid a damp trail over her inner right leg. "Don't be the way I was, so intent on proving myself to the whole damn world that I lost the joy."

Joy? More like sexual hunger so powerful she was certain she'd scream. She'd seldom had time to indulge in sexual fantasies, and what she'd repeatedly slipped into this afternoon went far beyond anything she'd ever imagined. The men were trying to tell her something they considered important, but the words meant little. They'd taken her from her world and placed her in theirs.

Yes, theirs.

She concentrated on Master Ken's mouth as he nibbled and licked. He came so close to her pussy that she barely noticed when Master Jeff crossed one of her wrists over the other and held them in a single hand. His other hand found her left nipple.

"Right now your body is everything," he said. He pressed down, rotating his palm as he did. A molten river sped from her breast to her hot, ever-dripping vagina. She groaned and arched her spine.

"Your speed is fleeting," Master Jeff continued. "Believe me, I know. Don't miss a moment of the experience. Breaking a school record isn't the goal. The journey is."

"Journey," Master Ken muttered with his mouth against her beyond-sensitive thigh. "Step after step. Emotion piled upon emotion. Occasionally stopping so you can exist in the moment."

Oh God! "I, shit, I can't think." Her useless fingers fluttered.

"Maybe not consciously, but the lesson is sinking in." Turning his attention to her other breast, Master Jeff applied a little more pressure, moving his palm about as he did. "Pleasure. Nothing but pleasure."

When Master Ken slipped his hands under her buttocks and lifted her off the table, she forgot everything else. Strangely, she'd never felt safer. At the same time, she'd never faced a greater challenge.

The big man let her back down followed by placing her legs over his shoulders. Fortunately the table was tall enough that she didn't feel as if she was being bent in two. What she felt was deliciously helpless.

And a moment later, his tongue gliding over her labia.

"Oh God!" Unable to stop herself, she fought.

"Easy, Runa, easy. You know you want this."

Even though Master Jeff was right, she couldn't dismiss the unnerving sensation snaking through her. A cramp in her right hand pulled a little of her attention there, and she realized she was clenching her fingers. The men weren't helping her relax, damn them! Not Master Ken with his all-knowing and all-invading tongue. Surely not the man behind her who'd laid claim to her breast.

Caught between them. Their sexual toy. Existing for their pleasure.

"Your body," Master Jeff muttered, "is an incredible gift given only to a few. Celebrate everything it's capable of."

Everything? Only her growing, growling need to climax mattered. If she could speak, she'd tell them she'd do whatever it took so they could get off, but right now that would be a lie.

"You and I have been here before," Master Ken said, his words tearing what remained of her thoughts apart. He kept his mouth near her core so his breath bathed her there and drove her crazy. "The last time I handed you a climax. Now you have to earn it."

She still couldn't find her voice, didn't care about trying to communicate until he lowered her back onto the table, and she needed to know what he intended to do next. Silent, he positioned her legs so they dangled off the table's side.

"Did you hear him?" Master Jeff reinforced his question by pinching one nipple and then the other. "What do you intend to do in order to earn another climax?"

Think. Give them what they expect and deserve.

"Ah, if you let me up I'd be more than happy to, ah, stimulate you." She aimed her gaze in the direction of Master Ken's cock. Because of the way they'd positioned her, she couldn't see it, but maybe it was better this way. Easier on her nerves at least.

Chuckling, Master Ken slid what felt like his little finger inside her. "I appreciate the offer, but if I simply wanted to jerk off, we'd already be there."

Still on the hard bed with her limbs immobilized. Her masters are no longer fucking her fore and aft. Someone has moved her about so she kneels. Hot with sexual frustration, she studies the two naked men who stand side by side looking down at her. Their gazes intensify and their eyes darken. A whip suddenly appears in their hands.

Fear touches her, but she shakes it off. Half-crazed with anticipation, she lowers her head until she falls forward. Her forehead lands on the spread. Sweating from the effort, she forces more distance between her knees. Her tied ankles twist one over the other.

"My gift to my masters." She wiggles her ass at them.

"A gift?" The asker reinforces his question by swatting her buttocks. "You belong to us, slave. We take. You don't give."

As the stinging sensation slips into pleasure, she again wiggles her ass. "This is freely given, my way of showing gratitude for showing me how to be a slave."

Instead of abruptly pulling out of her fantasy as she'd done before, her last words stayed with her as she heaved herself into an upright position. Master Jeff still had hold of her wrists, and Master Ken's finger remained nestled in her vagina. Logic said she wasn't a sex slave, that this was part of some well-thought-out plan the men had devised for reasons she was still trying to wrap her mind around. Did they know she was as free as she wanted to be? Master Ken's nudity mirrored hers, but strength surrounded him while she'd never felt more exposed or weaker.

"I've been having some crazy thoughts," she admitted. Her throat ached as if she hadn't spoken for a long time. "Bondage fantasies."

Master Ken nodded. "Go on."

"It all—every fantasy revolves around a sense of helplessness." *Sexual slavery.*

"Like now?" Master Jeff tightened his hold on her left breast. Fire danced through her.

"Even more so," she admitted through clenched teeth. "Ropes and chains and a cage." Stopping, she tried to remember if she'd already admitted this. "You—I want to pleasure both of you, but it needs to be right for all of us."

"I do believe," Master Ken said, "that she wants us to remain in charge."

"Otherwise she'll feel cheated."

Much as she wanted them to understand that, for her, everything about this afternoon felt perfect, talking would have to wait. Hard, swollen veins stood out on Master Ken's cock. She wasn't sure her vagina was large enough to accommodate him, but she'd try. Hell yes, she'd try! More than that, she'd do everything she could to bring him release.

With half a plan in mind, she tried to pull her arms free. After a moment during which Master Jeff let her know who'd win this battle, he let her go. That done, he pressed his forearm against her shoulder blades to stabilize her. Master Ken's little finger continued to drink from her sex juices.

Embracing her strength and weakness, she cupped her fingers around Master Ken's erection. Raw energy surged through her. The all-encompassing slavery fantasy threatened to envelop her again, but she fought it off and concentrated on rhythmically pressing her palms against the big man's cock.

"Oh shit, yes," he growled.

Slipping fully into her task, she let go of him long enough to run her fingers over her sopping labia. She acknowledged his hand against and in her with a downward glance before focusing on coating his cock with her fluids.

"You have so many skills," she told him. Her mind kept skittering off to thoughts of fucking. "I only have this." Gripping his juice-coated erection, she held him steady while scooting closer. Instead of abandoning her pussy and making room for his cock as she'd thought he'd do, he continued to plug her. A look into his eyes led her to believe he was challenging her, so she grabbed his wrist and pulled. His finger slipped out of her. Lonely and wanting, she placed his hand on her thigh.

10

The world seemed to be waiting for her, at least the world that consisted of these two men. Courage gathered, she reached out and gripped Master Ken's buttocks. He didn't resist her weakened strength but arched forward in response to her fingers against his ass cheeks.

His cock touched her entrance, and the world started to fall away. The slave world still clinging to her subconscious began to take over. She could almost feel her bonds.

"Not yet, damn it," Master Jeff snapped. "Come on, Ken, you know what you have to do."

Cursing, the former football player effortlessly twisted out of her grip. Her flesh on fire and her mind screaming denial, she watched him walk away and into what she assumed was the bathroom. Furious and frustrated, she swiveled about and glared at Master Jeff.

"Watch," he said. "You'll understand."

A minute later she did. Instead of leaving her as she'd feared, Master Ken returned wearing a condom.

"Thank you," she whispered. "I should have—I've always insisted—"

"We understand. It's the same for us."

Much as she appreciated Master Jeff's admission, she didn't see how she could have lost touch with the real world as much as she had. For some reason, seeing Master Ken ready for sex made him appear more vulnerable to her. Up until now he'd been in charge. Now he was an ordinary man intent on one of life's most basic acts.

How little she knew about both of them, she realized as she reached out for him. Tears filmed her vision.

"Is something wrong?" Ken asked.

"No." She gave him a weak smile. "Everything's right."

"Then—"

"Sex, please. Now. Talking later."

The living warmth behind her wrapped his arms around her shoulders, silently letting her know she could rely on his support. As she leaned back, Master Ken planted her feet on the table and closed his fingers around her ankles.

Held by the two men.

The three of them together.

She didn't care whether these moments of equality would last. Master Ken's hard, heavy breath left no doubt that the time he'd spent getting her to this emotional place had exacted a toll on him. Even though she wasn't sure she'd been granted the right to do this, she reached between her legs and separated her labia lips. That done, she caught his sheathed penis and brought it to her.

"Take her." Master Jeff sounded equally aroused. "Make her scream."

Closing her eyes, she kept her fingers on Master Ken's organ as long as she could. Finally he was inside her, a hard force promising both destruction and salvation. Yes, she'd already climaxed today, but that seemed like a lifetime ago, something that had happened to another woman.

Slave or free, it didn't matter.

The darkness she'd created carried her to a place where her body became weightless. She lost contact with her arms and legs and no longer touched reality. A powerful, all-knowing man was fucking her, grunting with every thrust. If he wanted, he could tear her apart with his strength. Instead, he kept a fierce hold on his strength, one that might not last much longer.

Invasion and retreat, feeling him deep within her followed by tightening her sex muscles around his cock in an attempt to keep him there.

Invasion and retreat, growing more heated as the attack continued. Perhaps it would all become real if she opened her eyes, but this unreal sensual place was better. Her flesh became more and more sensitive, her breathing less controlled.

"Do me. Oh shit, yes, do me!"

Master Ken drove into her with such force that he slammed her back against Master Jeff's chest. Desperate to let him know she approved, she reached for him. Before she could finish the task, however, Master Jeff captured her wrists and lifted her arms up and back.

Caught again. Gloriously imprisoned.

The chain attached to the nipple clamps jerks about and sends fire deep into her helpless body. After securing her wrists behind her, Master had commanded her to stand motionless while he placed the familiar and painful clamps on her. When she'd first become his possession, she'd hated and feared this act, but now she understands it for what it is, a prelude to sex.

Fucking. Being taken and taking.

She straddles him as soon as he positions himself naked on his back on the massive bed that, for her, has only one use. Wise in what he wants from her, she slowly settles herself onto his cock. It plugs her as she bounces up and down, his pleasure as vital as her own. Head back and thigh muscles straining, she performs for her master. He doesn't care whether she climaxes, and at first she hadn't been able to. However, endless sessions designed to please him have trained her body.

Pleasure and pain, exertion and anticipation, those things and more had turned her from the shy woman she'd once been into a wanton sex slave.

Her teeth clench against what feels like daggers digging into her breasts as she fucks the man who owns her. Pain comes in waves but is always there, a core part of what her system experiences. Repeatedly pummeling his cock gives her a fleeting sense of superiority so she feeds off it. Her vagina weeps, growing more desperately hungry with each second.

At first he lies there, tired from whatever his day beyond her has been about, but she knows how to take away that day and turn him back into a man.

A man being fucked by his slave who needs the same.

"Where the hell has she gone?"

Runa fought to remain in the world she'd created from her sexual fantasies, but Master Jeff's question pulled her back to reality—that and the glorious burn escaping her vagina and spreading over her.

"I think I know," Master Ken's voice rasped. He slowed, went deeper into her, demanded her full attention.

Somewhere between alarmed and curious, she opened her eyes. Master Jeff's hold on her arms had expanded her chest so her breasts appeared more prominent. The big man pummeling her was staring at them.

Master Ken stilled. "Helplessness really turns you on, doesn't it, slave?"

The word *slave* stroked her mind. "Yes, Master."

"But it alone isn't enough," he continued in that rough tone, "so you, ah, designed a world that gives you—everything you need."

Master Ken was red-faced. The muscles on the arms anchoring her feet stood out in hard relief. He studied the union between them and then slammed into her.

"Yes! Yes, again, please," she managed.

"What is it like?" Master Ken asked a moment later, or was it a demand? "You're back in that cage with a collar around your neck?"

She couldn't think. Hell, she wasn't sure she could speak. Her lids again drifted down, and she arched her spine. The cock buried in her shifted so it touched the top of her vagina. Shocked and hungry, she tried to lift herself even more.

"You about there, old friend?" Master Jeff asked.

"What—what the hell do you think?"

"Good. Look, I'm going to try something I think will get her to the same place. Let's see if . . ."

What Master Jeff had in mind didn't matter. She was certain he was speaking a language she understood. Wild for the eruption, she rocked her tethered body from side to side.

Caught. Helpless.

Suddenly her arms were free. As they dropped to her sides, she whined in frustration. Where was her fantasy, the bonds that—

Pressure on her nipples! Fingers gripping them, holding them, claiming them.

Logic told her that Master Jeff had let go of her wrists so he could focus on her breasts, inflicting a measure of discomfort her body interpreted as pure sex. Unable to lift her heavy arms, she continued her sideways thrashing. Every move increased the awareness in her breasts. As the pleasure/pain expanded, she fed off it. Screamed. Cried maybe.

Came.

Her vagina gripped Master Ken's cock as it pulsed and jerked inside her, taking her even deeper into her climax.

"Don't stop, slave," Master Jeff commanded. "Push your limits."

Only two things registered: her nipples were still imprisoned and Master Ken continued pummeling her. A climaxing man couldn't keep this up for long, could he? Sensation told her he'd emptied himself. Instead of becoming exhausted, however, he kept after her. Helpless to quiet her quivering muscles, she mindlessly rode with him.

"I can't—oh please, stop!"

"You love it, slave. Admit it, damn it!"

It didn't matter which master had spoken. The thrill of pleasure's assault was giving way to something she couldn't wrap her mind around. She felt as if she was in a whirlpool and being thrown about, splintering, crying, maybe begging. Her hands dragged over the table, her head fell back against Master Jeff's chest, and Master Ken kept slamming himself at her. She couldn't find a way out, couldn't free herself.

"Please! Masters, please."

"What do you want, slave? To fully enter your new reality?"

Master Ken didn't sound as out of breath as she felt. Before she could open her eyes so she could study his expression, he pulled out of her. His wet, shrinking cock dragged over her entrance, touched her clit, sent her off again.

He was done. He had to be, she desperately comforted herself when she could think. Peace and relief was coming. It had to! She was too exhausted for—

Master Ken pressed his calloused finger against her sexual trigger and she screamed. Her body exploded. Only fragments remained, all of them on fire.

"Help me, please. Someone help me."

"Take it," Master Jeff ordered. "Today is just the beginning."

11

When, after what felt like half of her life, her masters granted her spent body a measure of freedom, she curled up on her side on the table. Sticky sweat coated every inch, and her pussy felt as if it had been attacked.

Deliciously pummeled.

At first all she wanted was to be left alone, but after what might have been a few minutes or an hour, her mind started to stir. She wasn't back in the world of slavery she'd designed, but the pieces were beginning to come together. Her wonderfully sore nipples reminded her of how they'd felt clamped, and her arms and legs might as well be tied because she didn't have the strength to move them.

"We aren't done," a deep voice announced.

One of her masters. Demanding something of her.

Determined to respond to the best of her shattered ability, she opened her eyes and propped herself up on her forearm. They stood over her, making her wonder how long they'd been studying her.

"That's right." Grabbing her shoulders, Master Ken hauled

her upright. He pulled her arms back until her elbows briefly touched. "You've serviced me, but that's only half of the job."

The fantasy world she'd fallen in love with again moved over her. Surely her masters knew she was willing to pleasure Master Jeff. There was no reason for Master Ken to restrain her.

"What do you want me to do, Masters?" She kept her eyes downcast.

"To serve." Master Jeff slapped her breasts, setting off delicious shock waves. "I make the decision, got it?"

"Yes, Master."

"Good. Ken, prepare her."

A moment later ropes circled her elbows behind her. The former football player tied them so she felt pressure and not pain. When he was done, she tested the bonds. Her arms were useless.

"Get up, slave. Present yourself."

She felt awkward sliding to the edge of the table and nearly fell when she eased herself off it. Neither man made a move to help.

If she remembered correctly, Master Jeff had still been partly dressed. He must have prepared himself for sex while she was recovering.

"On your knees."

Yes! This time she lost her balance but didn't feel embarrassed as she worked at righting herself. Master Jeff was several feet away, Master Ken behind her. She squeezed her legs together while lifting and lowering herself to rekindle the simmering fire.

"You'd like that, wouldn't you?" Grabbing her hair, Master Ken pulled her head back. "To care about nothing except your selfish pleasure. Sorry, that's not what this is about."

Either he didn't fully grasp how much his rough treatment excited her or he was deliberately feeding a shared fantasy.

"What do you want from me, Master Jeff?"

"Your mouth."

She shivered and tried to focus. Even with his runner's body, she was hard-pressed to remember what the man had been before he'd taken ownership of her.

Ownership. His possession.

When Master Ken eased his hold on her hair, she obediently opened her mouth. Master Jeff's smile didn't extend beyond his mouth. She wondered if only his hard-on mattered to him.

"What is this?" he demanded. "You think I should come to you. You're damn wrong, slave. Remember your place. Do what you've been trained to do."

Trained. Yes.

Keeping her lips parted and her head straight so Master Ken's hold on her hair wouldn't hurt, she knee-walked over to the owner who had need of her. Vaginal juices ran down her inner thighs, and even though nothing was touching them, her nipples knotted.

Finally she reached her master, but as much as she longed to begin what he had every right to demand, she knelt with her mouth still open, waiting. Obedient.

"A well-trained slave is an amazing sight." Master Jeff patted the top of her head. "Makes all our hard work worth the effort."

"We aren't finished with her. She needs a great deal more work."

Yes, thank you.

"True, but at least she's come far enough to be of some use. We have plenty of time to mold her into what we want her to be, and what satisfies her." He chuckled. "Do it, slave. Show me what you were born for."

On the brink of diving back into the world of her mind, she instead focused on the familiar bodies flanking her. Today was only the beginning. A thrilling adventure lay ahead of not just her, but all of them.

The tension on her hair let up even more, giving her the freedom she needed to close her lips around Master Jeff's cock. Before long they'd meet at the university track, where she'd have to pretend to be someone she no longer was. For now she was what mattered, a kneeling and bound sex slave.

Master Jeff needed the gift of her mouth. Maybe he'd claim her entire body. He'd gone without sexual relief and then stood on the sidelines while she administered to his friend.

No more. His turn.

Determined to make the moments perfect for him, she leaned forward and took him deeper. She'd crossed a line. For as long as he needed her total obedience, she'd give it to him.

Her useless fingers clenched, and she felt her toes curl. *Deeper. Deeper still.*

She teased and suckled, occasionally ran her teeth and lips over his length. Intoxicated by the feel and size of him, she repeatedly pressed her tongue against Master's gift to her. On a soul-deep level she knew she had no right to his male organ. He had every right to deny her the pleasure of administering to him, and that made every moment and touch precious. Her body became so heated she started to pant. Afraid she'd lose contact with him, she closed her mouth around him.

His tip pressed against the back of her throat, startling her. Her eyes burning and throat convulsing, she arched away. He started to slide out.

"Watch it, slave. Believe me, you don't want to do that." Master Jeff reinforced his warning by grabbing her nipples. "Stay in place."

Later, maybe, she'd tell him she'd been afraid she'd gag. For now she'd seek redemption by turning her head so she could bathe his length with her saliva-moistened tongue. His hold on her breasts remained all-powerful, and she started to sink back into the world she'd created.

"She isn't learning her lesson," Master Ken muttered. "One last attempt, slave. If you fail—well, you won't like it."

A hook connected to a chain dangling from the ceiling has been placed around the rope between her elbows, and she has been pulled onto her toes. Another inch and she'll dangle. If that happens, she'll cry out from pain and fear. However, her masters might not hear because they'll gag her with a large black ball.

She'd failed at bringing her masters to climax within a short time frame, and they are punishing her, robbing her of the ability to try to make amends, robbing her of the chance to fill her mouth with a swollen cock. They might make her hang for hours. Teach her the consequences of failure.

"I'm sorry, Master. Please let me try again. I want—I'll do whatever it takes to satisfy you."

"Think she deserves it?" Master Ken asked. "It looked like a piss-poor effort to me."

"Not the best, that's for sure." Master Jeff shook her breasts so pain seared her from throat to belly. In a desperate attempt to escape the sensation, she sank down on her haunches, but there was nowhere to go.

And nothing else she'd rather do.

"Forgiveness," she whimpered. "And patience, please, Masters."

Master Ken patted her head as if she was some dog he was training. Between what the two of them were doing, she floated in wondrous captivity. However, all too soon the heat in her breasts cooled because Master Jeff had released them.

What could she do to prompt him to again capture and *abuse* them?

Lost in the male bodies that had changed her perception of life, she straightened and opened her mouth wide. When Master Jeff didn't immediately accept her gift, she touched her lips to his cock. Hands on his hips, he waited. She took him deeper, swallowed him, felt his tip against her throat.

"Keep going," he warned. "Don't you dare gag."
Yes, Master.

Instinct dispensed with, she sucked and suckled. Worshiped not just her master's cock but his entire being.

His breathing turned ragged, and he repeatedly pressed the tips of his fingers against her shoulder blades. He arched into her.

Mouth fucked. Taken in a way reserved for trusting lovers.

Lovers?

Was—could—

"Ah shit."

A powerful hand landed on her chest and knocked her back. Even as she landed on her useless elbows only one thing mattered.

Her mouth was empty.

Had she failed him?

Master Jeff straddled her and looked down at her as if she were some animal he'd just bagged. Her body burned, begged.

"Let's see if that little exercise we just went through did to you what it did to me." His announcement over, he leaned down and swiped his hand over her exposed pussy. "Yep. That's a damn river."

A sex slave's offering to her master, and herself. A world away from the runner she'd once believed defined her.

"On your feet, slave." Grabbing his cock, Master Jeff aimed it at her. "You know what I'm ready for."

The truth was, she wasn't sure what he had in mind, but as long as it involved the two of them and sex she didn't care. The elbows' tie made her desperately clumsy, and her masters chuckled as she fought her way to her feet. Spent, she stared at the ground.

"We need to teach you grace." Master Ken patted her head. "That should be her next lesson."

"I don't know. I love watching her trying to obey without

the use of her hands. It'd be even more interesting if we hobbled her." Master Jeff held up his cock. "Shit, if anything I'm even hornier. Time to bring this little show of ours to a head. For now." He frowned and looked around, then smiled. "Over there." He pointed at the table. "Believe me, you don't want to try to escape." Lifting his arm, he pretended to snap a whip. "Hmm. There's an idea for next time, a little pursuit and capture."

Running barefoot through thick woods. Her breath puffs gray in the early morning chill, and her feet sting from striking the hard ground, but she keeps going. They are after her, on horseback or dirt bikes, determined to recapture her.

She escaped during the night, or did they deliberately leave the metal door unlocked?

It doesn't matter because freedom awaits. She'll no longer be forced to live within the small cage. Another mile, maybe five, and she'll be out of their clutches.

And then?

The question slows her, but she pushes it aside and plunges on. She doesn't want to be their sex slave. What woman would choose that existence?

A masculine shout silences her thoughts and she looks around, relieved to see a narrow deer trail. She hurries onto it and picks up her pace. She will outdistance them! They can't—

A rope tightens around her left ankle. She's jerked off her feet and up until she hangs suspended upside-down.

Her masters, riding beautiful white stallions, come into view. They acknowledge her, begin to laugh.

But she doesn't cry because this is what she needs.

Flushed with excitement, she hurried over to the table. Master Jeff had disappeared by the time she turned around. She guessed he'd gone into the bathroom for his own condom. No matter that they might disapprove and punish her, she repeatedly clenched her sex muscles. Having her arms restrained this way strained her shoulders, yet she wasn't ready for the sensation to end. Master Jeff hadn't needed to warn her not to try to run because even if she had somewhere to go, she'd be slow and awkward.

Hobbled? Would they really do that?

Curled on the floor next to the bed where Master sleeps. After recapturing her earlier, he'd ordered her onto it and fucked her, but now he has no use for her so he has forced her to this demeaning position. The metal bands around her ankles and connected via a four-inch chain are enough to keep her here, but Master has secured the hobbles to a ring bolted into the floor. She can turn from one side to the other or lie on her back, but if she stands, she won't be able to take a step.

She will be there when he wants her again.

"At least you can obey a command," Master Jeff said when he reappeared. "Having to punish you right now would get in the way of what's important to me." He made his point by indicating his sheathed cock.

Her body caught fire, forcing her to pace and rock. She arched her spine to accent her breasts and widened her stance.

Master Ken, who'd joined her near the table, chuckled. "The slave's in heat."

"Which is exactly how I want her, always."

Always. No end to the connection between the three of them. Endless days and nights of submission and dominance. "How may I serve you, Master?" she blurted.

Instead of answering, Master Jeff stalked over and spun her so her back was to him. He pushed her against the table, then lifted her arms and forced her to lean over.

"Looks a little high to me," Master Ken said. "I'll take care of that."

She didn't know what he was talking about until the table started lowering. After a few inches, Master Jeff pushed her arms up even more. She turned her head to the side and rested her cheek on the padding. Instead of letting her go, Master Jeff held her in position and reached between her legs. The moment his fingers touched her pussy, she tried to open her stance. Holding her in place, he repeatedly stroked her labia.

Mewling like a wild cat, she stopped trying to keep her mouth closed. Drool escaped. Master Ken brushed her hair back from her face.

"You were a good capture," he told her. "I believe we're going to keep you. Of course, you'll have to continue to prove yourself worthy."

"Which is exactly what she wants," Master Jeff said. "Damn it, do I know how to recognize a sub or what?"

"You do. Pleased with yourself, are you?"

"I'm not sure that's the right word. I'm learning, same as her."

Master Ken chuckled. "No problem. I'll teach both of you."

"We'll hold you to that, won't we, slave?" Master Jeff spread some of her juices over her anus. "It'd be interesting to see how she responds to this."

Alarmed, she tried to straighten. "No, damn it!"

"All right, all right. Relax."

Despite Master Jeff's surprisingly gentle words, she remained tense until she felt his mouth on her right ass cheek.

"I'm sorry," she whimpered. "I'm not—I can't—"

"It's all right. You have every right to express your boundaries."

"He's right," Master Ken said. "The rules—I'll spell them out once . . ."

Maybe one day she'd be ready for some back door action, but not this afternoon. Knowing they understood and respected her eased her mind and body. She settled back down and concentrated on sensation. Trusted.

Master Jeff's fingers returned to her pussy, where he found

and invaded her opening. She'd experimented with some doggy action with a man she'd referred to as a friend with benefits and had found it exciting. However, he'd found a woman he'd wanted to be more than a friend with. Since then, being taken from behind had been nothing more than another chapter in her imagination's arsenal.

"My guess is, you're not going to feel comfortable doing this for long," Master Jeff said and brought a second finger into play. "Much as I'm enjoying the view and experience, I want to keep your pleasure as much of a priority as mine."

Even as her stretching vaginal muscles threatened to capture her full attention, she appreciated being told that this afternoon was nothing more than play. Play and pleasure.

"I'm turned on, Master. Every—everything you and my other master do to me makes me excited."

He flexed his fingers. "Yes, I can see that it does. All right, here's what I want you to do, slave. Close your eyes. Imagine that you've been blindfolded. You can no longer see what your masters are doing and that both frightens and thrills you."

Locked in darkness, she imagined that the men were silently communicating with each other. She was their plaything, their toy.

A whine escaped her when he withdrew his fingers. Believing he intended to exchange them with his cock, she relaxed so she could get the full benefit. Instead, he slapped her ass.

"What—"

He shoved into her. At the same time he pulled on her arms and lifted her off the table. Totally within his control, she slipped into a space defined by sensation. Instead of the slave world built from her exploding awareness of herself as a sexual human being, she floated in endless colors. His every thrust took her somewhere new. Despite her helplessness, she'd never felt stronger or more free.

She grunted and groaned and twice shrieked. The sounds coming from the master fucking her weren't much different, only deeper. Masculine as a counterpart to her femininity.

Female. A woman. A sexual creature.

Always before she'd known when she was going to climax, always had time to climb onboard the impending sensation and cling to it. Today it slammed into her before she was half-ready. Shocked silent, she lost touch with everything except her exploding body. Lived for one thing.

"Oh shit! Yeah, yeah!"

A powerful male body pounded at her, his cock tearing her apart and making her giddy with pleasure. One, she thought. They'd become one.

Take me, use me, teach me.

Long, incredible moments later, Master Jeff let her down and drew away. His ragged breathing reminded her to do the same thing. As her body continued to treat her to electrical charges, she sank even deeper into wonder and joy.

"Runa? Runa, you okay?"

Not caring which of her masters had asked, she nodded. How had her body become so heavy?

Knowing fingers released her elbows. She tried to bring her arms up so she could rest her head on her hands, but she lacked the strength. Someone—probably whoever had untied her—took hold of her shoulders and drew her upright. Her legs gave way but before she hit the ground, her *rescuer* lifted her in his massive arms and carried her over to a rubber mat on the floor. She turned onto her side and looked up at Master Ken. Master Jeff stood near the table, looking as done in as she felt.

"Thank you," she whispered.

"No, thank you."

Epilogue

Stay in the moment. Keep the pace. Work your breathing. Listen to your heart.

A half-dozen other runners, each of them wearing their school colors, pounded behind her. In the past, feeling the competition nipping at her heels would have tightened her muscles, but she felt loose today. Joyous.

She ran, not because she was determined to win the district meet, but because this was what she did. What made her feel most alive.

They were watching, feeling her joy because they knew her body as well as she did.

Turn the page for
a sizzling special excerpt of

NO MERCY

by Jenna McCormick

An Aphrodisia trade paperback
on sale now!

1
_____

"Another drink, Gia?"

Gia dragged her gaze away from the well-muscled arms of the bartender, Los, and looked up into his pretty brown eyes. "I'm not sure that's smart. I'm starting to fantasize about you naked again."

He winked at her as he poured a shot of some green liquid into the bottom of a coffee mug. "How about a hit of wake-up juice?"

She cradled the cup between her palms and inhaled. Though it was cool to the touch, it smelled like the richest French roast she'd ever had the pleasure to drink. She thanked him and didn't even try to present her credit chip. So far from Earth, this planet didn't exchange currency, instead relying on the barter system. Scratch my back and I'll scratch yours. Unfortunately her back wasn't the part of her anatomy in need of attention right now.

"Do you want to come back to my ship for the night?" It had been weeks since she'd enjoyed male company, and with no missions to fly she was totally out of her element. And Los was as fine a specimen of male perfection as she'd ever seen.

He placed his warm hand over her cold ones. "I told you, I'm looking for something more. A real connection. Until you have that to offer, I must regretfully decline."

No surprise there, yet she was still disappointed. Gia's up-front, no-strings-attached approach had helped her out all her adult life. Men appreciated her candor, enjoyed her body, content with the knowledge that was all she was offering. Not Los though. The first time she'd hit on him he seemed flattered, but disinterested. She'd asked if he was gay and he'd assured her that wasn't the case, even as he'd provided her with another drink to ease the sting of rejection. The same held true for every other man on this planet, or at least those she'd propositioned. They all wanted more than a quick nail and bail. More than Gia had to give. So she'd changed her strategy and focused on Los, thinking she could wear him down. Unfortunately, it had the nasty side effect of making her feel pathetic.

He smiled at her kindly. Los was too nice for her. Everyone on this world fit into that category. *Too kind for the likes of Gia.* A reasonable person would love this place, filled with honest, caring people who wanted nothing more than to be close with their friends and family. Gia shuddered at the prospect. "Are you sure I can't pay you for the drinks? I have plenty of supplies on my ship—"

She cut herself off at his shaking head. He knew what she intended, and she felt like some sort of letch for even trying it, a pervert offering candy. This whole place, full of decent, honest people, made her feel like a shallow slut. Grabbing her jacket, she headed toward the door before she disgraced herself further. "Night, Los."

The cool breeze off the shimmering ocean lifted her hair off the back of her neck. She inhaled deeply, savoring the salty tang off the purple sea. She focused on the distant landmass, another island of some sort. The topography of this planet was filled with various size islands, interconnected like an archipelago.

All tropical all the time, the world having found a perfect balance within itself, just like its inhabitants.

Well, most of the people here had found balance. Pivoting on her heel, Gia started back toward her ship, kicking stray rocks out of her path with a viciousness born of sexual frustration and general ennui. She needed to *do* something, be active and have a purpose. Daily runs on the beach kept her in shape, but in shape for what? A few cargo shipments a month swallowed by a host of mind-numbing downtime? What was the point, other than feeling like an outcast, the serpent in the Garden of Eden?

A high-pitched, distinctly artificial chirp woke her from her reverie. She fumbled for a minute, retrieving her comm link from her jacket pocket. " 'Lo?" The word came out slurred. Maybe she should have had another hit of Loss wake-up juice.

"Hey, Gia, how are you?" Gen's smiling face filled the small screen.

Gia couldn't help but smile back. It was so nice to see her best friend really happy after all she'd been through. She took to this place like a duck to water, more than suited to Rhys, the empath she'd fallen for and his touchy-feely way of life. "Not as well as you, I imagine. How's Rhys?"

"Divine." Gen breathed the word like a woman coming off an orgasm. Which she probably was. Jealousy reared up, the ugly green eyes burning through to her soul. Not that Gia begrudged Gen her happiness. Her friend had gone through a dry spell for most of her adult life, where Gia had bathed in the pool of decadence. Until recently anyway.

"Why don't you fly over here, stay out on the island? It's private, and we could spend some time together. I feel like we've hardly talked at all in the last month."

"I didn't want to interfere," Gia hedged. Or be the useless third stabilizer on a two-engine rig. Gen had finally found her bliss and Gia didn't want to sour her daiquiri. "You guys are like newlyweds, or the empathic equivalent of it. You need alone time, to bond."

"If we bond any more we'll be permanently fused together."

"Show-off," Gia said with a wink, to take the bitterness out of her quip. "You know what I need? To be fucked good and hard by someone who doesn't give a fig what's going on in my head. Abstinence is total balls."

Gen winced visibly. "Maybe you could try getting to know someone. It's better when there are feelings beyond *oh baby, right there, that's the spot.*"

Gia stopped and leaned up against a large rock. "Hey, that was pretty good. Maybe you can talk dirty to me and help me out of this funk."

Shaking her head, Gen sighed. "You're hopeless, you know that?"

"But you love me anyway, right?" Gia hoped so. Alienated from everyone and everything familiar, Gia needed her friend now more than ever.

"Of course. I know what you gave up to help us, Gia. Your career and your home, all your friends—it's all gone because you chose to side with us."

"At least I still have my stinger." Gia gazed out at the empty field where her stinger-class starship waited patiently for her return. Pride made her chest expand, just like the first time she'd seen the stealth weapon that would become her home. Small and streamlined for maximum efficiency, the stinger could travel for over a billion miles on its cold fusion energy pack. The weapons and navigational systems were state of the art, and while she couldn't take down an armada, any single ship in the galaxy would think twice about messing with her. Providing shelter, transportation, basic foodstuffs from the synthesizer, and protection, the stinger gave her an instant family. It was the only thing Gia let herself count on. The one constant she couldn't afford to lose.

Gen spoke the truth. She *had* sacrificed a great deal. Not just her place in the stinger squadron, but her reputation as well. By going against orders, Gia had branded herself a traitor. And given the choice she'd do it again, no matter the personal cost.

Refocusing on Gen, Gia said, "I promise I'll come over soon. Now I need to take some time to figure out what my next move ought to be. Send coordinates to my comm unit. And say hi to Rhys for me."

"Will do." Gen's face shrank to a tiny point of light and then blinked out altogether.

"And then there was one," she breathed, unsure of whether it was relief or disappointment in her belly.

"That ain't quite true." The deep timber of a male voice spoke from behind her, rumbling with menace. Gia shivered even as she reached for her laser pistol. Whirling around, she met the golden-eyed gaze of the one man she never thought she'd see again.